ISBN 978-1-7390876-0-9

Typeset by Goldsmith Publishing
Book cover artwork and design ©Samantha Sanderson-Marshall www.smashdesigns.co.uk

THE
STAND-UP
MAM

KAY WILSON

love ♡
Kay x

♡ love

xoxo

For my mam, Peggy Stewart, who always encouraged me to write

ONE

Then

In the windy wastelands of Newcastle, a concrete-clad comprehensive hummed to the marching tune of 1,000 pupils' flat shoes as they made their way into the buildings. They were braced to be bored as usual.

Most pupils had 'Roll With It' by Oasis in their heads until the bell rang. Then they all tore themselves away from each other's manic chat to sit in morning registration. Dinner money at the ready. Pens on desks.

Georgie Smith took her time climbing the stairs. Each one seemed to have a magnetic pull to the centre of the earth. Her scuffed shoes (with the permissible one inch heel) seemed to stick themselves to the steps, stopping her ascent.

Her breathing became heavy. Through each deep intake of the cabbage-and-mince-filled air she felt her stomach heave. She wiped her tears. Stopped thinking about missing her friend.

Georgie kicked the broken security door open. An endless expanse of sky and light welcomed her like a giant spotlight on the grand stage the top of the building was to become. Far below the flat roof of the science block she could see 7C, 11F and 9E making their way to their classes.

It was harder to walk to the unwavering sharp line of the building's edge than she had thought, as the wind blew like a whirling dervish. It pinched her cheeks tight as if the devil himself held them and wouldn't let go. Her wild, white hair, her one pride and joy, stood on end as if she was already upside down.

She felt each step was made with moonboots, slow and heavy. All the planning and fear had lasted the whole weekend. Suddenly there she was. On the edge. Toes perfectly level with asphalt, a very pleasing 90 degrees.

'STAY. WHERE. YOU. ARE.'

So, she did. For a moment. Georgie obeyed and stayed still. Her worn, black school jumper with its chewed cuffs, shiny with snot, pulled over her wrists.

While the usually-calm Mr M was screaming at her to not move, she remembered Reuben's Sunday tea. Despite the wind around her ears, she was back there again, sitting at the long table, trying to swallow morsels with a bone-dry mouth, over and over. And then their stupid mistake. She was the one paying the price. A baby.

This is it then. I'm going to count to three and jump.

One. This One is for the baby in my belly, making me sick, trying to get all the badness out of me.

Two. Two is for both of us. My Reuben and me. But really not mine any more.

Three. The three of us. Not playing happy families. A triangle of love, hate and pain.

She closed her eyes and was about to lean into the wind when she thought an angel had swooped her up. A giant, warm cloud engulfed her. Suddenly all the wind and noise stopped. She was in a cocoon of safeness.

'You're OK now.'

Mr M wrapped the massive blanket around her and led Georgie gently down the emergency stairs. *It is an emergency,* she thought.

Her baby, thrilled with the adrenalin rush, twisted in her womb. Instinctively she stroked her belly then Georgie's heart broke into pieces. *It thinks it's here to stay. If only that could happen but I'll never be allowed to keep my baby.*

TWO

Now

The Shaker kitchen was the heart of Georgie Chancellor's world. A clean and tasteful structure exactly right for when she felt like she had no backbone and wanted to dissolve into its framework. This warm, family hub would stop her deception being discovered, for now. She wasn't really a perfect mother. Not in her heart.

Georgie was damaged and living a lie. Oh, how she tried to be a caring mother. She always stopped herself from screaming at her children when they made demands, even though their words were sometimes like nails scratching on metal. The problem was made worse as she was so bad at reading people, there was no way of knowing how they felt about her either.

This relentlessly middle-class mother and wife, in a posh Tyneside suburb, had a veneer as thin as the ones on her teeth. Yet sometimes her reinvention, even after 20 years, gave her a sharp scratch. What lay beneath was something entirely different, darker, dissembling.

She ran her fingers over the gleaming worktop. It soothed her demons.

The other, original Georgie never got a chance to rise up. Thank goodness for that. Georgie Chancellor had too much to lose. No matter how much family love she put on display she always felt it was returned in short supply. *Not a complaint though*, she told herself whenever it crossed her mind.

Be grateful for what you have, Georgie. Remember where you came from and where you could end up. You don't want to turn into your mother, pissing in the yard, too drunk to get to the bathroom.

But today was always the worst day of the year.

She opened the Mother's Day card from her teenage daughter Lily first, carefully, as if it was going to be a treat.

A fat Mr Toad from Wind in the Willows was overloaded with washing. A standing joke. Georgie loaded up the washer as soon as anyone's clothes hit the floor. Dirty or not. Her family laughed that most days they only saw her feet as the rest of her was hidden behind the piles of laundry in her hands.

To Mam, thanks for doing all the rubbish jobs in the house, tough life but someone's got to do it! ☺ *Love you loads. Lily, your little lamb. Xxx*

Even the use of Georgie's pet name for her daughter didn't soften the impact of those words. Just for once she would have liked some appreciation and to be seen as more than the house slave. The butt of all jokes. That is until she turned the tables and had them laughing at something she'd told them, to try and get some self-esteem.

Lily's Molton Brown body cream gift smelled lovely but brought her out in hives. She was sure she'd mentioned the rash but it was Lily's favourite, so that might have slipped her mind.

Georgie made herself laugh loudly at the message on the card and rubbed some body cream on her hands. *I mustn't forget to wash this or I'll be scratching my skin off by bedtime.*

'Thanks so much. You're so thoughtful. My gorgeous girl. And hilarious.'

'Not as funny as you Mam, to be fair. And you're welcome. You bloody earn it. If we had to pay you for everything you do, I couldn't afford to drink all those cocktails with my mates!'

'It's always a pleasure, m'lady.' Georgie gave a mock curtesy and forced another laugh.

Nat, her 19 year old lanky dreamer of a son gave Georgie a huge hug and began scoffing his breakfast.

'What's the card for, Lils? Let me see? I've not forgotten your birthday again, have I, Mam?'

'It's Mother's Day, pillock!' Lily laughed.

'Oh shit. Sorry Mam. I'm useless.' He got up, planted a kiss on Georgie's head and gave her another long hug. 'I love you Mam.' The tear in her eye passed him by.

Her past misery was buried yet it could still burst through like weeds pushing through concrete. She clenched her hands and forced herself to get control of her emotions. *Don't dare break down. Think of this as just any day. Stop remembering. What's done is done.*

She began loading up the dishwasher. *I hope Lawrence doesn't give me smelly lilies again just because his mother loved them.*

'Happy Mother's Day, my darling.'

'Lilies! Perfect. Thanks Lawrence.' She smiled, on automatic pilot, and stuffed them in the nearest vase. *Why was I persuaded to call our daughter Lily when I dislike them so much?*

A smile was fixed. Truth squashed down. Honesty terrified her with its potential to cause upset to her family, and in turn, her safe life.

Georgie's tousle-haired husband, now the shortest family member since Nat's growth spurt, handed her his encrusted porridge dish.

'I've had an email about that huge property deal. Any chance we could put off going out for lunch today? It's going to be an all hands to the pump job. Need to call into the office to pick up some papers.'

'Fine. No bother at all. Totally understand. Mother's Day is always really hectic in restaurants anyway, isn't it? All those happy families celebrating.'

She picked at her cuticles and drew blood.

After a few minutes loading up the dishwasher she asked, 'Now what shall we have for lunch?'

No-one was interested so she began finely dicing sweet potatoes, onions, aubergines, courgettes and grinding the spices for a Masala sauce.

Lily bailed first. 'Actually, if we're not going to that Casa Mia restaurant I'll just head off to Jasper's house.

He's got a vintage Japanese film he wants to show me.'

Nat followed her lead. 'Yes. No offence Mam but I need to see Sam about some college work. I bet it's going to be lovely having the house to yourself anyway. No need to cook for me.'

Once they'd left Georgie stared hard at the prepared vegetables and sauce. She scraped the whole lot in the bin. *Get over yourself. It's just one day.*

But there was a shift. She realised the rare peace in the house was intoxicating. She curled up on the sofa and read a women's author she loved that Lawrence dismissed as 'chick lit', whatever that was. Then she dozed off before realising it was after 1pm so made herself a white bread crisp sandwich and tried to forget about all her children. Just as she assumed all three wouldn't be thinking of her.

*

Georgie walked around the house barefoot, still soaking in the silence. She put hair removal cream on her upper lip, legs and big toes. Then she remembered the plants in her front lounge needed watering.

With perfect timing, Sophie from next door was looking into her room through the window. No doubt she was going out for her Mother's Day lunch. Her husband had his arm around her waist and their two young children were running ahead. Everyone was immaculate in matching, well-worn Barbour jackets.

Sophie gave her a wave, pointing at the white cream on her face and laughed. Then thoughtfully distracted her husband from Georgie's embarrassment, by encouraging him to run after the two tearaways.

This was the first time she'd felt seen and understood for a long while. She stopped wanting to pick her cuticles and smiled.

The freedom to spend hours how she pleased was such luxury Georgie then took a taxi into town. She'd never done that before. Her life consisted of a long jobs list including giving the rest of the family lifts or picking them up.

Lawrence offered her the chance to buy expensive

clothes but she always felt embarrassed to try them on and be the centre of attention.

Yet today she spent a week's housekeeping budget on two designer shift-style dresses. Another first. They were in brilliant emerald green and shocking pink. She hoped they would make her feel happy. Before heading home, she had a Pornstar Martini, just so she could say the name.

By six o' clock that night she thought *I've enjoyed one of the best Mother's Days. And it was mainly without my family. Weird.*

She had even managed to subdue her mind's regular torment, always worse on Mother's Day, about her first son's life and whether he was happy.

Her evening was the same old routine. Once Lawrence and Nat were back home, she made them laugh with her tale of being spotted with the hair remover then it was back on the motherhood work track. And just like that, Mother's Day was nearly over.

Then Lily rang, sobbing and slurring, 'I've had too much. Bloody cocktails. Bastard Mojitos. And. And. Jasper's…'

'Jasper's what?'

'Gone!'

'Gone. Gone where?' Georgie struggled to understand what Lily was saying.

'Left. Me. Meeting.' More sobbing. '…rugby mates. And I couldn't get into the cocktail bar with Sophia and everyone.' Then she blew her nose loudly, followed by a burp.

'By myself. Tyne Bridge. No taxis. I'm scared, Mam.'

'Oh no. Don't panic. I'll come straight down. Don't worry. Won't be long. Stay put.'

'Hurry, Mam.'

'Ok. Ok.'

When they got home Lawrence had switched off work mode completely and ordered in Georgie's favourite takeaway to save her cooking. They had fish and chips with vinegar and batter, even though he thought they were common.

'You've looked after yourself all day so now it's my turn

to care for you. My gorgeous Georgina.' He hugged her tight and she relaxed into the safety and warmth of his body, enjoying feeling loved.

By 10 o'clock the whole family were fed and sitting on the settee watching TV, squashed together in what should have been a lovely huddle. But tonight, rather than comforting it began to feel claustrophobic to Georgie.

'We're such a happy family,' said Lawrence.

'Aren't we.' Georgie replied.

She was last to go to bed as the kitchen needed tidying up from the takeaway boxes. When she was about to shut the coat cupboard under the stairs, she saw one of her old art pads had fallen against the door. Lawrence had wanted to throw everything stored there in the bin the previous week but she'd insisted on keeping them.

Hunched down on the floor Georgie flicked through her drawings and felt proud. She had real talent. And knew it. Everyone in the school art department said so. They'd told her about art college. She dreamt about going. Imagined drawing and painting every day. Exhibiting work in actual galleries not just school walls. People buying her pictures signed by her. Georgie Smith.

Then she buried her head into the coats and screamed.

THREE

A chance for change flew into that controlled life when Nat got a funny email. Georgie had been 'talking rubbish', as she put it, as usual, about the PTA meeting. It had got so fractious the whole school became a mad riot of furious, middle-class mothers pelting each other with home-made Viennese whirls.

She mimicked their posh voices. 'My Annabel says there are some first years' mothers who are refusing to use organic flour for the fete baking stall. And, worse still. There's supermarket saver jam in their sample cakes tonight. I could smell the cheapness from across the lacrosse court. It literally stained my teeth more than my usual fine Shiraz.'

She was re-enacting the whole scene, impersonating everyone from the headteacher to the ancient, fiercely-loyal secretary who was trying to calm things down.

Lawrence, Lily and Nat were helpless.

Nat looked up from his laptop and slapped the table. 'My mate Matt has just sent me info on a comedy competition, Mam. But I can't tell jokes to save my life. Why don't you do it?

'It's an Edinburgh Festival course and gigs, with a London final. You get paired with a professional comic to help.'

Georgie smiled, 'Well that's ridiculous.'

Nat banged the table again.

'No. It's abso-bloody-lutely not.'

Lawrence joined in, 'You're cute and hilarious darling. Very....'

As usual she had no idea what the end of that sentence might be.

'42?'

Lily didn't look up from her A-level sketchbook, doodling gothic animals.

'Yep. Like cosy crime. You can do cosy comedy. Just think of all the jokes about Mary Berry, gardening, weight loss club and all that. Should be fine, tbh.'

Georgie stared at her. 'Yeh. I'd tell you what I mean but I cba.'

All of them laughed, apart from Lily who just said, 'Not bad. But we all know you're using the initials as Dad wouldn't be happy if you ever said arse!'

Their reaction to her humour made the hairs on Georgie's arms stand up with the strangeness and pleasure of it. A real buzz. She'd not had that for a long time.

Nat tutted. 'There's likely to be some stiff competition but forget about them Mam. And ignore her. She's just being a pain. We need a three minute clip of you speaking. Let's start and write some stuff down that's happened, like the PTA thing and that dog at the wedding.'

Georgie and Lawrence burst out laughing again.

'Yes, Brock was so brilliant, what could possibly go wrong with him being a ring bearer. Apart from him also being great at chasing things. But not great at bringing them back! And he was so fast.'

Lawrence added, 'By the time they caught him he was nearly in Scotland!'

She said, 'I could do something about our Forest Fun holiday. You remember when they said everyone had to get out of the swimming pool because there was an unacceptable level of urine in it. What on earth is an acceptable level? We all showered for ages afterwards, didn't we?'

They all laughed at the memory.

Georgie smiled at Nat. 'This might be fun for you all. Laughing at me. But I don't know the first thing about stand-up!'

Lawrence said, 'Well. How about a family trip to the Comedy House in Newcastle on Friday night to see how it works? I think live is probably better than seeing it on TV.'

'I'm up for that. How about you Lils?' said Georgie.

'Ok. Not busy then.'

'Right. I'll book the tickets. How exciting.' Lawrence smiled.

'Yes. Exciting.' Georgie repeated on automatic pilot with butterflies in her stomach. They were all going out to help her do something. *Lovely. And what a change.*

FOUR

When she wasn't running after her family Georgie was office manager for Newcastle marketing agency, Luminos – Shining a Light on You. She thought it was a terrible brand but no-one ever asked her for her views on creative things. So, she kept them to herself.

The day before the family comedy gig trip Georgie was at her desk setting out the project plan for the month. She was allocating staff, marking holidays, deadlines and making sure everything was in order.

But as the sun shone into the glass and steel Quayside office, she gazed across her desk to the river beyond. She let thoughts wander to the comedy club and the competition. *I wonder if there will be any women like me on stage?*

She was the first employee of Brett Callaghan, the owner of Luminos. Over 20 years ago, she was an administration apprentice. Now she had the running of the office at her fingertips. Yet Georgie was almost as invisible here, as at home. But she got more respect at least.

'Georgie. Georgie,' said Brett as he burst into the office. He was looking like the archetypal agency head in his tight white shirt and even tighter designer white jeans. As he marched over to her, he was rubbing his shaved head.

She was bolted out of her reverie.

'I'm right here Brett. No need to shout across the room. What's the problem? No. Don't answer that, I know.'

'Man. Don't pick today to get all hormonal. Please. For fucks sake. Please.'

She didn't blink and handed him a pink file with Perfect Pitch across the top.

'There.'

'Oh, thank Christ for that. Lifesaver.'

'I've arranged for the design team to meet you in the studio at 10 to go over their ideas. They've got some great ones.'

'Fantastic. If I wasn't married to a guy I'd definitely marry you.'

'I know. I know. Now bugger off and let me get on with running your business.'

Two new graduates, Stephanie and Dominic came and sat beside her.

'Yes. What's the trouble now?' She smiled through gritted teeth.

'Well. We're having trouble with our laptops and IT don't seem to want to help. The word programme won't load up.'

Georgie took the computers and switched them on and off again. Word loaded up immediately.

You're a genius', said Stephanie.

'Nah,' said Dominic. 'She's just watched the IT Crowd re-runs on TV. They do it all the time.'

'I am still here you know. Calling someone 'She' in front of them isn't very nice.' *Happens all the time at home however.*

'Sorry Georgie.' They said in unison and slunk out.

The morning followed the same pattern. People stood by her desk asking questions while she tried to get on with her own work.

By 12 she went to the kitchen to make a coffee and shut the door firmly behind her and rested her head on the bench.

'My God. This is becoming just like ....'

Brett came in so she stopped speaking.

'Are you talking to yourself? Well. Anyway. I've been looking for you. Everywhere!'

'The office isn't huge for goodness sake. What is it?'

'That design idea shakedown isn't the best. Is it worth having a call with Robert, that freelancer? But we need to keep it hush hush. Be subtle. No-one needs to be offended.'

'So. The design team aren't to find out we might have ideas from someone outside? And they need to think you've come up with them.'

'Exactly.'

Brett hugged her.

'I don't take all this for granted you know.'

Georgie's smile was pinched but she still fixed it in place.

'I know.' *Yes, you do. Sometimes I wish someone would just give me some proper credit round here.*

*

It was rare for the whole family to agree to go somewhere together. Georgie was both apprehensive and excited for the Comedy House trip. The club was a former warehouse in Newcastle city centre. All stripped back bricks and wooden boards. It was packed with everyone from stags and hens, to students and locals.

Lawrence managed to get seats to one side of the stage but far enough away to avoid being picked on. Georgie thought the microphone looked like the gallows. Making it worse was the huge spotlight shining on it.

Settling in with the glass of Pinot Grigio that Lawrence always bought her. She fixed her eyes on the stage.

A young Geordie comic, Wayne Watson, started the gig.

'Any families in tonight?'

Lawrence was about to raise his hand but Georgie grabbed it and brought it back down.

'Don't Lawrence. It's not a good idea to speak to them I've heard.'

Wayne said, 'Thought not. It's going to get a bit sweary. So, buckle up everyone. Any Newcastle United fans in?' And off he went with his comedy set on dating, sport and trying to get a six pack.

'I said to my best mate, oh, she looks fit. Stupid guy went over and asked her if she was a runner!'

Nat laughed. 'I should tell him about you going to do this competition video!'

'You'd better not.'

Lawrence added, 'Don't tease your mother Nat. Why

not just take in some tips. We can then all keep her right.'

He was shushed by people around him. *Embarrassing*.

All through the act Nat would whisper to Lawrence something that he thought was useful. They'd then look at Georgie and nod.

Lily sat stony-faced. 'This is not my thing. Hope the others are better than this. Football jokes. Urggh. Rubbish.'

None of the comics were older than 30. And only one was a woman. She joked about internet dating and avoiding serial killers.

'I don't think I'll fit in to a comedy competition. There are no people like me on this bill.'

Lawrence was dismissive. 'Don't worry. There's no expectation of you. No pressure, darling.'

The headliner was the funniest. Jaz Jones was slightly-built. He told stories about his Indian heritage and the conflict between what was expected of him and how he'd turned out. Part of his set was also about looking for love and trying to avoid an arranged marriage.

'Young women my parents set me up with are so ambitious. They always want me to change career and become an accountant. I'm just looking for the simple life.

'An older woman who's funny and my equal. Or even better than me. Won't be hard! I don't earn that much. Can't cook. And could possibly die every night in public. Or maybe not today. You seem a great crowd.'

He got a big round of applause at the end.

'I liked him.' Georgie smiled.

'Not bad.' Lawrence agreed.

'Hmmmm. Bits were funny but good luck learning how to do that Mam', said Lily. 'Although tbh I have faith in you. Think you'll be fine.'

Georgie stared at her daughter with disbelief. The praise was rare and lovely.

'Well, what do you think about doing the video when we get home Mam? Less scary? Surely?' Nat beamed.

Georgie threw the remainder of her wine down her throat. Dutch courage.

'Yes. Let's get home and do this.'

Nat gave her a high five.

Lawrence helped Georgie on with her coat. 'Don't get carried away Nat. If your mother decides not to do it then that's fine with me.'

I don't think he wants me to do this.

The crowd were still cheering the comics as they all got a final round of applause. Everyone was happy and supportive. It made her feel part of something. Connected. And with her family.

'I think I'd like to have a go. And thanks for bringing me Lawrence.' Georgie kissed him on the cheek and hugged him tight. 'You're very thoughtful.'

Back at home, Georgie fixed a smile on her face. She began talking to Nat's phone camera, as she nervously tucked her blonde cropped hair behind her ear.

She ran through four quick stories about everything from her slimming club to mispronouncing names and hardly drew breath.

'Well. I used to think muesli was called mu-es-lee and and mange tout was mangey towt until I met my husband who put me right. And don't get me started on malapropisms. The number of times I said someone was green behind the ears. Or I have a hot spot for a film star only to be told it's a soft spot!'

'Perfect.' Nat gave her a thumbs up.

'I've no idea why I let you talk me into this.' *I've no idea why I feel better after saying these stupid little stories either.*

Lawrence and Lily had left them in peace to record the clip. He gave a small knock on the kitchen door. 'Can we come back in yet?

Georgie remained standing, arms folded, looking at her family. They looked normal on the outside. But she knew all their inner schisms, including her own, could rise up and bite at any time. All she ever wanted was a family and its security. She hadn't realised the price to be paid for it all.

This night had been a change from that.

Nat loaded up the video and wrote Stand-Up Star Competition Entry, G. Chancellor, Newcastle.

The closing date was the next day and winners would

be notified two weeks later.

Georgie was still unsure why she'd agreed to enter the competition. As usual it had been easier to go along with her family. But now her worry was how uncomfortable it would be to get through and have people listen to her. If they did, what might accidentally come out of her mouth?

*

On competition results day, Nat was in the kitchen constantly checking his emails. He had done a black cross on the kitchen calendar counting down the days to the result. It was a source of endless teasing. Georgie had no idea why he felt such confidence in her. His noisy run-up to logging in was also driving her crazy.

'I'm opening up my lap top, tip top. Typing in my pass code, pass code.'

'Stop it Nat. Just stop speaking and being a prat please. For a minute. Just for me.' She rarely asked for anything as a rule. On top of doing a stand-up video, that was another first.

The kitchen was reflecting sunlight on every surface but she polished some more, while her son refreshed his laptop for the 10th time.

'I didn't stand a chance Nat. Let it be.'

'Mam. Listen. If you get through we're all going to have such a laugh. There's a mentor. A trip to a comedy workshop in Edinburgh. A series of gigs. A series. Can you imagine?'

'Yes. I can and you're not selling it to me to be honest. Doing a silly recording is one thing but nothing more. Thanks very much.'

'My mate has been trying to get some advice and a gig at Joke Junction in town. Really hard to get one.'

Georgie banged her Mr Sheen on the kitchen table. Then immediately regretted the scratch she'd made, as well as the noise.

'You're being daft Nat. Joking with you three is one thing. How am I going to leave you all? If I went away for the weekend, imagine. You'd try to make toast and burn the house down.'

The minute the words came out of her mouth her dark side, always whispering, felt a certain pleasure in the whole immaculate structure being reduced to ashes. *Bliss.*

Lawrence was always trying to help her. Being kind and protective. He said they should have a cleaner, gardener, handyman. The list was endless but she preferred being in control, which meant doing things herself. Despite the boredom of it all. There was also less time to think.

She appreciated his concern and loved him for it. He got a heart-shaped sandwich on Valentine's Day. His golf clubs ready for his regular session. Neatly-ironed boxer shorts every day.

Georgie did these tasks without thinking about whether or not they were appreciated. Sometimes she knew they were, as Lawrence said so. But lately they were just taken for granted. On those days she allowed herself to feel a moment's sadness. Then it was gone. *Good.*

*

A stampede thundered down the hall. Lawrence and Lily crashed into the kitchen after their boxing training. Red-faced and full of hot energy, they drummed their hands on the kitchen table.

'News. Have we news?' Lawrence boomed, pumped up with adrenaline.

Lily was a close second. 'News. We. Need. News.'

Georgie shrunk under the attention and pressure. Craving invisibility once again. Melding into the walls. Down the plughole, anywhere but there.

'Ah Mam.' Nat banged the table beside his computer. 'Sorry.'

'NO!', said Lawrence and Lily in unison.

Georgie felt a huge sense of relief, then grabbed her son and hugged him hard.

'Thank goodness for that.' She flopped onto the nearest kitchen seat.

'I think I'd rather have had my teeth pulled out than do it to be honest.'

'Ah Mam. You nearly could've had your own stand-up

viral fame. It's such a shame it's not meant to be. Not this year anyway.'

Nat gave her arm a rub. Lawrence kissed her cheek.

To distract them from giving sympathy she began her relentless chopping of vegetables for sushi.

'No need to feel sorry for me. It's the best news I've had. Ever.'

Then family life as Georgie put it 'TikTok'd' right on as if there had never been a possibility of a change. No-one mentioned stand-up again and her daily routine returned. She was invisible and busy looking after everyone. At home. At work. Repeat.

But over the next few weeks she kept wondering what it would have been like to be picked. Centre stage. Imagine. It was years since there had been a hush when she spoke and people heard her right to the very end.

The feeling of making her family laugh had been lovely. It connected them. And now it was missing again.

It made Georgie sad.

Life went back to normal. Yet for reasons she couldn't put her fingers on she kept thinking about the funny things that happened in her life and made a note of them. One stood out in particular when she'd persuaded Lawrence to see an old rock band she liked. As they'd been famous in the 1960s Lawrence and her were the youngest by a long way. The light bounced off the audience's predominantly bald heads and when a great song came on to dance to, people stood up like creaky zombies. The track had nearly ended by the time they were on their feet! *Could that be part of a comedy set?*

As time moved on, she always intended to remind them of the stories, making them laugh again. But there never seemed to be the time for her to be centre stage any more.

*

Two months after the rejection she was staggering down the stairs with the daily pile of dirty washing when her mobile rang with an unknown number.

She tripped and as the clothes cascaded down like an

avalanche Georgie flopped down onto the last step. Fed up.

'Hello. Is that Mrs Hilarious?'

'Excuse me. Who is this?'

'Ah. It is you I'm after. Mrs Georgie Chancellor, I presume.'

'Who's speaking please?'

'Saul. I run the Stand-Up Star comedy competition. And I have news!'

'Ok.' Georgie was hesitant. Intrigued and still fed up.

'Unfortunately, for them, one of our winners has broken their leg in several places. No doubt a comedy caper... Ha, ha. So, fortunately for you. You're now IN. Get a bag packed. Edinburgh is CALL. ING.' He said the last word as if it was part of a song. It grated on Georgie's nerves, which had become very tight.

Sunshine danced around her feet and the pile of washing still spewed around her. Something was digging into her bottom. It was the funny anecdotes notebook, tucked into her jeans pocket. She pulled it out and spoke softly.

'This is a. I don't know. What's the word. Shock.'

'I can imagine but are you a 'yes' to join us, that's the thing?'

Her heart thumped madly. Words wouldn't come.

'Emm. I'm....'

'I'm not sure what 'Emm I'm..', means. But if it is a no. I need to know with a K N O and W, or I'll have to ring the next runner up.' Saul huffed.

'No. It's not a no but do I have to say yes right now?

''Fraid so Mrs Hilarious.'

She looked at the washing then through to the kitchen and the shopping list pinned to the notice board. The school letters' pile and Lawrence's various committees' paperwork. And then to the joke notebook.

'I'll do it. Send me the info.'

'Fantastic. You'll not regret it. I promise.'

'No. I don't think I will.'

Georgie hung up and put all the washing back in the basket. But this time there was a big smile on her face.

*

She needed everything to be perfect for when everyone got home. Perfection gave her courage.

The sun bounced off all the surfaces which had been polished to rare gem status. Delicious fresh Asian vegetables like pak choi and mouli radishes were making the room smell like a Far Eastern market.

'Tonight, you're having tofu on a bed of chilli noodles and vegetables. You're welcome.' Georgie did a mock bow before passing the steaming plates around.

'You've really gone a bit over the top Mam but it looks lush.' Nat began to eat before Georgie had a chance to sit down.

'Yes darling. This looks almost as good as that Michelin-starred place down the road. Well done.' Lawrence patted her hand.

'Not bad for an old lady.' Lily smiled and pinched the largest tofu piece from Georgie's plate.

Georgie put down her cutlery.

'I've got some news.'

No response.

'I'm doing the Edinburgh comedy course.'

Lawrence didn't look up and continued to eat.

'No, you're not. You weren't good enough. Or something like that…'

'I've had a call. Someone broke a leg.'

'That's comedy for you,' laughed Nat. 'Surely that didn't actually happen? What the actual f….'

'Nat! Language.' Lawrence boomed.

'They needed a reserve and I was the next best.'

Georgie's courage started to waver and her voice didn't sound much like a comedian. More like a faint hearted, maligned PPI claim line assistant.

A huge sense of unease sat deep in her belly as she felt physical change as well as the rush from the news. And what she'd agreed to do. It was terrifying to think of doing stand-up, at her age.

People will look at me. My wrinkles.

Yet fear was mixed with determination.

'You'll be great Mam.' Nat smiled.

Lily said, 'Yes. Good for you. You will leave us plenty of food though, right?'

I'll not be invisible but I might wish I was.

'Yes. You must go. Go.' said Lawrence, the mind-reader for once. Even though the decision was already made and not by him.

'I've talked to Brett and he's fine. So that's work taken care of.'

The dynamic of the family shifted, silently, towards her. And it felt great.

Georgie, with her off-the-cuff daftness about home life and PTA stories was going to the Edinburgh festival and getting a comedy writing mentor. It was quite mad and the penny was slowly dropping. Scary, but exciting.

'What if all stand-ups are young blokes, talking about sex and beer. Or women talking about periods, Tinder and the patriarchy. What on earth are they thinking of having me in with all of them?'

Lawrence kissed her on the top of her head, as he often did. 'You're different darling.'

He always said that and she never took it as a compliment. But she had no time to worry about that now. *Am I really going to do stand-up comedy?*

*

Two weeks later Georgie re-read the comedy course instructions, checked her train ticket and hotel reservation. Then she checked the fridge was full, kitchen tops spotless and zipped her immaculate suitcase shut.

Her comfort zone was never breached. Now her very bones were breaking loose from chains.

As she stepped out of the front door Nat and Lily gave her a huge hug.

'Good luck Mam.' Lily's goodbye was not as warm as Nat's but as usual Georgie chose to ignore it. She loved her daughter with all her heart, didn't she?

Lawrence pipped his BMW's horn. That was her signal to crack on.

Let's do this.

The familiar smell of her home disappeared as the front door slammed shut. She felt the old Georgie was locked behind it. This new woman was heading to a comedy course. At the bloody Edinburgh Festival. Like a more confident twin to the real her.

'Seat belt please', said Lawrence even though she always buckled up. Georgie took a slow breath in. Calmed her nerves. Kissed her husband on his cheek.

'What's that for darling?'

'Caring that I'm not going to crash through the windscreen. And taking care of me in general.'

'I love you.' He said, 'It's that simple.'

'I love you too.'

She gave him another kiss goodbye at Newcastle Central Station. The air blasted through it like a mad wind funnel from the Tyne. It made her shiver with nerves and cold.

Lawrence looked at her squarely in the face. His eyelid twitched as it did when he was worried.

'We've not been apart at night when I think about it …'

'Yes. That case in London you did. When was it…'

'Oh. The Glover one. My, that's a while….'

'Yes. Bet you never thought I'd be the one going away. And to do stand-up.'

'Indeed. I know. I'm going to miss you so I'm making you sit here for a few more minutes darling.'

'Bless you Lawrence. But I need to go…'

'Yes. Yes. I know.'

He jumped out to get her suitcase and hugged her hard. It reminded her of how lovely and safe he made her feel.

'Don't break a leg. That would be awkward. If you and the original comedian did it! And don't put yourself under pressure. You're perfect as you are.'

Georgie really appreciated his praise but it didn't make her feel perfect. And was pleased when the train pulled in.

'Bye' she mouthed through the window as he was blowing kisses to her, running along the platform. *I wonder if I'll feel different when I next see him?*

FIVE

On top of never having done stand-up comedy, Georgie rarely travelled on a train by herself. As a result, she snuggled into her seat and decided today was more full of possibilities than any other time she could remember.

The beautiful expanse of fields and North Sea was a seamless, hypnotic palette of green and blue. She was relaxed, which surprised her considering what was coming her way.

Not on demand, feeling free to order carbs and talk in my own voice. No need to fret about it being 'lunch' or 'dinner' time. Or have I said 'pet' rather than 'darling'? Is my sentence going in the wrong order as in, 'I like it, that wine'.

The train service trolley was a good bit lighter when it left seat 12b Coach B. Georgie feasted on her forbidden fruits, tutted at by Lawrence. Common food. And fattening. Cheese savoury sandwiches, pickled onion crisps, Mars bar and a strong latte with white sugar.

She gorged herself and read the tackiest women's magazine she could find. *I married my step dad* had particularly piqued her fancy.

The announcement it was only 10 minutes until Edinburgh suddenly reminded her why she was on the train and set nerves into overdrive. She re-read her competition email for the 100th time, while trying to stop picking her cuticles.

There were so many questions running through her head. *What were the other winners going to be like? There were six of them on this course, with a grand final in London in three months' time. What would they learn? Would she be rubbish compared to the other five, who were all picked first?* The pressure was building.

Georgie remembered the video with Nat. Her pithy, funny comments at home didn't seem like anything suitable for other people.

She imagined, for the first time staring out from a stage into strange faces, unresponsive....

Oh no, I can't do this.

Her stomach ached. It might be nerves or all the trans-fats. She wasn't sure. As the train made its way into Edinburgh Waverley station and the monumental stone terraces faced her like soldiers, she held her breath. Then she realised, with a pleasing buzz of excitement, that outside the course, she was also free to do whatever she wanted.

*

After checking into her hotel, Georgie clutched her leather bag and peered at the map to find the course venue.

She then read her directions three more times before arriving and gathering enough courage to go through the tatty door. The black cavern reeked. It was so dank it made her shiver both with nerves and a very real chill.

The walls were wet. She tried not to touch them as she eventually reached the top of a stone staircase and stared at three closed doors. Each had a peculiar name. Whacked Out, Ab Normal and Pinch Gin.

She jumped as Pinch Gin slowly swung open.

It had the damp, historic atmosphere which oozed from the very pores of Edinburgh. The cheery August day seemed to have accepted defeat and had disappeared altogether by the time she sat down.

Georgie grabbed her handbag so tightly her knuckles were white. A million things flooded through her head. But at the front of them was the burning question. *What am I doing here?*

She was last to arrive and the five other winners were already sitting around the room's edges.

The place was so tight with all their nerves, even the overhead lights were twitching. She had never been to an Alcoholics Anonymous meeting but the room was set out like the ones on TV.

A semi-circle of wooden chairs was facing a lone black plastic one and a Formica table with notes on top. They all stood up and shook hands with her then sat looking at each other nervously. A door tucked away at the far end flew open making them all jump.

'Fuck. OMG.'

Saul Sykes, who had rung her about her place, was in his 50s. Tall. Immaculate short black hair and beard. Dressed in a tight black t shirt and faded designer jeans. His voice was deep, like an actor, Home Counties and smooth. Everything about him got right up Georgie's nose.

Snapping a look at his watch he acted like he had been given a lightning surge of power. He rushed round the wannabe comedians giving everyone a high five.

'Willkommen. Pleased to meet you. Welcome. Welcome.'

'And congratulations on winning our Stand-Up Star competition places. You look hilarious guys.'

Georgie and her fellow comics all stared at each other aghast. *Is he for real?* Georgie mouthed at a female student-type who shrugged and slunk further down her seat.

She felt ancient and so out of place it was making her skin crawl. In her head she may have been still in her 30s but she was older than these people.

The night at the Newcastle comedy club had been full of young comics. They were attractive. They had stage presence. They were able to speak without faltering or waiting their turn.

This is not me. Standing on a stage, microphone in hand coming out with jokes. Impossible.

Saul switched on spotlights. The room became so bright it made her blink.

'Let's have a look at you properly you lucky, lucky guys.

'I'm your leader. So to speak. Sure you'll have seen me on TV. Well, it's hard to see me on the radio to be honest. Ha. Ha.

'How's about we all introduce ourselves. You first, with the red hair.'

'Hello everyone.' The female student sat up straight then waved like the Queen and stood up.

'I'm Clem. First year at Uni. Not travelled far today. Just from Edinburgh's New Town. Or as we call it. The posh part. Where everyone has their own clan tartan. And men always grab any opportunity….'

'Keep it clean' said Saul.

'…to wear a sporran!' She added with a giggle, sitting down. Then she smiled at Georgie, who was pleased to smile back. *I might have an ally here. Despite the fact she's got a fancy background.*

The next woman was from Southern Ireland, around 30. Saul waved his hand instructing her to speak next.

'Well. I'm Anna. Not from the posh part of anywhere. As you can tell. It's Dublin I'm from. And my stories are all about me Mammy and Daddy, as well as the daft things me whole family's done. We all had such a laugh at a wedding last weekend.

'Everyone did a turn and me Daddy sang so loudly his false teeth shot across the room. And then…. '

'Brilliant. Well done. Next.' Saul waved at a middle-aged man who looked funny in a good way, with a waxed moustache.

'Hi. Pat, 32, Yorkshireman. Looking for a Yorkshire woman. Or anyone really. To be fair. Thought this stand-up skill would add to my charm. Kerb appeal. Type of thing.'

'Great to meet you Pat. Perfect.' Saul pointed at a young man with long hair tied back in a ponytail.

'Hello ladies. Matthew at your service. I'm a proud London boy. Love a good cocktail. Not a euphemism. And a lady with immaculate taste. Who will no doubt like me. Ha. Ha….'

'That's ok but don't laugh at your own jokes son.' Saul was a smiling assassin.

What on earth is a euphemism? Nat would call him a bit of a cock thought Georgie.

'Next.' Georgie thought he had pointed at her so she stood up with trepidation.

'Not you.' Saul said. 'Yet.' Then smiled. Georgie sat down with a thump. She wanted to die.

'You. Second last. With the curly hair. Let's hear your story.' Saul sat back and folded his arms. 'Begin.'

'Student. From Cornwall, half dead from a fuckin 20 hour coach journey. Had to pee in a bottle. Now dead. Man. I mean DEAD. People call me Will.'

Saul laughed briefly. 'Well, you're not really DEAD are you. Will. If that is your real name. He mimicked his Cornish accent. 'Cos you're here with all of these other lovely, very much alive, peeps.'

Maybe I won't have to speak. Please God. This is horrific.

'Now. We're ready to meet your mentors I think.'

Clementine said, 'What about that lady there. We've not heard from her. Hello.'

'I know. I know. I was just messing around. Here's your minute of fame darling. Give us the low down. But stand-up. As that. Is what. We're all here for!'

Georgie swallowed hard. Gathered every bit of her inner strength. She stood up slowly.

'Hello everyone. I'm Georgie. I live in Newcastle.'

'We know that sweetheart. Can't mistake a Geordie accent. Love it.'

'People seem to find my silly stories funny. I feel better when I make people laugh. That's it.'

'Well. We all hope to make the audience feel better after a gig as well as ourselves. Don't we?'

'I didn't mean that…. What I think is…'

'Teasing. Darling. That's me. Just teasing. Now sit down.'

I'm going to fail.

'Right then. I'm going to introduce you to your Stand-Up Star comedy gurus who'll help you on the path to success. Slippery slope. Whatever you'd like to call it. Hah!' He laughed like a car engine backfiring.

Behind him six figures entered the room and stood beside him. The professional comics, without exception, looked sleep-deprived and scruffy. There were three men, one was brown-skinned and slight, the other two were white and short. The three women were by contrast, very thin, tall and looked driven. One was a goth, one an English rose and one a free-spirit hippy type.

Georgie recognised Jaz Jones from the Comedy House straight away. It made her feel better. Even though she'd hoped she would recognise all of them from TV for the tale to tell back home. She was embarrassed to not know who everyone was, as the other wannabes all seemed to. They nudged each other and were impressed.

Saul gave each of the professionals a high five. Then he stood legs apart and stared intensely at each finalist, holding Georgie in his sights the longest.

I wish the ground would open up. Right now.

He shouted out a comic's name then pulled out a name from a cardboard box on the table.

'Mark, the shark, you're paired with', and he did a small drum roll. 'Anahana.'

She smiled and Mark smiled, then they stood at the room's edge.

Comic Louise was paired with Pat. Henry was the mentor for Clementine. Matthew was linked up with Felicity. Will got Marie. That left Georgie, fixed grin, staring at a dot on the wall behind Saul's head.

'Only you left Babe. So heeeere's Jaz.'

Georgie's teeth were so clenched the smile was never going to let her cheeks slide back into place. Jaz came over and formally shook her hand, making a little bow as he did so.

'Enchante', his accent was soft Brummie.

When she held his hand briefly Georgie felt instantly relaxed. He squeezed her fingers for a quick moment and grinned.

Everything was going to be all right. Wasn't it?

*

Saul clicked his fingers above his head and the strange group paused their awkward conversations.

'What an arsehole. For God's sake!'

Did I just hear one of the professionals mutter this?

'Before we start, I'll just go over some of the competition's details, as in the mentoring and final of this comedy feast. You've each got a series of gigs locally to build up your confidence before the grand final in London in November.'

Every one of the winners was fidgeting with empty note pads, to varying degrees, depending on self-confidence.

Georgie could have gnawed her fingers down to the already bright red cuticles. Jaz looked sideways at her and smiled sympathetically. He quickly patted her hand as she had often patted her children when they were small. Because she'd seen other mothers do that.

Saul planted his legs wide apart again and grinned at the captive, motley audience.

'The Professionals. Using that term loosely guys. Are here to help you. The first step of comedy is to get great material. Find out what makes you mad. And to kick off your training we're going to have a little go now.

'They'll get you to drill down that very thing that's infuriating, to get a great visual image to sell the joke's idea. Now crack on with your mentors and see what magic comes along. A quick-fire round, if you will.'

The professional comics took their proteges off to the corners of the room whispering in their ears urgently. Each one wanted their trainee to be a success, even at this first stage. There wasn't a moment to lose.

As Jaz Jones guided Georgie towards the edge of the room she brushed against his arm. Her stomach fluttered ever so slightly but she ignored it. Obviously.

The unlikely couples grabbed the nearest chairs to them. Georgie was still quietly terrified as she watched the room's inhabitants shuffle round like chess pieces but it took her mind off the comedy scenario for a moment.

Focus. Focus. She grabbed hold of her nerves and stayed glued tight to Jaz. It was the closest and neediest she had been with a man other than Lawrence, for a long time.

He swung one of the chairs round and grabbed one nearby for her. He placed them facing each other, so close their knees nearly touched. Everyone else was more formal, side by side.

When he leaned in she could see pores on his nose, a trace of mayo or butter at the corner of his mouth and flecks of violet in his brown eyes.

His converse trainers were worn down at the front, almost into a hole. *How much money do comedians make? Could I survive on their pay?* Then she wondered why she was wondering that.

'Tell me about yourself Partner and I'll share my tales before we get into this angry business.' His voice was warm.

Georgie began to relax and told him she'd seen him at the Newcastle gig and how impressed she'd been. Then she talked about home life. Shrunken jumpers in the wash. Yoga classes. Cooking. All the while he quietly nodded, giving nothing away and wrote brief notes in a tatty, leather notebook.

'Right. Now. What makes you really furious?'

Georgie didn't want to seem rude or dishonest, so sat for a few seconds, conflicted.

'I'm sorry. I never allow myself to get mad at anyone. Apart from myself. I don't think that much about me. Maybe I'm just not funny?

'Don't believe you. Try harder. We need something Georgie'. His smile was less warm. *This competition is not just between the wannabes.*

'Tell me about yourself. Does your other half slob around the house? No washing up? Always at the footie match?'

'No. He's more rugby than football.'

'Underpants on the floor?'

'No, always in the basket.'

And so it continued then suddenly there was a light bulb moment.

'Got one about myself!' Georgie's face grew hot at the memory.

'All of the mothers in the PTA are obsessed with Mary Berry. I know so much about her I could write her autobiography. I'd call it 'They think it's pavlova'. If it got published that would definitely be the icing on the cake.'

'Ok. That's an interesting start.' He smiled in encouragement.

'And all the boring discussions about bloody soggy bottoms. It's my saggy bottom that worries me! And saggy boobs. I've always wondered why bra sizes are 'A' 'B' and so on. Well, I think it's how far down your body they go. A is for arm pit, E is for elbows as that's where mine are likely to be in another few years. It's all the way down to K for knees. Should be P for pancakes as they're as flat as them.'

Georgie suddenly shut up. *Why on earth am I talking about these personal thoughts with a total stranger?*

'Great. That's the business.' Jaz nodded enthusiastically.

Then she found she couldn't stop what Lily would have called 'oversharing' and words just came out of Georgie's mouth as if they were somersaulting down a hill.

Jaz scooped them up, writing them down at breakneck speed.

'We're getting material. Georgie. Well done.'

She flushed with pride and started to feel a bit relaxed for the first time that day.

*

Saul put his arms around Clementine's shoulders and whispered in her ear in the much-needed lunch break. Flirting finished, he addressed the room.

'We're all going to have so much fun. This is just the start of your stand-up journey ladies and gents. Wait until your practise gigs. But I am ahead of myself. To continue with more advice. The secret to good stand-up comedy as well as gathering up that fury, is….'

Georgie held her breath for his golden words of wisdom.

'Timing! It is all about great timing people. Oh. And talk from the heart. Punters can tell false rubbish from a mile away. And give LOADS of eye contact to as many people as you can.

'Also make sure you have local references. People love hearing about where they live. So, remember to mention Edinburgh when you're doing a set here. Which you just happen to be tonight!'

The collective gasp was probably heard all over the city.

'You're kidding', said Georgie, terrified to her bones.

'Absolutely not. No messing about. Right, you've got another couple of hours here. Work up some more material with your mentors using what I said. See you here for the gig at 8, plenty of time to prepare and practise people.'

Georgie took herself off to the darkest corner of the room with Jaz, where the chilling air wrapped around her shoulders.

Jaz calmed her down and took charge. Georgie chewed on her Stand-Up Star pencil trying to stop her heart exploding out of her chest.

She had hoped against hope this course gig was a vague do-it-if-you-want to type of thing. But it seemed it wasn't optional after all. Her panic attack didn't feel optional either.

After the afternoon session and a quick salad, she went back to her hotel room. In no particular order, stomach churned, head thumped and fear had a tight grip on everything but her bowels.

'Hello Edinburgh.' She ran through the five minute set as she blow dried her hair but her voice sounded as if she was hungover, hoarse and sore.

Getting dressed in her black t shirt and jeans she hoped it would settle down. Half an hour to go and the real horror of doing stand-up live in front of people began.

A text flashed up from Jaz. *I'm staying round the corner, but will be with you in five to walk you round, don't be...* followed by a chicken emoji.

A slick of red lipstick and vigorous backcombing of her hair created a small illusion of being sassy. She didn't know if that was going to be helpful.

Jaz looked handsome which surprised her as he had just looked tired and tatty earlier in the day. He was friendly, cocky and surprisingly good at keeping her mind off what was going to happen, as they walked to the club.

'Right. You're going to be just fine. Some last minute tips help?'

'Oh God yes. I feel sick.'

'You're really funny. And warm. You'll hold the crowd no bother.'

'I'm just so scared Jaz. Really. On a different level.'

'Tell me one of your best punchlines again.'

'Molly won slimmer of the week. The prize was a hamper full of food. It's the club you can never leave.'

Georgie realised they were walking in perfect rhythm.

'Ahh, sweet. That's lovely Georgie. Most people have dieted and will enjoy recognising that. You're going to be just fine.'

The walk to the club was too short for her nerves.

When they arrived at the Flying Duck there were half a dozen people outside but no-one under 30.

'Don't you dare duck out.' Jaz gripped her elbow and directed her inside the mock Tudor entrance. A typed sign said Comedy Nite, free admission, upstairs, 9 -10.

The other competition finalists were sitting on a table at the side of a tiny stage in the upstairs room with a small audience in the front row. Clementine and Anna looked like death.

Georgie looked at them. They shook their heads. So did she, then said, 'I'm not doing it either.'

She had assumed the men were punters but they all stood up as one.

'You can't…' The tallest one said.

Georgie blinked at him. Then the closest woman to her spoke.

'…back out. No. You've got here. Well done. It'll be over so quickly. Stay. You'll be fine. We're all comics and doing a few minutes each.'

'I don't think I will be fine. It was a daft competition. I did it for a laugh but it's stopped being funny.'

All of them looked at her and the two girls before speaking to them with more encouraging words. Then Jaz appeared beside her with a Diet Coke.

'You can do this. Sit there with the other comics. I'll go over the gig and we'll double check your set.'

Jaz was also the Master of Ceremonies or MC as it was called and went through the running order, Georgie was in the middle of the middle section. She paced outside during the first break, wishing she smoked.

All of them then sat around the table that classed as a green room, trying to memorise their scripts which were now short and crisp. Georgie's brain was struggling with it all as well as the attempt to be funny. The more she tried to pin down what she had found quite hilarious when she had written it down, the more it disappeared before her eyes. Jokes were dissolving. Confidence at a similar rate.

By the time the gig started the room was half full of tourists, all ages and types as well as a handful of young students. It had a lively atmosphere which Jaz had got going with an introduction and plenty of audience banter.

First finalist on stage was Clementine. Her hands were clearly trembling as she held her script tightly, but her voice was strong and determined. She did well. Although the stories of student parties and waking up in a pool of someone else's vomit, did not appeal to Georgie's humour, she laughed loudly to be supportive.

'Last night the student hall manager came and knocked on my door in the middle of the night. He boomed, 'Have you got a man in there?' So, I squeaked, 'No.' He then shouted loudly, 'Don't worry. I'll get you one!'

Anna was charming. Her comedy persona was more subtle than her real life character. She recounted tales of her family and their competitiveness about everything from, who gets up first, to her brothers' regular 'Who has the longest willy?' competition. Richard, the eldest, always won.

Matthew's jokes were funny and he was so confident everyone listened intently. He finished with a long story about losing his virginity to a friend's older sister on a South of France trip. His punchline made people laugh.

'We were drunk. What can I say. It was my first taste of coq au vin!'

Big burly Pat's tales were the contrast of a rural life in Yorkshire to going into town and looking for ladies who he wanted to be dirtier than his pig shed.

Then it was Will who was hilarious about his native

Cornwall and how tourists spent most of their holidays being terrorised by locals driving down tiny single track roads at great speed.

Rather than really listen to their sets properly Georgie's head felt full of fresh air. She had never known her thoughts to be so hard to rein in. In her mind she was actually a rider pulling on a harness, to keep her comedy set on track.

Jaz controlled the crowd well. He got them to clap around the room, getting louder and louder, before Georgie went on.

As she stood on the white-taped spot she sucked her stomach in, took a slow breath out and carefully unhooked the microphone. Her heart and bowels were competing again to see which part of her anatomy was going to explode first. Then the introduction came out.

'Hello Edinburgh.

'I love your city. But it's never dry. I don't mean from the whisky it's all the bloody rain. The steps down from the Royal Mile to the gardens are like Niagara Falls.'

Her breathing steadied.

She talked over the PTA mums' obsession with Mary Berry, her body and its many failings.

The audience were all listening. *Phew.*

By the time she finished her joke about the weight loss club prize she realised the room had warmed up. A little bit. The audience gave a low chuckle.

Georgie allowed herself a grin as she walked back to her seat. Her facial muscles relished this new direction. Clementine, Anna and Jaz each gave her a big hug and she made her way to the chair, almost collapsing on to it with nervous exhaustion and relief. Job done. Thanks goodness it was over.

But she did it. They all did it.

Now they needed to do it again. And again. For the competition.

The minute she switched her phone back on it buzzed furiously with text after text.

Where's my new blue t shirt Mam? Lils x

Can Greg come for tea on Thursday? Nat ☺

Missing you darling. What did you say we should have for supper tonight? L xx

Sorry, should have said, hope it goes or is going well. L x

Georgie replied to them all with a new 'bravura' as Lawrence would have said. Bolstered by her formidable new friends she replied to all the family's texts with. *Presume you're all sorted out with everything. Having a great time. See you tomorrow. X*

As she was typing the last word Jaz touched her arm.

'Coming to the pub? You've earned it.'

'Absolutely.' She beamed.

The Robbie Burns was heaving but the comics, professional and amateur, had managed to grab a corner.

'What would you like to drink?' Jaz led her through the crowd to the huge bar.

'Treat yourself. Your favourite tipple. Go on. Saul's put some money from the Stand-Up Star organisers behind the bar.'

'Pornstar martini please.'

'Really? Interesting choice. I had you down more as a G & T type of woman.'

'Used to be but getting more adventurous just lately. For some reason. Don't know why?'

'Really? Nothing out of the ordinary to see here. Just a fearless mother doing stand-up for the first time!'

They laughed and sat down with the rest of the stand-up crew. They all thought it was funny Georgie drinking a Pornstar martini but it was good natured banter.

'There's got to be a great gag in you having that drink,' said Pat.

'I don't think we should mention gag and porn in the same breath,' said Anna.

'Keep it clean people. You've been told', added Jaz.

Georgie had another two cocktails loving the post gig camaraderie. Everyone was praising what worked in all their sets, with the professionals giving more tips.

'You were punching above your weight tonight. Definitely got potential. Hasn't she?' said Jaz.

'Yes' Saul agreed. 'Did pretty well for a first go.'

'Maybe just a bit more energy. Don't you think?'

'Yeh. But that'll come with confidence. You didn't bottle it either. We've had loads of runners. Haven't we Saul?'

'Hell yes. You're the first ones that have lasted the whole session and gig.'

Georgie was open mouthed. 'Women ran away?'

Jaz smiled, 'Well. Not exactly. More of a fast walk. But yes. We've lost a few along the way.'

'You must be made of sterner stuff Gracie', said Saul.

'Georgie,' she said firmly. 'The name is Georgie.

And this was just the start.

SIX

The journey back to Newcastle from Edinburgh was packed as if the festival itself was moving South again. Families returned to England after their fix of culture and fun.

Performers tired out from long nights and endless beer, fell fast asleep across the tables as the train raced them back to the cosy familiarity of the London circuit. Street entertainers struggled to squeeze their extraordinary kit of chains, bikes and paraphernalia into stuffed overhead shelves.

Georgie felt a sense of euphoria and dread in equal measure.

She hadn't slept and the other comics' voices were banging around her head. They had been kind but stand-up was going to be a dog eat dog adventure, she could see that.

The train pulsed its way back to Newcastle and the domestic perfection of her life. Her phone had buzzed and vibrated as if it was having a fit throughout the whole weekend. Names flashed like a ticker tape warning of impending doom. Lily. Lily. Then Lawrence. Lily again. Nat. Nat. The incessant red light in the top corner flashed like a police siren, unrelenting in its persistence.

She knew she should answer it in two rings like normal but she was enjoying not being at everyone's beck and call. Their neediness was laid bare before her. A platter of queries, requests and in Lily's case, the odd rant, were squirrelled away in the 3 x 6 inch piece of metal sat before her on the train table.

My kids aren't kids. Lawrence has more qualifications than I'll ever have. They should manage without me. For two days.

Her phone did its vibrating dance again. This time it was Lily's name flashing across the screen. Georgie clicked reject. One more hour of peace couldn't hurt, could it?

*

The dank air from the River Tyne was like a miserable spirit breathing on the necks of everyone leaving Newcastle's Central Station. Georgie lifted the collar on her leather flying jacket to keep it at bay.

A sharp horn blast made her catch her breath and there in front of her was Lawrence. His imperious command cut through the crowd like a referee's whistle, 'Get in! Georgie. Get in! It is survival of the fittest here.'

As she climbed in, he leaned over to plant a welcoming kiss on her cheek and gave her hand an affectionate squeeze.

'Well, my comedy heroine. How was the course? Tell me all about it and how brilliant they all thought you were!' Lawrence smiled at her. His driving was disrupted by loud honking from a growing line of taxi drivers behind them. He pulled on to the hectic one way system through Newcastle's night-time streets.

Georgie looked at him, his smooth-skinned face and intense expression. She took in his carefully pressed white Ralph Lauren shirt meticulously tucked into Gant jeans. All in perfect order just as he said he was taught from being a tiny boy. His father would spit on his hand and smooth down his son and heir's hair, to ensure his 'little soldier' was ship shape.

'It was very cool. I did OK Lawrence. Yep. I did OK.' Georgie stretched out her legs, relieved to have space after the cramped train journey. Tipsy women in tiny skirts or second skin shorts, waved at them as they stopped at the numerous sets of traffic lights on the way out of the city centre.

'Drunken tramps. Look at them. Off their heads, the whole lot. The lads are no better. See that group over there Georgie?'

Lawrence pointed to a group of six young men around 20 years old, two were peeing against a brick wall. All of them were wearing tight t shirts. Tattoos looked like they had been stripped of flesh to reveal their real selves underneath.

He wound the car window down to Georgie's horror. 'Come on lads. There're toilets up the road.' All the group all turned round and looked at Lawrence as if he was a far bigger joke than anything Georgie had cracked in Edinburgh.

The leader of the group pointed at him and started howling with laughter. 'Look, it's one of the seven dwarfs!

'Definitely Dopey!'

They all collapsed with laughter as Georgie fixed a hard stare at the lights and willed them to change. And they did. As they moved along the street other people were now starting to stare at the car and peer inside, wondering who the men were shouting at.

Georgie's gaze took in the worse-for-wear women, holding on to their mates for support. They all collapsed occasionally like a rugby scrum in reverse. Bare bums and provocative underwear displayed without a care in the world.

She felt a shiver as one girl rose up from a particularly loud, drunken huddle and stared straight at her. The girl's tatty denim skirt and battered stilettos in neon green were exactly what she would have worn, if she hadn't been scooped up by Lawrence and reinvented as a middle class, professional woman.

'Better mind my step.'

Lawrence glanced at her sideways.

'Sorry darling. Didn't catch that.'

'I'm just talking to the wind Lawrence.'

'That's a comedy technique I presume. Ha. Ha.'

*

Georgie walking up the path at home was different to the one that had set off to Edinburgh.

She couldn't wait to tell them about the gig. All the fun. And people laughing at her jokes. Her brain was setting up the story and the punchlines.

But life is rarely how she planned.

'Hi Mam. How was it? Nat didn't look up from his PlayStation game.

Lawrence bustled in from the car and put her bag down in the hall before she could answer.

He said, 'Right. Lovely to have you back. Have an urgent call in the morning. Any chance of a cuppa as I read the report about it all? Darling? Missed you.' He kissed her and handed her his empty mug. The one with World's Best Husband on it.

'Ok. Yes. It was ....'

'Hi Mam. Glad you're back. These two. Have done. Absolutely nothing. Useless tossers. It was all 'Lily can you just defrost the meals Mam left? Lily can you just cook us some bacon for breakfast? Can you just answer the door?'

She linked Georgie's arm. 'We need to stick together Mam. It's us against the world.'

'Now. Before we hear about Edinburgh. What do you think about this new top? Too much boobage on display? They seem huge?'

It took all of Georgie's patience to stay in the house. She wanted to run. From the incessant self-interest and demands of everyone in her life.

Instead, she did what she had taught herself many years ago, when overwhelmed, Georgie got on with the tasks in hand. A small success in Edinburgh meant nothing now. She knew that. *Silly thing.*

The kettle was on for Lawrence's herbal tea. She answered Nat about the Edinburgh trip but knew he had long lost interest. And then she looked carefully at Lily's top. 'It's perfect pet. Just perfect.'

Then, she couldn't remember how it happened but she dropped her husband's treasured mug onto the floor. The noise exploded like a missile going off. It replicated what was going on in her head.

Am I really so invisible?

When she picked up the pieces, she noticed the letters instead of World's Best Husband now spelt Worst Husband. It made her smile. Ironic. *Maybe this could be a joke in my set?* She was brought back to earth with a bang.

'God. Georgie. How did you do that?' Lawrence was exasperated. 'You're just home. Rather than bringing order. You're making chaos. Chaos.'

'Sorry. I'll buy you a new one.'

Nat chipped in, laughing. 'Ah but will it still say Best Husband?'

'You'll have to wait and see.' she said to Lawrence's back. He was already heading up the stairs and had stopped listening.

The following morning interest from her work colleagues was slightly better. For a few minutes.

Despite her low key office presence Georgie had high hopes of her colleagues. She walked through the office slowly, nodding to people on the way.

'Good weekend?' A few replies but no questions.

Then there was Brett. In red tartan trousers. *Is this an Edinburgh reference?*

'Morning Georgie. I've been looking everywhere for the password for the Zoom meeting at 10. Any ideas?

She put her head down and tried not to be hurt.

'I said. Have you…' He then thumped his forehead on her desk.

'Sorry. Sorry. Sorry. I'm all about me. As usual. Come on then. How did you do? Meet anyone famous?'

As she was telling him about it two or three people heard and joined them, listening to the tale.

'Hmmm. Jaz Jones? Brett said. Saul Sykes? Not sure. I've heard of them. Is that the Irish one. From Father Ted. What's name?'

'No. That's Ardal O'Hanlon. I think.'

'Well then. Give us your best joke.' Brett folded his arms. There was now a small group of colleagues gathered. Intrigued. They knew Georgie as the quiet but efficient right-hand woman for their extravert boss. Not a stand-up comic.

Georgie realised Brett never dreamt she would actually open her mouth and tell a joke. But Jaz's words of encouragement came to her. So, she plucked up her courage and stood up.

'Well. The one that went down best was about me mispronouncing words. Then I told them the story about how I felt about my body getting older.'

She rattled through the first minute of her Edinburgh set and everyone laughed in the right places politely. Then Brett gave her a brief clap.

'Amazing. And you can organise us all as well! Which is obviously handy atm. Now where's that pesky password again?

And with that Georgie's world went back to normal. Pretty much. There was a comedy tuition session with Jaz but that wasn't for a fortnight. *I wonder if there is any point in going?*

She went back on automatic pilot. Home to work. Back to home. Most days she didn't even remember the drive there or what she'd done.

*

Then everything changed.

When she got home from work the day before her session with Jaz, Lawrence was already in, opening up his briefcase, loosening his tie.

'Apparently we're to go into the front lounge. Lily has requested our presence!' Lawrence was amused.

Lily and her boyfriend Jasper were hugging in the lounge. Nat was leaning on the door frame, ready to bolt.

The minute they saw Georgie the children all spoke at once and it wasn't to ask how her day had gone.

'Mam.' said Lily.

'Lily's up the duff' said Nat.

'What!' said Georgie and Lawrence together.

'Oh, and that means I'm going to be an uncle. Cool.'

Her daughter looked at her with her usual confidence and a new touch of vulnerability.

'Surprise. And that was my news, you stupid thing.' Lily snapped.

Jasper hugged her to his worn Fair Isle jumper and then moved across to hug Georgie, who was silent and ashen. Her hand shot to her mouth as she thought she was actually going to vomit with shock. Jasper stopped dead in front of her, quizzical.

No words would come and everyone was staring at her.

Georgie couldn't think what to say so said the first thing that came into her head to fill the void, 'I've only been at work for a few hours. How's all this happened?'

Nat blurted with laughter 'I think we know that!'

Georgie felt as if she was stripped naked in front of her children and gnawed to the bone. She would give anything to be back in Edinburgh and disconnected from this horrific, electric tangle of problems. But she had to stop Lily feeling like she had all those years ago.

'My poor, poor Lily. How are you feeling?' Georgie held her daughter tightly and Jasper enfolded both of them in his arms. The security of being held was just what Georgie needed. She also knew it would be a comfort to Lily.

The silence was broken by Lawrence. 'The most important thing is Lily's future. I personally don't see how she can have a baby at 17. Her University place, Durham, St Chad's College like me, then the Bar....'

Georgie stood in front of him, finding her inner strength. 'Lily will still have her brilliant career. Our daughter is determined and works hard...'

'And it's not down to you, really. Mr Chancellor. I think. With respect and all that...' said Jasper.

Georgie breathed deeply. *What can I say to them? This whole situation is madness and here was Lawrence suggesting what? A termination, an adoption.*

Her whole body shook with memories and trauma. Yet she had to cope with this.

'I know the timing is not ideal but look Lawrence. They're...' She paused. '...very happy. Well suited.' The words stuck in her throat but she forced herself to stand in front of the blooming couple, hands on either side of their shoulders. A bricklayer cementing them into one unit.

'Suited and happy. Suited and happy!' For Christ's sake Georgie. Who the hell has a baby in their teens and makes a success of their life?'

Jasper wiped a tear from Lily's cheek.

'We know we're young but we're really in love, for real and everything.'

Georgie wanted Lawrence to leave so she could talk to Lily quietly, but he started up again. 'You've both got major exams this summer. Lily could be vomiting all over the papers, which is not the type of 'additional material' her tutors advised. And I didn't pay a huge fortune in school fees for her to blow it all on a bastard.'

Georgie's brain was screaming with the thought of her young daughter being pregnant with no preparation or maturity to cope.

'I know, you love me and have given me everything but I want this baby.' Lily started to cry more and snuggled into Jasper's jumper, looking more like an eleven-year-old than a teenager. Georgie felt her own tears come.

She had built the perfect family and life. Whether Lily could keep the baby or not was one of those damned decisions. The past made her want to scream in pain.

Georgie looked from the young couple, moon-white with emotion, to the back of her husband as he headed out of the room to the kitchen. Now she had her chance to give comfort and support.

She sat on the settee and patted the seat beside her. Lily sat down and rested her head on Georgie's shoulder. They held hands and quietly discussed when the baby was due and what needed to happen to keep her well.

'I'll do anything you need to keep you safe and cope with this Lily.'

'You are such an amazing Mam. I know I'm tricky but thank you. I love you. So much.'

'I love you too.'

They hugged and Georgie drew strength from being able to show love and kindness to her daughter. She would control Lawrence and ensure the baby stayed in the family.

He was still furious when she joined him in the kitchen, 'She can't have a baby. It is just not happening. But I can't get my head around it now. Awful timing as ever. I've got an important American client call to make then I'll be back down to discuss it properly.'

She sat in the dark kitchen staring at the garden, her deepest fears darting back and forth in her head. *Lily was too young to have a baby. How hadn't she realised she was having sex? This comedy thing was ridiculous. Especially at this time. And yet.*

The stand-up world beckoned as a relief. Her head couldn't allow thoughts of babies and teenage pregnancies. It would destroy her. But her daughter needed her and it was important to be there. A cruel dilemma.

Was it too much to ask to have another chance to enjoy being the centre of attention. It was intoxicating. People staring at you to improve your self-esteem?

She realised you had to be over 40 to understand the true need for this. And the corresponding horror of being rubbed out of the world. Paler and paler, right from the edges, then puff out you go.

SEVEN

Then

Georgie had known something would happen that particular day. Reuben, her saviour, had tried to head off the boy she called Bastard, but in a second there he was, on his tip-toes, in her face.

'What's the weather like up there, King Kong? His breath was strangely sweet for such a repulsive thug. A peculiar mix of chocolate and mint gum.

'Don't even think of running. I know your timetable as well as my own. Now where's my two pounds?'

The silver coins were slippy with sweat in her hand as she dropped them into his school bag. The day would come soon when this money would be missed by her dad. Then who knows where she would get his ransom.

Bastard gratuitously spat on her shoes and shot off with his gang. She wiped off the slime and slowly made her way over to the football pitch grass when her boyfriend, Reuben, bounded into view.

'Shit. Sorry I couldn't head him off. McCann stopped me.'

Her fingers were still moist. She hoped he wouldn't try and touch them while half hoping he would.

Reuben was the blonde school super-hero, rather than the slightly seedy nightclub owner he was to become. The boy-man parted groups of the younger girls like a God on earth. It was a like a Royal visit. To Georgie, he was absolutely everything.

After her usual miserable week, the weekend promised to be so much better. She ran to his house, bursting to see him again.

The run had made her sweat. She slowed down to wipe her face before quiet terror worked its way up from her toes. Adrenalin which had been booming around her body slowly evaporated. The usual skin chill was creeping over her skinny legs, sunken stomach and smooth ribs.

She imagined a strong hand picked up her own and placed it firmly on the gatepost of Reuben's large, detached house, clamping it so she couldn't spin round and set off again at a breakneck pace. It was though she was connected to her bedroom by a giant elastic band. Twang. And she would be gone.

Georgie thought she stunk. Her feet. Her armpits. Even her hair. She wished she had blasted some Impulse perfume over her denim jacket so the stink would be masked. *If I was a colour, I would be rancid yellow.*

Without looking up, she sensed him looking at her. Slowly, slowly, she raised her head. Her fringe protected her eyes so she could see him looking at her for a quick second before there was the usual electric charge. It felt like petrol was poured between them and set alight.

The house was posh with grey-green watercolour paintings of Italian landscapes and a large photo of Reuben taken with his parents in a professional studio, all posed and composed.

'You smell.'

Her very guts heaved. She had to pretend someone had a tight hold of her throat to stop a yelp from escaping.

'...absolutely amazing. All new puppies and meadow hay.'

'And that's a good thing?'

'Absolutely. I hate the smell of that Impulse everyone wears. You smell of you.'

There is a full bucket load of my smell at the moment.

His mother, smooth skin and blow-dry (not a perm and set), waited by the door to the dining room. Her jeans were a bit too tight for her age, but she looked almost attractive for someone middle-aged, she thought.

'Come in.'

His father was already sitting down at the head of the

long table. It was laden with tiny sandwiches, delicate, almost transparent cups and saucers and home-made treats.

Reuben looked remarkably like his father which was unsettling. Like seeing a possible future husband. Georgie sat down and throughout a very long half an hour, she ate. She ate one lone scone, one piece of cake and drank one cold cup of tea.

'Well?' his father said, 'How are we all doing? Busy days?'

There was then a long discussion about Reuben's father golf game and his mother's trip to the supermarket.

Despite the monotony of it, Georgie was delighted to put down her tea cup and swung round to listen to his father's small talk. She was sure every single mouthful of her food's passage down her skinny throat, past her her very tight windpipe and chest to her almost-always empty oesophagus, had been amplified around the room.

'Well, young lady.'

'Mum. Dad. Don't start asking loads of questions.'

But dad continued.

'Well. What do you think of the Government?'

'Dad!'

'Only joking. Joking. You know. Funny.'

The mam chipped in.

'Funny peculiar if you ask me.'

All three of them then laughed, more than it warranted in Georgie's eyes. *Are they really just laughing at me?*

The tea-drinking did become slightly easier with the scented water she would later know as Earl Grey, slipping down a treat.

'Reuben's off to St Leonard's Sixth Form. Oxbridge. No doubt.

His mam spoke to her. 'Aren't you an artist? Where are you going?'

Georgie opened her mouth. She knew her lips were moving, but no words came out, so she snapped it shut, took a breath and tried again.

'I'm not sure I can go to college. My parents can't afford to send me. They say I need to get a job.'

She was talking to herself. His father had lost all interest. He was talking to Reuben's mother and ignoring her.

'Dad!' He patted the table in front of his father to no avail.

'Well. Been nice meeting you dear.' And with that his father strode out of the room, closely followed by his mother, moving as quickly as her jeans would allow.

Reuben also jumped up and stood behind Georgie. She felt even worse than she had at school if that was possible. Her head was heavy cement and try as she might she couldn't lift it to meet his gaze.

Before she knew it, he was behind her, rubbing bony shoulders and playing with bra straps.

From the hall his father barked loudly, 'We are just popping out to see Grandpa, back in an hour. Nice to meet you, Gail.' Then he whispered to Reuben's mother, 'It is Gail that one, isn't it?'

Her humiliation was complete. He stopped fiddling with her straps, pulled out her seat and swung her round to face him, crouching down till their eyes were level.

'I am not Gail. I'm Me.' She whispered.

Something deep in the pit of her very being twisted in agony. Her shrunken stomach was trying to turn itself inside out.

'We finished two weeks ago and he just keeps getting confused, forget it. Now where were we?'

She had never felt so ugly in her life. His beauty seared her senses while his intensity made her shrink with horror at her own repulsiveness. He seemed oblivious.

'I know what will make you feel better.'

He gently parted her hair and kissed both her eyelids in turn before cupping her cool fingers in his own, oh so beautiful, hands. She knew what was coming. A thawing of the ice-maiden and a fumbled lovemaking. Not forced but probably not what she had really wanted either.

Boombastic by Shaggy was on repeat. She heard it through twice.

*

Her father had given her a hard slap for being 10 minutes late to cook his tea when she got home. But unlike normal, the white, hot smarting had actually made her feel better, like scratching a healing wound.

He would give her a harder slap when she was four months late and fastening her school skirt with a cat's cradle of safety pins and ribbons to conceal her swollen belly.

'You're a fat cow and a failure.'

The words could have been tattooed on her forehead. *That's what everyone thinks of me.*

EIGHT

Now

Georgie's world was still a whirlwind when she went to see Jaz. It was her first comedy mentoring and gig after Edinburgh, in a run-down Newcastle pub's upstairs room. It was dingy, matching her mood.

'All OK with you?' He said.

'I'm doing fine. Thanks.'

'Let's crack on then. I'm not here to be a shrink but to be honest. You look like shit.'

'I'll work it into the act shall I?' Georgie managed a small laugh and Jaz smiled as well.

'Could do. But not sure it'll work. Come on. Put whatever is going on out of your head. And be brilliant. As I know you are.'

She flushed with pleasure. Praise a rare treat.

His sacred, leather notebook was placed on the wooden table, riddled with beer and slop.

Georgie put her own moleskin one opposite it. 'Checkmate.'

'Hah.' He smiled, then put on his concentrating face. His creamy, pale brown face was near her own as he leant in. Deep brown eyes were fixed on her own blue ones.

He seemed to be suddenly aware of her and jumped back in his seat, making her jump back into her own.

'Oh my!', he said.

'Sorry. That was my fault', said Georgie.

'No. No. It's me and lack of respect for personal space! Right.'

There was an awkward pause.

'We need to get cracking.'

He deliberately moved his chair back a couple of paces. 'What's been funny in the last week or so? Any more mix-ups in the ironing pile?'

'Ironing pile?'

Georgie's mood shifted again. Touchy. Then she felt cheesed off. *I'm not putting up with him being condescending like Lawrence, not today.*

'Actually I don't want to talk about house stuff like that today.' She spoke sharply. Which she never did normally. Always held in. Perfect wife. Perfect mother.   Perfect comedy student.

'I want to get how I'm ignored off my chest. Everyone takes me for granted. At home. At work. I have no time to myself. And I feel like a piece of rubbish. No matter how hard I try.'

Jaz jumped up.'Brilliant. That's what we need.   A bit of anger. Sass. Come on Georgie. Use the stage over there and spit it out!'

'This is really hard for me you know.'

'I do know it's awful you're ignored. I'm so sorry. But also, not sorry as it's great material.'

He took her hand and led her over to the tiny black stage in the corner and helped her up. She didn't want him to let go, not just because it felt exciting but because it stopped the fear.

'I can't speak from up here. It feels too high.'

'A foot. It's nothing.'

'Seriously, can't I do it from the floor?'

'Listen Georgie.' He stood in front of her, eye to eye, 'You're not going to fail.   Just start by shouting all those things you said make you …'

'Mad!' Georgie finished the sentence.

'Exactly. We also need to have a character to work against. You wanted to be a slightly goofy mother. But there actually could be a great bit of bite about things coming out of your mouth.'

'Sounds tricky. I don't have any character. I'm the typical middle-aged invisible mother. Don't forget my family put me up for this as I'm plain daft.'

She then realised that 'being normal me' wasn't going to be help her act be funny.

Jaz shook his head. 'No, no, no. We need you to create a comedy persona. Tell you what. Write down the things you hate. That'll build on what we've already done in Edinburgh.'

'Kids who stare.'

Georgie, if she was being honest didn't really like children, possibly because of her own childhood, but was never able to admit that.

'I really don't like the type that haunt you silently in supermarkets. It's like they deliberately pick on me and then follow me around the various aisles, standing at the end, like Damien in the Omen horror film.

'You can't win. If you smile they tug at their mother's coats and shout about the strange lady grinning at them and being 'scary'. And if you ignore them, they smile until both their mother and the check-out assistant realise you are ignoring a cute, small person and you are indeed a hard-faced bitch.'

Maybe I am a hard-faced bitch?

Jaz scribbled down some notes. 'Hmm. Interesting.

As she paused, fingers at the ready, she shuffled on her seat and gave herself a wedgie with her knickers.

'Thongs. I hate them.'

'Ok. Go on?'

'The tiny, scratchy knickers are like cheese slice wires ready to cut us women in half.'

Even the thought of the nylon, lurid coloured underwear made her skin itch. How anyone felt sexy in them she would never know. Her hate list grew.

She bit her pencil. 'My family make me furious sometimes. Her hand flew up to her mouth. 'No. No. I don't mean it. Sorry.'

'Don't apologise. I can imagine how hard it is. Yours are teenagers, aren't they?'

'Yes. Difficult age.'

She desperately didn't want to start to talk about them.

Every thought of Lily especially was giving her a huge lump in her throat.

Then Georgie blurted out a passing thought.

'Coffee café chain toilets!'

Jaz sat still, shut his eyes and waved his arm for her to continue.

'They faff on with your drink for ages putting grated chocolate on the top with a hint of vanilla, this and that. It's put in a recycled, compostable, energy-free disposable cup but the toilets are also usually sprinkled with 'grated chocolate' and it's vile.

'They have a smell of eau de wee, overlaid with cheap as chips, strip your skin hand wash. Topped off with a dose of as many germs as you can breathe air freshener and a pathetic poof of hand-drier.

Jaz scratched his chin. 'Hmm. Not bad but we need a bit more. Let's see what else is going to come out of your mouth about your charmed life in middle-class suburbia.'

'I'm not ready to talk about much of my home life.' She sat quietly for a moment. 'Although maybe I could talk about Mother's Day? Lawrence's World's Best Dad mug smashed and the letters spelt out Worst Husband instead. That was quite funny.'

'Hmm. Might work. Any more?'

Georgie suddenly remembered. 'Yes! There's another one about something my daughter said when we were at the cinema years ago.'

'Great. We'll work it in. Don't worry. You will want to talk about them quite a lot at some point. I'm sure.'

Georgie looked at him in disbelief. *He can't possibly think I'm going to talk about my family in front of strangers and make a joke about them. That's mad.*

*

The pub was packed when they were ready to move to the downstairs bar to try out the material at the open mic night. Whether the punters were there to hear comedy or just catch up with mates wasn't obvious.

Georgie felt her stomach do her stand-up heave. It was

horrific and made her want to dive into the toilet. She would have done if they hadn't been so awful.

Jaz put his hand in the small of her back to help guide her through the crowd. *I feel alien in this place with all the scruffy tables after eating in gorgeous restaurants for so long. But I don't belong in those places either.*

Her eyes scanned the room like she used to when she was 18, looking for someone who might buy her a cider in return for a sloppy kiss and a squeeze of her bum. Everyone looked like bikers and there were so many beards. Long straggly ones, short tufty ones, plaited and even beards neatly fastened into a ponytail.

Lawrence would have a fit if he could see her, cutting a swathe through the rough crowd. He thought the comedy training was just sitting about swapping ideas about runaway dogs, baking and PTAs. Her brain was racing and she was stressed knowing she had to be funny. Very soon. Funny.

As she pushed her way through the crowd, several people were given unconscious digs in their ribs from her elbows, out to attack.

The Stand-Up Star organisers had booked the rehearsal space and gig. Jaz said they were lucky to have somewhere that wasn't a complete hole. Georgie couldn't imagine any place worse than this.

He was on the edge of his seat when she left him to do her set. 'You need to nail this first one Georgie. Go get them. For both of us!' He smiled and winked.

Did he just wink?

Even standing at the side of the stage scared her to death. She stood rigid. Her eyes strained as she tried to see into the dimly-lit room beyond. Then the smell of too many unwashed men hit her. A blast from the past. And it was showtime.

She bounded on, blinking at the surprisingly fierce, wonky spotlight.

The landlord was doubling as an MC. It always surprised her that people (mainly men) thought they could do the job, confident they were hilarious despite stunned silence sometimes showing otherwise.

She began, 'Hello Ouseburn. You're looking very, well, Ouseburn to be honest. Which is on the edge of Byker/ Heaton vegan but within Mongolian throat-singing distance of the trendy part of the Quayside.'

Her introduction had been her set pieces about Mary Berry, Lawrence's mug and the coffee shop toilets.

Jaz and the Edinburgh course rules were glued to her brain. She repeated them like a mantra. *Make a local reference – tick. Make a remark about yourself comparing you to someone famous – tick. The final was coming. No time for messing about.*

Georgie joked 'I'm like Sarah Millican's little sister' and got a laugh.

Then she swallowed hard. Gave herself a moment to check out the expressions of the front row. Apart from a couple who were holding hands and entwining legs as best they could, despite the shape of the table, everyone was still listening.

Then a small group of young men began talking to each other and laughing at something on their phones. They ignored Georgie and the 'shhhh' hissed by the people behind them.

She recognised them as a type, taking in their expensive trainers, scruffy yet artfully-ripped jeans and designer t shirts. Only one of them, blonde, skinny, unlike the rugby-build of the others, seemed uncomfortable. But even he didn't shut up.

Her set was becoming harder and harder to remember but she tried her best to keep the rhythm right, speaking more loudly. She repeated her strongest material about Lily at the cinema.

'It is her own fault. When I first took her to the cinema to see Frozen, she embarrassed me by asking for cock porn, really loudly. So, I told her Disney didn't make that type of film! I really should have Let It Go!'

There was a small chuckle from the room apart from the group of men again who continued to talk amongst themselves so she crouched down at the front of the stage in front of them, speaking slowly and loudly, 'My. Daughter. Asked. For. Cock. Porn. Something you four would no doubt know about as you're all total dicks.'

They shut up and looked up at her for the first time.

'Look at the state of you. You're in a comedy club and it's you four that are the jokes. Rude. Didn't your mam tell you children should be seen and not heard?'

They looked at their feet so she continued.

'So did she tell you that?'

The blonde one muttered, 'No.'

'What do you all do?'

They mumbled something unintelligible.

'Students? Well, how typical, I bet it's in something totally useless like how to identify a left-handed screwdriver.'

The blonde one looked embarrassed and smiled sheepishly.

They sat in shocked silence. Georgie realised she had terrified them and changed tone. She had taken out her frustration about her family life out on these men.

'Bless you. Look I'm new to this so, let's both of us just enjoy the benefit of being famous for a minute.' She laughed nervously.

Her pre-gig nerves were nothing to this feeling. She knew she had to run away or take control. If she wanted to be a success there was only one way to go. At the top of her voice she delivered the rest of her set.

It shut everyone up but she felt as though she was dying inside. She put the mic on the stand. Left the stage to quiet applause. Determined not to cry. Jaz patted her arm and it made her feel better.

He said, 'Well done for sorting out those hecklers. Not easy. Not easy at all.'

Then she got a text from the competition producers asking for an update on how it had gone. It included a countdown to the number of weeks to the final. *Shit, only 12. Shit. Shit.*

The competition WhatsApp group pinged with updates. Clementine. *Died darlings!* Anna. *Holy shitting hell, that was terrifying!* Pat. *They liked me :)* Will. *They didn't understand my Cornish accent. Weird.* Matthew. *Gig is getting me laid!* Georgie texted *Stressful. Very. Very.*

By the time they left the pub was nearly empty. The bar staff said bye to them. There was Jaz's light touch on the base of her spine again. Even when his hand moved away, she still felt it.

NINE

The next morning Georgie was busy in the kitchen which she felt had its own pulse, matching her heart beat. Pans were bubbling with aromatic food. The sound system was pulsing with Planet Rock and the table was under fear of its life with her fierce chopping of any vegetable within grabbing distance.

Lily came in softly rather than her usual bounce.

'Mam?'

'Yes?'

'I know you are worried about me but I've made a decision.'

Georgie put the knife down, for the moment.

They sat down opposite each other and held hands across the table. Lily reached for her hand first. These details mattered to Georgie.

'Talk to me about how you are Lily.' *No-one ever stops to ask me about how I'm doing.* But she knew today was not that day.

'I've decided I can't keep the baby. I am too young. Dad's right. Anyway, it's just a butter bean and not a real person, not yet.'

At that moment Georgie wanted to howl with distress but that was not Lawrence's wife's way. Stiff upper lip at all times. Instead, she plucked her stand-up courage, ignored her husband's wishes and calmly worked through how to stop her daughter having an abortion.

'Is that what you really want? Talk to me honestly. Your father isn't here now.'

'But Dad said that…'

'I know you'll be scared. Vulnerable. But with our support you'll manage.'

Lily twisted her hair round her fingers. Thinking. Worried.

'I'm doing what you call my flip flopping Mam. Sorry.'

'No need to say sorry. For anything. Shit happens. Trust me. I know.' Georgie felt so sad she decided to be quiet in case she cried.

More hair twisting from Lily. After a minute she sounded firmer. 'Jasper's happy, obviously. And going to help. But my mind's going mad with questions. How will I go to uni with a baby?'

'We'll sort it out. You can live at home. We'll get a nanny. Where there's money, your Dad always says, there's a way.'

'My boobs hurt. Already. Is that normal?'

'Yes. Don't worry. It's nature getting you ready for….'

'OMG. Literally. Don't say another word. Mam. Seriously. I can't even think about THAT. '

'It's all a long way off, Lily. The most important thing is not to worry. It's a change but a lovely one.' *Unless you've no-one to look out for you or your baby.*

'I always thought it was people who were a bit thick or slept around who got pregnant when they were young. You know, like that Erica at school. She was always a real sad case.'

Georgie related to Erica but kept herself focused on Lily.

'Sometimes babies come when they are least expected so we're not to judge anyone. People won't really judge you either. And if they do say anything they'll have me to answer to!'

Lily hugged Georgie. 'Thanks for being you Mam. Always a fighter for me.'

Then Lily shut up and looked at Georgie with shock. It was if she realised for the first time her mother had also had a life-changing time.

'Sorry. How was your gig.'

'I was hilarious!'

'Really?'

'No. I was terrible. Well, not all bad.'

'That's good for such early days, isn't it? I thought you'd struggle at first.'

'Don't sound so surprised. You're one of the culprits that put me up to it.'

'Yes, but we all expected you to come home from Edinburgh and pack it in.'

'Oh, that's not happening.' Georgie surprised herself at her resolve.

*

Lily was 17 while Georgie had only been 16 when she got pregnant but it was still too young and devastating. Throwing yourself off a building type of devastating.

Georgie's head was somersaulting through space so she grabbed hold of the kitchen bench. Lawrence and her were about to have The Talk about it all. It has been put off for 24 hours but needed to be done.

He was pacing.

'We can't let her have the baby Georgie. She could be ill with all of the stress of a pregnancy at her age. Also, there's so much at stake. University places. Grad schemes. A future without Jasper. We hope.'

'Stop it Lawrence. I'm overwhelmed with the news as well but she must decide herself whether or not she wants to have this baby. It's horrifying for me to even think of her terminating it. But it's not for us to say that.'

Georgie's head was like a pressure cooker about to explode.

'Let's just have a sensible talk here Georgie. Lily will recover from the situation being resolved quickly. She'll be in and out in a few hours and all will be well. She'll not get into Oxbridge if she has a baby in tow, will she?'

The normally submissive and perfect wife stood straight. Without hesitation, a rarity in their marriage, Georgie spoke eloquently and with a strong conviction of her own, rather than one that was foisted upon her.

A late summer sun was sliding down the back of the garden. As conversely Georgie's strength was rising up.

'She's having this baby and keeping it if that's what she wants. Make no mistake Lawrence. I'm going to be here to support her at every step along the way.

'And don't forget we had our own similar situation all those years ago. And we wouldn't be without Nat. It'll be hard but I'm serious. I couldn't bear for this baby to either not come into this world or be brought up by other people.

'Don't fight me on this Lawrence.'

He looked at her for a moment and she held her breath, wondering what was going to come next. But then he held her hand.

'You're right. I'm sorry. Sometimes I can't help but want our children to have a life laid out in straight lines. I know your path was anything but simple and I would have loved to help you avoid those painful times.'

She squeezed his hand and looked her husband squarely in the face, knowing he didn't know the half of her hard path. Seeing herself differently, and her past coming back to the front of her thoughts, had given her strength.

TEN

Comedy was a perfect way to take Georgie's mind off Lily's pregnancy. She couldn't get enough of it. Jaz was coming round to continue her tuition and when the doorbell rang it was like plugging her into an electric socket.

Even through the glass hall door Jaz was striking. Despite being slight in build, he held himself tall. He was neat, wearing all dark green and clutching a battered leather satchel which had a sheaf of paper poking out.

They both stood still unsure if they should shake hands or hug, so they did neither. Georgie just waved and pointed down the hall.

'Hi. How are you?' He spoke first.

'Nervous but pleased to see you.' She smiled, small and tight.

'Let's go to the kitchen. I'll put the kettle on.'

As they drank their coffee Jaz went over the plan for the next gig and showed her Sarah Millican's videos. Every now and then he would stop it and point out different styles of humour and techniques.

'Here. See.' He paused the clip. 'She asks the audience questions, then repeats funny answers people have given her. That's a great idea. You're getting other people to give you set ups for a gag.'

'What types of questions would you use if you did that?' Georgie stared at him blankly.

At that moment Lawrence walked in even though he had promised to keep out of the way. Then, as her father had broken ranks, Lily followed.

'Hello.' Lawrence beamed, a bit too brightly. 'I'm Lawrence, Master of the House.' He punched Jaz's arm in jest then went to shake his hand.

Jaz looked at it, paused briefly, then smiled back, while accepting the handshake. 'That's not what I've heard Sir!'

Lily also shook his hand. 'Lily. Mistress of the house.'

Jaz smiled again. 'Now, that I have heard.'

All four laughed politely as Lawrence put the kettle on. 'More coffee anyone? Please continue your little talk, don't let us keep you. We both want Georgie to be an ENORMOUS success don't we Lily?'

Lily grinned, 'Yes, Mam's hilarious.'

Georgie stared at the floor.

'That's what I think as well.' Jaz then slapped the table, 'Let's get to work.'

Lawrence seemed reluctant to leave his wife alone with Jaz but Lily kindly bustled him out. Georgie was relieved to see them go, more than she felt was appropriate, and for a very confusing set of reasons.

Jaz read and scratched through half of her first set notes.

'Not. Funny. Enough. Yet. The yet is very important. It's what give us our staying power.'

Georgie sighed. 'If I'd known it was this hard to be funny and not invisible, I would have just streaked across St James Park.'

Jaz laughed. 'Right, what's the most extreme part of your life and can it be funny?'

Georgie just sat and stared at him. He couldn't know about Lily. Not yet. She wanted to talk about safe, mundane things.

The first thing that came into her head was her relationships with different, terrible men before she met Lawrence.

She suggested 'Could we do a ratings joke about my exes maybe?'

Jaz bit his thumb nail, 'Perhaps. How could that be developed?

Georgie sat still, thinking, then it came to her. 'How about doing it as a spoof Tripadvisor review?'

'Perfect.' He gave her a high five. And her stomach did a flip.

She went through a few past boyfriends and listed their faults and attributes. Jaz scribbled furiously. Afterwards they worked together, heads almost touching, then when they realised, quickly moved apart, pulling out the stories with the most potential.

They looked at the real Tripadvisor reviews and matched them with the old flames or as Georgie thought of them, the dregs of the earth. Jaz tweaked and added, taking in Georgie's comments.

'I think we've got a good, funny minute there G.' Jaz was pleased with her and she felt an unusual feeling of pride. She read out their script, then a second time, where he suggested pauses, different tones of voice for dramatic effect.

It worked. She could see honing it in front of a live audience where ad libs and facial expressions for emphasis could come into play giving it even more impact.

Laughing she said, 'I don't know what Big Pete from Bensham is going to think about being only 1 point for cleanliness and no points for customer satisfaction. Hope he never hears about this!'

'He'll assume he's a 10 and you're talking about someone else so I wouldn't worry.'

'They're all like that to be fair!'

'Now. What else can we talk about?' Jaz asked.

'I think I can maybe talk a bit about my family with just one story.' She bit her lip.

'Excellent. Go on.'

'When my mother-in-law died, we tried to scatter her ashes and it didn't go to plan. We put the box in the sea but it kept getting swept back in land. We ended up asking a fisherman to scoop up the container out to shake it them out instead. But they all got caught by the wind and covered us in her grim remains from head to foot.'

'I like it. What could the punchline be?'

'It was like she was letting us know we were never going to get rid of her easily! The granny that wouldn't die?'

'Hmm. That could work.'

Georgie went through the story a second time and Jaz made notes again. He helped her add more punchlines and emphasis to draw out the dark humour.

'Two minutes under our belt. That's OK, right there. Well done. Only another three minutes of material to go to add to your Edinburgh notes that are strong enough.'

'Come on. Now just go for a big old rant again. Anything. Remember. Feel the fury. It's comedy gold! And maybe we can also talk about something you really love?'

She rolled her shoulders to ease comedy tension out of them. It was starting to dawn on her how stressful this was going to be. The writing was bad enough. How to make it work on stage though?

'Chocolate. I really love chocolate.'

'Right. What would be funny about that?'

Georgie chewed on her pen. Then slapped her hand on the table.

'I've got it. A piece on different chocolate bar names?'

Jaz shut his eyes and waved his hand for her continue with a huge smile on his face. 'This could be interesting.'

'Right. How about…. adding a bit as part of the weight loss club section?

'Go on.'

'There was a major incident the other week. Let's call her 'Marjorie' had to confess why she'd put on two pounds. Turns out she ate some chocolates. Everyone was sympathetic when she explained how much stress she had been under. She just couldn't stop. One sweet led to another and another. Then, the killer question. 'How big was the bag Marjorie?' A whole selection box. The whole room turned on her. Bad Marjorie!

'Then to be honest we all had a Snicker about it. I could throw one of the bars into the crowd.

'But she still tried to Fudge the issue.

'She had been 'Lion' to us all. 'Revelling' in her greed. Because I tell you dieting is no 'Picnic'. She was just not giving a 'Daim' about slimming. So, we all decided to take a 'Time Out'. She must be living on another planet, probably 'Mars'!'

'Hmm I'm not sure about that. If you throw those bars into the crowd we could get sued for injuries. Imagine death by chocolate!'

'There are worse things.'

They both grinned at each other.

'I'm sure.' His phone pinged. 'Right. We've now got your next gig. Thursday, 25th, we've got two weeks but you'll be fine. Don't worry.' Jaz smiled as he had done for most of the two hours, which had flown. Georgie's heart beat a little faster. She must get hold of these nerves.

'Two weeks. This is mad.' Lily, Nat and Lawrence had come in and were standing beside her, not realising they could well end up being part of her set. They were enthusiasm personified, for now.

ELEVEN

The next evening Georgie was drinking wine, making supper when a noughties pop song by Britney came on. It jumped her back in time to when she had her fortune told.

She had been at a fair with three friends who had clutched their precious pocket money tightly, wondering how to spend it. They were all slightly bewildered by the lights pulsing manically and the frenetic music which blasted so loudly it merged into the next ride's different mad beat. They had eyes on stalks and mouths like gargoyles. This was both heaven and hell.

The gypsy's caravan was a tiny oasis amongst a vivid brash landscape of machinery and kinetics. Georgie carefully put her right plimsoll on the first rickety step. The delicate structure quivered even under her skinny 12 year old frame.

'Go on' her friends hissed. 'Knock on the door.'

A massive nervous lump was stuck in her throat. As her left foot was about to plant itself with more authority than she felt, the caravan door swung wide open nearly knocking her over backwards, revealing Gypsy Rose Marie herself.

Georgie still remembered the shock at seeing her. She wasn't the witch from Hansel and Gretel about to feed her gingerbread. This fortune-teller was more like one of her friend's aunties who sang in the local social clubs at a weekend. She was camouflaged in top to toe leopard print. Hair black as a mud pit. Lips red as fresh blood. Smile as broad and friendly as her form teacher Mrs Lyle, with the added touch of an Embassy Regal cigarette dangling out of the corner.

A low rasp from the pit of the Gypsy's stomach warned her some words were coming. Across a cigarette induced low timbre she said, 'Get yourself in and ...' delicately drumming her beautifully painted long plum finger nails on the lace tablecloth, '...put your silver down here.'

The cigarette was plucked from her lips then dramatically, and yet carelessly, thrown out of the door. Georgie gazed in wonder at all the lace frills and what her nan had called 'nicknacks'. They smelt of strawberries and sugar. There was not a spare inch in the tiny room which was not a mass of white froth and nylon.

She had wondered if it was a good idea to be the guinea pig but she was here now. Her future was about to be laid bare. A million questions rushed through her head. Did anyone fancy her? Would Ronan Keating notice her through the TV if she got dressed really smartly and put on her eyeliner? Would she be a pop star?

'Give me your hand sweetheart.' Gypsy Rose Marie's own hand was very hot and moist. Georgie didn't like it much but tried to concentrate, not wanting to spoil the moment.

'Oooh. This is interesting. I see a very handsome man in your future. He is tall and thin, like a Victorian gentleman. I also see babies.'

'I don't know if I want babies.'

'Tough luck love. They often come to people who are just meant to have them whether they like it or not. And there's three of them.'

'Three babies! But am I going to be rich and famous?'

'Not sure but you are going to be outspoken. Let me see. Oooh. I can see money. Lots of money. Hmmm.'

Georgie didn't like 'Hmmm.' 'What can you see now?'

'I think you need to be careful who your friends are. That's all I'll say. Mind your step on the way out.'

*

The kitchen clock beeped and brought Georgie back into the room. It was Aga-warm and smelt of her special Moroccan couscous in the oven. She hugged her knees to her chest, finished the glass of wine, relished the comfort of her sweat pants and leant back in the armchair. The radio was still playing in the background and she hardly noticed it until a Bruno Mars pop song started about how amazing the singer's girlfriend was.

She turned the lyrics over in her head and thought of the two men who had declared her amazing. Love of their lives. Staring out at the garden she caught a reflection of herself in the long French windows. Even in this translucent glass she could see the dark circles under her eyes and the start of a heavy jaw and even heavier boob lines. They lay like envelopes. *Not amazing at all* she thought and before she knew it, tears filled her eyes. This was slow sadness from a crappy pop song.

The front door cracked shut like a firework making her jump out of her skin. She grabbed kitchen roll to blow her nose an important second before Lily strode in, switching off the radio as she passed it.

'Not Bruno Bloody Mars! Mother. Mrs Chancellor. Really? Get some chuffing taste.'

Georgie could tell that Lily was momentarily non-plussed by her lack of quick funny reply but continued.

'Get a life Mam. And a decent radio station. You like Motorhead. Talked Dad into going well out of his comfort zone and taking us all to see Iron Maiden. Find Planet Rock for God's sake!'

Lily slammed her massive leather satchel on the table missing Georgie's nose by a whisker.

She hated either of her children to see her anything other than in complete control of her emotions. It was source of great pride to her that she never cracked, even when she was battle-worn after work or stressed by the limiting grind of domestic duties. She was the perfect mother, giving out warmth usually when it wasn't genuine.

Georgie suddenly caught her breath. Lily was a mirror-image of herself at that age. Her pale eyes and alabaster skin only broken up by two tiny red dots high on her cheeks and a flash of rose lipstick.

Lily sat down on the seat beside her with a big sigh and

nervously tucked a stray piece of her ash white hair behind her ear as Georgie unconsciously did the same.

'I need you Mam. This baby thing…'

'I'm here for you. Lily. Promise. We'll talk it over tonight.'

*

Georgie, Lawrence, Lily and Jasper sat in the lounge, sinking into the huge comfortable armchairs but each one felt ill at ease. Lawrence took charge.

'I thought we needed to have a proper talk about this pregnancy situation. Now. Lily. Jasper. Have you really thought about the….'

'Yes Dad.' Lily was first. 'Whatever you're going to ask me. 'We've talked about it all day and all night since we got the test result. Haven't we?'

Jasper put his arm around her shoulder protectively. '110 per cent Mr C.'

'It's 100.' Lawrence corrected.

'Sorry?'

'You can't have over 100 per cent. It is. Not. A. Thing.'

'For God's sake Dad,' said Lily. 'Let's just talk about it and not stress about every single word.'

Lawrence stood up. 'What do your Mam and Dad think Jasper? Are they in favour of you being a father? At such a young age?' As he said it, he looked at Georgie.

Jasper put his arm around Lily's shoulder and she snuggled into his huge jumper.

'They're cool. Anything that keeps old Jasper out of trouble is fine with them. The band might have to take a break but they're all for that! Dad's happy to pay for everything as well. What evs. Cot. Other stuff.'

'Cool? Cool?' Lawrence spluttered.

Georgie interrupted him pragmatically. 'You must tell your parents thank you. That's very kind.'

Then Lily stood up. 'I think that's enough chat don't you Jasps. We're keeping this baby. There's only you wondering if it's right for us, Dad. So, we both think you just need to buckle up.'

Georgie knew she needed to stop Lawrence from exploding, so quickly jumped in. 'That's not quite how I'd put it but I get you. Why don't you make Jasper a tea. Dad and I can talk over the details, like who's going to tell the school etc.'

'Fair dos,' said Lily.

'Laters,' added Jasper. And with that the happy couple wandered out to the kitchen, holding hands.

As soon as they left Lawrence jumped up and stomped up and down the room ranting.

'Laters. Bloody hell. What is he? Ten?'

'Stop it. Please Lawrence. What's done is done...'

'Well, not necessarily...'

Georgie cut him off. 'Yes, we're not going down that road. Lily wants to keep this baby and so does Jasper.'

'So that's the end of it is it?'

'Yes. Please just accept that it is.' She went over to her husband and rubbed his arm in sympathy. 'We will all get through this. I know there are worse things in life.'

'Well, it's the worst thing to happen in mine.' And with that he went to leave the room. 'I'm going to accept this but I'm not happy about it. At all.'

Once he closed the door behind him Georgie let out a sigh of relief and gave herself a hug. She couldn't calm down that night. Without thinking she walked past her bedroom and into the small office at the back of the house, overlooking the garden.

She felt a strong sense of fight or flight in the top part of her chest, pulling her in two different directions. Then a small part of the lifelong sadness began to fade.

Georgie thought and wrote. She wrote reams of material. Part of her had never felt so miserable yet she was writing about the funniest things in her life. From Nat's obsession with food and sex but not both together, or so he said, to observations on the hot TV soap storylines.

When she had finished, she felt a rare sense of peace. Satisfaction and hope combined in a potent mix. It was now one o' clock in the morning. The house slept and she would sleep now too.

As she walked past Lily's bedroom, a mix of pink baby girl fluff and gothic independent woman, she did her usual quiet entrance. Holding her breath tight as if her life depended on it, Georgie crept up to Lily's peaceful body and knelt beside her bed. She picked up her hand carefully, just as she had done every night when her daughter was a tiny girl.

Georgie shut her eyes tight. She prayed she could learn to love her daughter properly. Love her as she had done for a fleeting second when she was born and their fingers had locked tightly in the delivery room. Flesh forged in hope. The two of them interlocked stars in a mad, black galaxy.

Her eyes felt wet as she got up and carefully put Lily's hand back on the bedclothes. She watched the teenager settle into a deeper sleep and a contented smile rest on her face.

I'm sure she senses I am here, but she doesn't know everything and never will.

It didn't cross Georgie's mind that if Lily knew her past, she might have understood her and her occasional coldness so much better.

TWELVE

For the next practise gig Georgie drove herself to the Dog and Duck beachside pub on the Roker Promenade in Sunderland. The seagulls were dancing under the luminous street lights. No doubt they'd eaten their weight in discarded chips.

Jaz was there already. He hurried over to meet her, then put his arm around her shoulders. Very quietly reassuring her it was going to be all OK, they walked to the comics' reserved table. The crowd was quiet and sparse. Georgie felt it was a shame after all their work, but at the same time, she was relieved.

And pleased when she heard she was in the middle, first section, a good slot. Once on stage the crowd's faces were fixed, rictus grins, willing her to be funny so they could have a good night.

She started the set with the carefully prepared material and then began on newer jokes that had come from her session with Jaz. She was as proud of them as if they were her babies. As she'd been taught by her mentor, she forced her voice to be calm, and authoritative rather than stressed and squeaky. After a few seconds she realised the confidence trick had worked. She had fooled herself into thinking *I can pull this off.*

There were a couple of older women in and she deliberately talked to them the most while remembering to also include the other audience members as well. Jaz's advice again. What a lifeline. *There's no way I could pull this off without his support.*

She did her jokes about her saggy bottom and long boobs.

The older one of the women joined in laughing and shouted. 'And don't forget N for nipples!'

Georgie jumped on the interruption. 'Exactly, thank you. Anyone think of any others?'

The women nudged each other and her friend said, I've been told mine are bit like fried eggs.'

'Oh no that's awful. Isn't it everyone? Well, you don't look like you've had your chips to go with them, so everything's fine!' The room all muttered agreement and gave a small chuckle.

Georgie had found her stride so she decided to do her Tripadvisor gags on old boyfriends.

It got a low but positive rumble around the room. She cracked on.

'As you can see, I'm a woman in her 40s and a real help with heating bills. In the winter the family can just heat themselves by being near me. In fact, you could cook toast on my face. The peri-menopause is just a gift that keeps on giving.'

She could see a couple of male students in the front row looking at each other, neither having any idea what she was talking about.

'It's called the men – oh – pause because when women are going through it, men really need to pause, stop and think about what they're saying to us, or we could kill you.

Someone said, 'That's a joke?' and another punter joined in, 'Yes, you're literally, fucking joking!'

She had to learn how to handle this. Gathering her spirit and a chunk of courage in a split second she said,' I know that's a fucking joke. I was just checking you were awake.'

'Hah hah hah.' Came from the very back of the room and that was the end of it. She got a small clap and was then off the stage.

Georgie wanted to leave straight away after her set, with the embarrassment of not being that funny but Jaz insisted she stayed to see the other comedians. She crossed her arms and smiled but inside she was disappointed to have not nailed it.

The other comics gave some tips and tried to persuade her to talk about more relatable things like TV celebrities.

Dave, the MC for the night said, 'I'm not sure people come to gigs to hear about that type of women's stuff. It's a bit niche. Mind, that's only my view.'

'I'm doing my set on what matters to me.' Georgie said quietly.

'Fair enough. We've all got to talk about the important stuff to us. I get it. And don't mind my advice. Hat's off for trying and all that.' He then gave her a patronising rub on the arm.

Rather than put her off, this dismissal of what was a priority to her, made her more sure her material was right. Even if doing a set successfully was so hard.

'Early days Babe. Early days', said Jaz kindly, realising what she was thinking.

THIRTEEN

The two weeks to Georgie's next gig passed by far too quickly.

The Grey Parrot was near the industrial relics of Newcastle's Quayside and stunk of beer slop, sweaty punters and too much aftershave.

All these smells were particularly vivid for Georgie as the room was pitch black and unfortunately silent, for a stand-up comedy night. *What am I doing here? My daughter is pregnant. And still at school. I've got 101 things to do, for everyone but myself. I don't have time for this. But. I'm starting to enjoy it and feel happy here.*

Jaz patted her hand and got her to go through the stand-up rules.

'What's your local reference?'

'I don't understand the famous song The Fog on the Tyne is all mine all mine. Why on earth would you want the fog? It's thick, grey and miserable. Bit like this man in the front by the look of him!'

'Good. Now, who are you comparing yourself to?'

'Sarah Millican's sister again?'

'Yes. Let's keep that.'

Georgie only realised Jaz's hand was resting on hers as he gave it an encouraging squeeze.

'You're going to be fine.'

'I hope so.'

Patrick from Ireland, who had the most experience, opened the gig. He talked about how his ancestors were more intelligent than Geordies.

'Our family had the sense to get further away from Southerners than you lot. Those posh people from down south can't get across the Irish sea that easily so they just visit here in Newcastle and the Lake District then go back home.

'Taking their patronising attitudes in their Fortnum and Masons bags with them.'

The crowd didn't like his tone and the front row crossed their arms. Mouths tight shut.

'Not funny. Prick.' shouted a heckler.

Patrick didn't last long and looked relieved to hand over the microphone to the MC.

Georgie's throat did its quick-drying-cement routine. *Come on.* She mentally urged it to work again so sound could come out and save her life. *I'm going to be as bad as Patrick.*

To her right, a glass was banged on a table with a loud mutter from a couple of metal-heads.

'It's one of them crap women comedians…'

The host and MC, Keith, who was hosting the night introduced her kindly and didn't say she hadn't done many gigs which was the kiss of death. A small but polite amount of clapping started from around the room, echoing against the concrete floor and brick walls.

Georgie tucked her hair behind her ears. Then her legs developed a life of their own and propelled her towards the stage, a hostile no-woman's land and the fierce spotlight.

Keith gave her a high five as he swept past. His fingers were moist. She wanted to pull him towards her, have a brief hug, anything to stop the sheer blind terror.

A quick check of her top lip for sweat. Clear.

She put her glass of water and notes on a table then grabbed the microphone, too high up as usual, with confidence that was a lie.

Repeating each set time after time was the logic. She'd been told that, time and time again, ironically. But she hated repeating part of the first gig as it felt stilted. The waiting for the laugh at a certain point, then sometimes not getting one. The horrible, lengthy pause of emptiness where people knew they should have laughed but didn't.

Georgie sucked in her stomach and felt the dread of going blank. Then off she went as Jaz had taught her. Act confident even when you don't feel it. The crowd senses fear like Romans and gladiators.

Georgie began her faked bravado. 'Hello Newcastle. I'm like Sarah Millican's sister.' It got a few laughs. Then she moved on 'Have we any students in tonight? Actually, it's a rhetorical question. I might not be able to see you but I know you are there as I smell a faint amount of weed mixed with unwashed clothes full of hormones.'

A low mumble of 'Yeah right' was the room's only reply.
I need to up my game here. Be louder Georgie. Come on.

The student gag got a few chuckles from the crowd, not many, but enough to keep her nerve.

'As you can see, I'm older than most of you. When you're a woman in her 40s your shape changes but I can't stand these Southern words for everything. Muffin top. Really? We need good Geordie words. I like to call them my stottie sides. Only wish I could cut them off. Maybe eat them with a bit of middle-aged spread.'

Her five minutes, carefully scripted, had gone in a curious mixture of great speed and mind-numbing slowness.

The MC bounded back on stage with two strides. This time the hand gave her a sharp tug off the stage. She had her time.

'Let's give it up for Georgie everyone.' And the crowd did.

Her legs buckled when she reached the table set aside for comics. Jaz, smiled and nodded his head. That was the confirmation she needed. The gig was ok.

She felt relieved and satisfied.

'Good job up there girl. I'm pretty proud of you.'

Jaz gave her a high five. And she became warm from the tips of her toes. Patrick also gave her a couple of mock punches in celebration.

'Canny craic up there Mrs C.'

Georgie smiled without showing teeth. A relieved grimace.

Patrick had been arrogant at the start of the night but seemed to have mellowed since his material bombed. He had done paid gigs. Only there to try out new material, or so he said. Sitting back in his chair, sipping his Guinness thoughtfully, he told her, 'You ...', he leaned forward for effect and put the tips of his fingers together. '...might be onto something there.'

Jaz nodded, 'Not many female comics your age on the circuit.'

Patrick added, '... and even fewer funny ones. How was it for you?'

'Terrifying. As ever. But cool. I got rid of everyone at home. No-one can ask you to make their tea or for money for clothes out there. I wasn't just a mam or a wife. Hurray. Definitely ready for the next one. Do you think I'm a bit old for stand-up?'

Patrick grinned, 'Nah. You're not even middle-aged yet so don't let anyone make you feel ancient. You're only a few years older than most comedians around. It's nowt!'

The comedians waited until the headline act, a 24 year-old call centre worker who had tales of debt and failed relationships coupled with a lactose intolerance, had finished.

Georgie's fellow Stand-Up Stars were also working hard. The WhatsApp messages said: Clementine. *Died again but got a few laughs.* Anna. *Great tips from other comics. Not sharing them!* Pat. *One-liners going down a storm.* Will. *Not sure I can keep on doing this.* Matthew. *I was brilliant as usual.* So, Georgie added. *Not the best. But not the worst.*

Walking out with the wannabe comedy stars, she felt her skin prickle. The Quayside air was cold. She felt like she was breathing metal fragments mixed with the oxygen.

Georgie leant against the railings beside the river which stopped people like her throwing themselves in. Her home life could fall apart due to this so why did she feel happy? Her comfort zone had been stretched and she had survived. It galvanised her but at the same time made her guts tighten.

And there was the pull of wanting to be a perfect

mother for Lily in particular. She surprised herself by how much she wanted to win, yet home was unrelenting. Everyone needed her. Didn't they?

Whenever she was home Georgie was at everyone's beck and call. After a comedy gig, it was like she was invisible when she got back. No-one even raised their head.

Maybe I'm not as indispensable as I thought I was. Isn't that a relief! But what's the point of me if I'm not the perfect mother and wife?

*

The next comedy mentoring was in a café's back room in the seaside town of Whitley Bay. Jaz was waiting patiently near the window nursing a cappuccino.

'Ok there?'

He smiled. And it unexpectedly lit up her world.

'I'm good thanks.'

Her stomach flipped with comedy nerves and what she now thought of as 'Jaz nerves' at a similar rate.

Bright sunlight poured through the one high window highlighting his profile and catching the tips of his dark eyelashes and perfect skin.

I wonder what he's thinking about? A girlfriend?

She was embarrassed to be caught looking at him and hoped he couldn't read her mind.

He said, 'Penny for them, or at least a cigarette?'

Jaz got up and walked towards her with his Barack Obama ease.

'Don't smoke. No sins. Sorry.'

He smiled. 'Hmm that could work in part of a set. No sins. Let's have a play around with it. Anything else in your notebook G?'

No-one else ever called her G. It felt odd, intimate and exciting in equal measures. He took her notebook from her hands without asking.

'Hey Jaz. There might be stuff I've to censor in that.'

'Well, I doubt it. So far all we've had really, to be honest, is Mrs Perfect Wife, Tolerant, Slave Mother and a fair portion of Mrs Dull!'

'Dull!'

Georgie felt a huff coming, something she hadn't had in years.

'Bloody dull.' She was cross and counted to 10.

'Yes. Don't worry it's fixable. I'm not here to help you bore people to death remember.' He smiled to soften the words' impact.

'Bore people?'

'You talked a bit about yourself in those first gigs but we need to up your game. More animated. Act confident. It's coming. But you can be better. Definitely got it in you.'

'I feel rubbish.'

'Well don't. You can do this. As we said in Edinburgh. Feel a fury for something other than being frustrated at someone not putting finishing rinse in your dishwasher.'

He handed back her notepad.

'God.' *I can feel tears coming, that's ridiculous. Maybe this is all stupid and I just need to pack it in.*

'God's not going to help you but I am. And. Don't even think of packing this in. You've got so much potential. You're unique out there.'

More than you're ever likely to know.

'And, my favourite female comic out of everyone I've worked with.'

The café had emptied so she felt free to stand-up with notebook in hand like an American evangelist about to address the crowd. This was her chance to be her own person. Not Lawrence's wife or Nat and Lily's mam.

Her world was all the piles of ironing, neatly folded, a fridge with vitamin-rich vegetables, low carb, high protein meals. The list of what she managed on behalf of everyone was endless, exhausting and grim.

There was also Lily's baby coming. More work. And more memories to keep under control.

But this perfection didn't mean what it once had to her.

Jaz took hold of her hand.

'Chaos. Cause chaos by telling the truth. I dare you.'

'Create uproar in my home life just for good comedy set material?'

'There's no just about it. We're in this Stand-Up Star competition to win it.   My career and yours are linked now. We're not missing a trick for anyone's feelings. Come and see me do a set tomorrow night in Newcastle. I think it'll be useful.'

He let go of her hand even though her fear meant she craved that anchor.

And so it was that an hour later Georgie Chancellor strode out of that café with some self-confidence and a bit of mischief for the first time in her life.

FOURTEEN

Twenty four hours later once dinner was done and dusted Georgie's coat was on and she swung her handbag over her shoulder.

'Where are you going, darling?' Lawrence stretched his arm out to catch her fingertips. Georgie then usually kissed his cheek. But tonight she was distracted. Jaz's gig was at the front of her brain. Learn from the master. Every chance to be better, grasped.

As she left the kitchen to get her shoes Lawrence was perplexed.

'Georgie. What's up? It's the National Theatre streaming live. I've a crisp Sauvignon chilling.'

'Shit.' *I never swear in the house.*

'Mam? Where are you off to?' Lily and Lawrence were now following her down the hallway.

'I'm seeing Jaz perform as part of a comedy night in Newcastle. I need to watch it to learn more.'

'But you saw him yesterday.'

'That was a development session.'

Lawrence was deadly serious when he spoke.

'We all encouraged you to do this funny stuff but it seems to have gone over into something more, what's the word? Extreme. You are definitely not yourself. Quite. Assertive.'

Lily gasped. 'Yes. That's it. Extreme. AND assertive.'

'We need you here, to be honest. Your support for Lily is going to be very important indeed.' He went over and hugged Georgie, kissing her cheek.

When he let her go, rather than the normal relaxation she felt from his warmth, Georgie swayed from foot to foot. Her body repeating the to-ing and fro-ing of her brain. Usually, she would have put her bag down and said, 'You're right' but the thought of missing seeing Jaz, the headline act, was important. *For my comedy,* she prompted herself.

She felt a thirst to learn that she had never had in her life. And now she knew why she'd sprung going out on them all.

'You all put me into this competition so don't complain about me taking it seriously.'

'But it's just something daft Georgina. You talking about dirty laundry and yoga classes on stage. Isn't it?'

Little did he know there was going to be real dirty laundry aired in the future.

*

Jaz sat back in his chair in their pub rehearsal space the following day and she enjoyed this switch of holding the power for a change.

'Well, what did you think? And more importantly what did you learn. If anything? I'm not that cocky!'

'I loved the part about all your different family members marrying into different cultures. That was funny. Especially the one living in Italy, insisting on making curried pizza to stop himself feeling homesick!'

'Oh. That's Aziz. It's become popular apparently… or so he says.'

'I thought the bit about the racism you've experienced at school was pretty hard hitting. Sounded a tough time.'

'Not the best. But it gave me the skills I use now. You hear comics often beat bullies through using humour. Worked for me.'

'I just can't imagine you being vulnerable. You seem to have your life totally together.'

'All an act. Well. It used to be. I'm pretty sorted now. Still get the odd P word thrown about. I've been seen as the underclass quite a bit of my life.'

I can relate to that.

'But enough about me! It's your turn.'

Jaz was brutal. But right. His comic timing and experience were like gold to Georgie. She ran through her original set. First minute. The set up. She needed to draw the crowd in to her story as she'd been told and use the local paper to pick up snippets to weave in. Then she launched into perceptions of herself.

'I'm a bit like a Real Housewife of Newcastle. Straightened hair, false eye lashes, whitened teeth.'

Jaz stopped her. 'But you're not, are you? Tell me who you really are, deep down and let's work on that.'

Georgie wanted to present herself as her family knew her, consolidate the perfect wife image. Something latent, however, nagged at her brain. *Is this the real me? Could I be a stand-up mam with a dark heart maybe?*

Meanwhile Jaz kept asking her questions.

'Do you like irony?'

'I've no idea what that really means?'

'Well, it's like turkeys voting for Christmas.

'Hmm, that's quite funny.'

'Thanks. Damned by faint praise!'

'That's irony!'

'OK. What about some anecdotes? I think we should include funny things that have happened. Maybe to do with the kids. Are you ready to do that now?' Jaz suggested.

They worked through more tales of small family dramas including details not usually shared. Lawrence snoring. Nat's breaking wind. Lily's dramas but not her pregnancy. Yet.

Then Georgie began speaking the truth about family arguments. This made her think of her Mother's Day disappointments. She told Jaz about her awful day but how she ended up enjoying it. It made her feel better.

'It could be made into a funny two minutes.'

'I might not be able to say this out loud so I'll just write it. See how I feel afterwards. Is that cowardly?'

Jaz hovered near her shoulder, making her feel both reassured and unsettled.

'Yes! I want the truth Georgie. No chickening out. Also keep it short and punchy.'

'Short and punchy.'

'Exactly! Cut. Cut and cut again. If you slow down the action the pace goes to cock.'

'… to cock?!'

'Yes! Now for the big finish. We need a really funny set piece that draws on the themes, then refers back to them.'

He sat down close to her, nudging her bottom to move on the seat. She could smell his sandalwood cologne mixed with some lived-in clothes scent. And there was a very specific battered old leather smell this time from his precious notebook.

The hairs on her arms stood up.

'Oh, sorry are you cold?'

He picked up his cord jacket and tucked it around her shoulders. It felt wonderful being safe, warm.

These thoughts were strange as she couldn't remember a time when she hadn't been safe since she married Lawrence. But this sensation of being enclosed inside Jaz's jacket was a different thing entirely.

*

The Stand-Up Star producers wanted an update on all their protégés and were ringing Georgie at precisely 10am Tuesday morning. This was causing Georgie stress as it was also 10 minutes before Lily's first scan and they were at the hospital entrance.

'Mam. Will you concentrate. Where in the hospital is the scan unit?'

'It can't be that different to when you had Nat and me surely?'

Jasper, Lily and Georgie walked up and down the hospital corridors, being told to follow blue lines, then yellow lines, before the scanning unit appeared before them.

'Thank goodness. I'm so excited for this. Aren't you?'

Georgie was about to answer when her phone buzzed.

'Hiya Georgie. Lou, the producer here. How are you doing?'

She walked away from her daughter to get some privacy.

'Jaz is great.' She nodded enthusiastically as if the producer could tell. Her breath was halting.

'The last two gigs were hard but I learnt a lot. Definitely.'

'Mam!' Lily was indignant.

Georgie's hand went over the phone speaker and she made a shushing noise.

'Yes. Everything is fine. Thanks. My daughter is just about to have a baby scan. Sorry.'

'Mam!'

Georgie kept her hand over the phone to her daughter's disgust..

'Lily. This may be a bit of fun but I need to check in and let them know how it's going. And your scan isn't for another few minutes.'

'Sorry about that. Yes. I understand. Next gig on Tuesday. Lovely. I think.'

She laughed not because it was funny but because it seemed the right thing to do. And Georgie always tried to do the right thing. At least she always used to try. Nowadays, not so much.

The waiting room door flew open and a nurse called out Lily's name.

'Showtime,' said Lily.

'In more ways than one 'said Georgie under breath, quickly saying bye to the producer.

She remembered her first scan at 16 where she willed the butter bean in her stomach to be just that, instead of a real baby.

And she knew Lily's scan photo was never going to be just a three inch square photo. The grey fuzzy image was a talisman for good luck to Lily.

For Georgie it represented a sad reminder of her past. She took the photo from Lily and said she would keep it safe. While all she wanted to do was rip it up and never see it again.

When they arrived home, the photo was also proving a point to Lawrence that he couldn't always be master in his own home. But he was honourable enough to accept the baby was coming.

'Get it out Mam. Show Dad. It was amazing. Wasn't it Mam?'

Georgie carefully handed over the scan picture to Lawrence. He put his glasses on and carefully studied the grainy image.

'Oh, look, it has your nose Lily. Like a little button. How cute.'

He clearly couldn't think of anything else to say so did his usual bustle out of the kitchen.

'Must just make a call. An important call.'

Lily flopped down onto the nearest chair.

'He's doing his avoidance thing again. He always 'makes a call' or hides behind the Telegraph when he's desperate to not talk about things.'

Georgie was overwhelmed. She wanted the freedom to say she was making a call as well. Instead, she sat with her daughter and listened. Every word a painful scratch, revealing a memory underneath.

'Now that I'm definitely having this baby I need loads of equipment. And clothes. Don't I Mam? Tiny, tiny clothes. How lush.'

'Tiny clothes. Yes.' *My heart is breaking.*

'And I need to tell school. Sometime soon. There's going to be some bitching. I'm sure. But I'll need to be strong and ....'

Georgie remembered the cruel comments directed at her only too well.

'We're here to support you Lily. No-one will hurt you. I promise.'

FIFTEEN

The next day the whole family sat down to the homemade sushi which had taken Georgie over an hour to make. She knew it would take seconds to eat but felt proud of making the beautiful rice delicacies. There was a more relaxed atmosphere than usual so she picked up courage and spoke out.

'I want to see if some of my new jokes work. Can I try them out on you all? And be kind…'

'Ah Mam. It's kinda cringey to be honest. Are you going to talk about getting old? Or…'

Georgie cut Nat off.

'No. Well. Sort of…'

Lawrence jumped in. 'Well, is it or is it not?'

Lily was next. 'Yes Mam. We don't really know what your set's about do we? It had better not be about all of us!'

Everyone laughed apart from Georgie. Which she found ironic. Now that she knew what irony was.

'As if.' She lied.

'No. I tell the same daft stories that made you put me forward. But Jaz said I need more punchlines.'

'Ok. Give it a go. But nothing about any of us please Mam!' Nat finished the last few bits of sushi in one gulp as expected.

'I've got a story about someone winning a hamper at the slimming club ….'

Lily burst out laughing. 'Oh, yes I remember you saying about it, that was Bethany's Mam. There were crackers, snacks. All sorts. I think I must have eaten quite a bit of that…'

'Bethany's really hot', said Nat.

'No, she's not. Anyway, you can't hit on her. It's all sorts of wrong. Imagine…'

'Yes. Meeting outside the bathroom door in a morning…Oooh Lily. How would that feel?'

Lawrence interrupted, 'No-one is staying overnight that is not a long-term partner. You both know that.'

'Didn't stop Lily getting preggers though did it Dad? Eh?'

With that Lawrence got up, 'Enough about all this. Off for a States call. And left the kitchen.

Lily hit Nat's arm and then followed Lawrence out of the room.

'Thanks for that sushi Mam. Mint.' Nat stood up, handed his plate to Georgie and left her on her own.

'Thanks for nothing you lot.' She spoke to the dishwasher as she loaded everything in. Then she remembered Lily being rude about an overweight man in a café. *I think I will use some of our funny family stories just to spite you all.*

*

That night Georgie had to put all the baby stuff behind her as she had another mentoring session back at the pub.

'You need some good punchlines.' Jaz was stern.

Georgie stood impassive.

'Sorry, that came out a bit tough.' He smiled at her and the skin around his eyes crinkled.

'Don't worry. I'm used to being told what to do.' She managed a small smile back.

Today the upstairs rehearsal room was gloomy and looked more tired than ever, matching her mood.

The wooden tables and chairs in the pub never looked as if they had been cleaned. Georgie started to notice the culmination of dust slowing piling up under the table's legs and corners. Spiders' webs became bigger each visit and one had a string of fluff like a trapeze artist hanging down. It didn't help her feel funny.

She clutched her blue A4 notebook and sat down opposite her mentor. He was wearing all black and concentrating on her face. She didn't dare meet his eyes.

There was something going on between them today that scared her.

He switched expressions and beamed at her. 'Come on Georgie. We're going to win this thing! You need to build, build, build. That's how you get a good reaction to a gag.'

Lawrence repeated himself but not like this. He was more of a 'I think I need a coffee, yes, need a coffee' type of man.

Nevertheless she trusted Jaz so repeated, 'I build, build, build.'

'Exactly!'

'How, how, how?'

He stared at her, punishing her sarcasm. Then burst out laughing. 'After that I don't think you need any help with hecklers to be fair!

'Often there are well-known phrases that you can twist like the headline pun, Man Bites Dog.'

They worked on different ideas and came up with a few that might work in Georgie's next set.

'What I hate about anti-climactic jokes …Then you leave a pause.' Jaz suggested.

Georgie added, 'I used to have a green iPod; I'd called it my peapod.'

They added to the list. Trouble was when Georgie tried to remember them, they were like dandelion clocks blowing away in the wind.

She remembered how uninterested her family had been at hearing her set and felt angry. *Maybe I will use what happens at home?*

There had been funny times that weren't too awful to share. Tales of Lily and Nat when they were younger saying daft things. Jaz thought they would work so she added them in. Then she rested her head on her hands. *Can I actually talk about my family or say what I feel about them to be funny?*

'I can't do this.' She had never felt this daunted and was about to admit defeat.

'My mind is just blank when I'm trying to remember these punchlines.'

Jaz suggested, 'We'll mix them in with longer stories so

if you lose your place you could just ad lib a bit with them. That'll help.'

'Hmm. A good idea. Now, how can I talk about my family without causing offence?'

'I know it's hard but you'll find your timing and ability to be honest gets sharper. It's like falling off a log. Everyone talks about their families on stage. Don't worry.'

He held her hand tightly. 'I promise you Georgie. Trust me.'

So she did.

'I don't always love my family. At all. I struggle with connecting to them. It's been a pretence. For years. And years. Not sure how that can be funny. I can see that so clearly now. Because of this.' She waved her arms around the room.

'Thanks for admitting that. Not easy. I'm sure. When you're ready, and not before, we can use your feelings. Keep thinking about it all. For now, we'll do the same one but there will be more to come I know.'

Georgie wasn't sure that day would come but got back into her current set.

He made her repeat it all until she was wholeheartedly sick of it. Now she knew how those dancers on Strictly felt. Practise, practise. The confusing thing was that every great stand-up comic looked like their set was easy. Jokes just coming out off the top of their heads.

'It's a big fat illusion. However, you only get to look that relaxed by actually doing some fierce rehearsing.'

Georgie was non-plussed. 'Well how do you know if what you've written is funny while you're practising?'

'That's when a series of low-profile, script in hand gigs come in. Every successful comedian does it. You do a short set and mark off with ticks when the audience laughs, and if you get a big belly laugh with a clap that gets two ticks.

She made a mental note. *I want two ticks on all my whole set or I'll never dare do the comedy final*

*

Georgie was stressing about the next gig and finding some more new material as Lawrence, Lily and her sat in the kitchen, drinking their usual artisan, finely ground coffee. Only Lily's was now decaff.

'Well. This comedy all sounds like it's getting a bit too difficult. We only suggested you did this as a bit of daftness, didn't we Lily?'

'You are getting all of our attention to be honest Mam. I really need you to be concentrating on me. With the baby. And everything. I think you're being selfish. Self-obsessed or whatever the thing is where you only talk about yourself.' Then she added. 'Love you all the same.'

'I'm still doing all the things I've always done. Nothing has changed. Not really.'

'It's the little things darling,' said Lawrence. 'The little things.'

Georgie was starting to realise being a mother who had the audacity to now be the centre of attention in the house, even some of the time, was not part of the deal.

Lawrence smiled, 'Pack it in m'dear.'

'No.'

Lawrence and Lily stared at each and smiled.

'Think about it for now Mam. For me and the baby. You said you'd support me, us.'

*

Georgie began to struggle more than normal to show love to her family. She also realised she hated this strong, posh coffee. *I want builders' tea with full fat milk instead. I want to do this comedy thing and do it properly. And I want to win.* All her life she had wanted to survive. But win. She had never had the luxury of that being a plan.

I'm changing. Before my very eyes. And I'm beginning to like myself for it.

A text lit up her phone.

Next gig. Black Bull. Tuesday. Be there or be square or at least a rectangle. Need more practise Jaz x

He never put a x. Weird. She wondered why she felt furtive as she put her phone away in her pocket.

Then a second text. *Sorry. Put x by accident.* Followed by the monkey holding its head emoji.

Georgie felt sad. The surprise of the day.

SIXTEEN

The Black Bull was a Tudor style whitewashed pub with fake black beams inside and out. Punters were middle-class and ate the 'famous' steak and kidney pies from posh pottery dishes with gusto.

Georgie stepped onto the tiny stage, set up in a corner away from the bar. She was still her apprehensive comedy self as she unhooked the microphone. But something had been unleashed by the conversations at home and she was going to speak the truth about her life.

The crowd was silent, but she threw out her words with what she hoped sounded like confidence, willing her churning guts to settle. Two blonde and botoxed women in the front wouldn't stop talking so she raised her voice to talk over them.

Staring hard at them she boomed, 'I've tried to be a good mother. But have you ever really listened to a teenager's problems. They go just go on and on. And on. And on. I've left the room and come back two days later. Never even noticed! Bit like BEING ON HERE.'

A few of the crowd gave her an enthusiastic clap for saying it.

The women shut up and stared at her impassively. Georgie wanted to die. But not on this stage.

She made herself look up and around the room, making eye contact with as many people as possible, just as she'd been told. There were about 30 people in the crowd, looking from quite interested to purely there for those pies and craft beer.

Georgie tried shouting again to own the stage. A phrase she hadn't totally understood until tonight.

After the cockporn joke she started new material.

'My son was just as daft. A few years ago he was at a new Catholic senior school and came home with his lesson planner.

He said, 'Hey Mam, there's a picture of the Statue of Liberty on the front.

'So, I told him 'You silly thing that's Jesus!'

And don't get me started on Mother's Day. What a disaster. Ignored totally. But I had my revenge. I had a porn star …(she paused for impact) …martini, I should add, not an **actual** porn star. That would be a bit of a stretch. And not in a good way.

'Plus as a bonus the World's Best Dad mug 'accidentally' got smashed and spelt out 'Worst Dad'. It was apt that day let me tell you.'

There was a slight murmur of appreciation from the crowd at the dark recesses of the room. She could have run over and hugged each of them.

Colin, 60 years old and one pint away from needing a liver transplant, was the MC for the night, he gave her a high five.

'Let's hear it for the Stand-Up Mam everyone.'

There was a very polite round of clapping and her legs buckled when she reached the comic's table.

Jaz was happy with how it had gone. No red marks beside the script afterwards, just a few ticks but one double tick. A double tick for the Statue of Liberty joke. God bless America!

The WhatsApp messages from the other finalists were also getting more upbeat. Clementine. *Got a big laugh. First one!* Anna. *Wales likes me.* Pat. *Big clap for punchline.* Will. *Hmmm. Don't love this ATM.* Matthew. *Loads of girls love me even more now.* Georgie added. *Got a grip of a tough crowd. Go me!*

*

Jaz's arrival to take her to her next gig was loud and proud. The whole street must have heard the tyres of his battered mini squeal to a stop outside Georgie's house.

She knew Lawrence was becoming less impressed by this comedy competition. It was taking her away from the house regularly. So, he kept Jaz waiting in the freezing porch while Georgie put on a last touch of her new scarlet lipstick, despite her shouting for him to be let inside.

She was wearing tight black jeans and a white t shirt with her old leather jacket, trying to look a bit rock and roll but hoping it was not too mutton dressed as lamb. A quick blast of L'Occitane's Lemon Verbena at her throat and she flew down the stairs, two at a time.

Lily was waiting at the bottom of them with her arms folded as if she was the mother about to chastise a wayward daughter. 'Where you are going with that …', she gestured towards the porch where Jaz stood like a trapped animal, peering into the house, '…Jaz man, who is most definitely not Dad?'

'Leeds.'

'Leeds! With Jaz!'

'Yes. Leeds. I'll back quite late so don't wait up. '

Georgie gave Lawrence the customary peck on the cheek as she ran through the porch and nudged Jaz out of the way to escape the house. 'See you 'bout midnight Lawrie. I'll tell you all about it.'

'Drive carefully. You have very special cargo in there.' Lawrence shouted after them, raising himself on his tip toes to try and give his instructions extra gravitas. Georgie had a brief shiver as she remembered how she left her house when she was young without her parents even noticing she'd gone. Not so much special cargo as dead meat.

Jaz was already holding the car door open when she stepped out into the early evening air. He was wearing his usual sandalwood aftershave and his crisp cotton shirt had a limey-fresh laundry smell.

'Jump in. We need to be there by eight at the latest. You look very cool, like a villainess from Batman.'

He hit the play button on his phone as he shot out of the street at full speed. Bad Company's *Greatest Hits* began to pulse through the creaky sound system. Georgie fumbled for her seat belt as Jaz began to sing along about being bad company.

'Earth to Georgie!'

She was brought sharply back to the present day as Jaz shot a look at her out of the corner of his eye.

'I used to manage a few bands alongside my early comedy work but way too young for Bad Company, just a lot of sound-alikes unfortunately.' His hand went to change gears and his knuckles rubbed against Georgie's leg as he did.

She purposefully crossed her leg away from him yet wondered if it was deliberate.

'What's the set up in Leeds then? What can I expect to learn?'

He thoughtfully stroked his chin with his left hand. She then saw him feeling the tiny bit of stubble with the tips of his fingers. And had the unexpected urge to touch it.

'Tom, the owner, is a great guy. It's useful to have his advice as well as mine. He'll give you an honest opinion of your set. Tips on how to write better gags, all of the usual stuff. Call backs. That kind of thing.'

'What's a call back again?'

'You know, when a comedian mentions something from earlier in their set. For example. In the opening you might say, 'My mother forgets everything and once even forgot to go for a memory test. Then later on you say when I was a baby, she left me outside the shops. At the end of the gig, you would do a gag again about someone you loved leaving you, but at least it wasn't outside the shops!'

By the time they arrived in Leeds the excited pulse was back in her stomach.

The Yorkshire Comedy Rooms was in a restored bonded warehouse beside one of the canals. Jaz shook the doorman's hand and pushed the huge glass door to the club back with a thump.

Tom Tripper was sitting at the bar, sipping a lager, deep in thought.

'Hello Doll. How the fuck are you Jaz man? It's been a while.'

Georgie noticed the respect Tom showed her mentor and the warmth Jaz showed, in return. They gripped each other's hands and hugged. Chest first. Only broken by Jaz giving Tom a hearty slap on the back.

After the ritual welcome they noticed Georgie again. Standing, picking her cuticles, looking around the room with tentative eyes.

She jumped when Tom put his arm around her and said with a loud laugh.

'I'm really looking forward to seeing your set.'

Georgie's stomach turned inside out but she knew she had to do this if she was serious. She breathed out through her mouth to steady herself. Tom stared at her as he drank the remainder of his beer. The foam catching on his grey, close-cut moustache and beard.

'We'd planned to have you in the middle of the second section for a quick five minutes or so. There are six of us on tonight and I am headlining. They're a good crowd, no stags or hens. Nothing to worry about. Some of them might even be our age.'

Georgie differences, being a wife and mother to teenagers, seemed to be magnified in this club. The table with the other comedians on it was a testament to the fact. They were all male, under 25, three Cockneys, a Yorkshireman and another Glaswegian who was also under Tom's wing.

'Thanks Tom. Excuse me while I check my set notes with Jaz and work out what I need to say as an intro.' Georgie dived into the Ladies toilets and slammed the door of the cubicle so hard it caused the whole cloakroom to quieten for a second.

She gathered her confidence and then sat with Jaz.

Think. Think.

They both realised the audience was the youngest yet and quickly went over the set. For an intro she rummaged in her bag for her comedy notebook, her Bible. There were a few topical jokes about Love Island and Strictly as well as her home life. She would do those. They should appeal to everyone.

Five minutes later she didn't know if she was going to be funny but at least she didn't feel quite as terrified. Jaz said he trusted her to nail it. That helped.

Tom smiled at her and tapped her arm. She liked him. He was a warm-hearted Glaswegian. His Led Zeppelin O2 gig in 2007 t shirt was worn with pride.

'You'll be fuckin' fine Doll. Dinnah fret yoursel'. Here lets' you and me go over to the quieter tables. I'll give yer the benefit of my small bit of knowledge, such as it is!'

He chuckled to himself as they walked over to the table where Nigel, the club's owner was drinking Bourbon on the rocks.

Nigel stood up as soon as he saw Georgie and shook her hand, giving Jaz a quick look and a wink in the process.

Does he think we're having an affair? Surely we don't give off those vibes?

Tom sat down beside her, their backs to the club and heads over her notes pile. He was as helpful as Jaz had promised he would be. He gave her a bundle of comedy tips, such as flipping a subject so something becomes funny as it is the opposite of what you expect.

'See Doll. You have this gag about your daughter saying 'Mam when you were born you must have fallen from heaven.'

The set-up is sweet and people will think 'Aahhh, isn't that lovely'. The flip is that you finish it by saying, 'And hit every branch of the ugly tree coming down. Have a go with some other gags as well. Let's see what else you have.'

Georgie showed him her draft set and he made notes and comments. She quietly ran through it with him until he felt she would be OK. Then she and Jaz waited while he did a countdown to the evening starting.

After the first group of comics had finished their sets, a lively atmosphere started to build up. It made Georgie feel worse. The buoyant happy vibe was increasing the pressure. It was as if there was something invisible in the room which could be so easily broken in her amateur hands.

She felt nausea rise up as the comic before her started his set. The Yorkshireman, Pete Walton, had the crowd in the palm of his hand with his charisma and solid one-liners about Leeds. His act was based on what it felt like to be a black Yorkshireman and proud of it.

Do I have time for another trip to the toilet, or do I need a quick drink?

Georgie couldn't decide, all she knew was that her fight or flight instinct was most definitely tuned in to flight.

Her hands instinctively covered her eyes as she willed a sense of calm to come.

Tom introduced her. She thought for a moment she might actually stay put and not stand. Only the pressure of everyone looking at her disconnected her bottom from the warm chair. So, she got up and headed towards the stage clutching her paper and diet coke as if her life depended on it. Jaz gave her a thumbs up. His smile gave her inner strength.

She tackled the horrible first part of a gig. The microphone. She had used one in her other gigs but tonight's seemed daunting. The cables. The on/off switch. Where to hold it? Where not to hold it?

Georgie tried to confidently remove it from its holder as she had seen the other comedians do. It wouldn't budge unlike her stomach which was moving at a speed of knots.

She moved it round and tried to free it from the stand. Finally, after a sharp tug out it came and banged her nose.

She noticed a hush had descended on the room and everyone was actually more transfixed than if she had taken it out smoothly. By accident she had them intrigued.

'Well. That should have knocked some sense into me! Hello Leeds.' Her voice trembled but she went on and enjoyed the crowd laughing.

'I'm a middle-aged mam who is doing this to stop being invisible. And make a bit of fun of my kids. Obviously, I'll change their names as it wouldn't be fair to tell you about them otherwise.

'As I came out, I reassured them. I said 'Lily don't worry, I won't tell them what you're called'.'

Georgie looked genuinely shocked to have said her daughter's real name but then winked at the people sitting near the front of the stage. She suddenly felt the heat from the spotlight had become too fierce for comfort, as she was already flushed with nerves.

Remember your jokes, remember your jokes. She willed her brain to work properly and sure enough the all-important punchlines came out in the right order.

'I have never let my kids talk slang. When my daughter was young, I never let her say she was having a wee. She made 'fairy liquid' and the upside was that we always had a clean bowl.'

Everyone in the club gave a chuckle and she relaxed, slightly.

Her set continued. Frozen cock porn joke. Double tick. The ugly tree. One tick. And so, it continued until the time was up.

'Goodnight everyone. I've been Georgie Chancellor.'

A quick wave and she shot off the stage. Tom got the crowd to give her another loud cheer and Jaz grabbed her to give her a small hug. As usual she collapsed onto a chair.

Tom was already at the side of the stage for his set and gave her a wink and a thumbs up sign before the spotlight came on for his 20 minutes. He strode confidently on to the stage and whisked the mic out of its stand as if he could do it in his sleep. The dreaded cable which she feared would wrap around her feet was professionally flicked to one side. Tom actually leaned on to the stand.

He was doing a series of short funny stories on Leeds and Yorkshiremen. The audience were enjoying the local humour even if it was from a Scotsman.

By the time his set finished the audience were clapping every joke with enthusiasm and he got an even bigger cheer when another of the comedians asked them to show their appreciation for him again.

Georgie gave a mock bow when Tom came off stage and sat beside Jaz and her.

She smiled at him and said, 'You're the man!'

He gave her a high five.

Jaz shook his hand as he sat down and said, 'Great set man. The real deal. It is going to be brilliant to see you down in the big City. It's the end of next month, isn't it?'

Tom grinned and took a deep drink from the pint Jaz had ready for him. 'Yep, the big city. I liked it here as well though. There was a good crowd tonight. Really up for it.'

Tom and Jaz discussed the various comedy clubs in Leeds compared to the ones in London. They picked over the good club owners, shady promoters who didn't pay and the partisan audiences who only liked local comedians.

She suddenly felt shattered with the nervous tension dissipated and genuine fatigue setting in. Luckily it was time to go. Jaz helped her on with her jacket and Tom gave her a small hug bye then they were out into the Leeds night.

'You did well, looking almost yourself as well.' Jaz lit up a cigarette, exhaled, then he stared at her through its smoke.

'I didn't know you smoked?'

'Off and on. When I'm feeling chilled. Want one?'

'I've not smoked since I was 15!'

'Really? I didn't have you down as having been a bad girl.'

'Not bad. Just different.' She sighed then decided to take the cigarette. He carefully lit it for her, moving in close to her mouth and her stomach flipped.

They finished smoking in companionable silence.

'Another one?'

'No. One's definitely enough, thanks.'

'You need to take risks in life Georgie. Get's you material. As well as into trouble. Sometimes.' He smiled.

'I've never seen you take risks so far?'

'Really? Time yet. Patience. G.'

She marched on ahead to the car, confident and feeling surer of herself than usual.

Jaz threw his cigarette down then ground it with his heel before following her.

'I can tell that you've always got self-control. Not a bad thing. Not a bad thing at all.'

Before she could think about what he meant and give a clever retort he had swung the passenger car door open and was helping her in. She decided to ignore it and just enjoy the journey home.

As they pulled up to her house the small table-lamp in the big bay window picked out the top of a curly hair mop. Georgie felt as if her bones were set in stone as she slowly stretched herself out of the car. She leant in to say thank you for the lift when she realised the seat was empty and Jaz was standing right beside her. It was like a vampire movie where the un-dead appear out of nowhere.

He was propelling her towards her front door when the sight of Lawrence in his silk dressing gown holding it open stopped him in his tracks. Georgie smiled as she took in her husband's slightly befuddled and teddy bear-like appearance. He must have dozed off in the chair while he waited up.

'Georgie, how did it go?' Lawrence ignored Jaz's offer of his hand and deliberately kept his eyes glued to his wife. 'Come on in and get warm. Get warm.'

She felt a pea-sized pot of warmth in the pit of her stomach for her husband.

'Love to!'

It wasn't like Jaz to be rude but he deliberately misconstrued Lawrence's offer, and calmly ushered Georgie past her husband and into her own house.

'Great style. I remember this. I really love all these stripped boards. You do it?'

The last question was thrown over his shoulder towards Lawrence who looked as if he was stuck physically to the front door, mouth agog.

Jaz smiled at Georgie, unseen by Lawrence and mouthed, 'See. Risky!'

Georgie's confidence was rising and there seemed to be a small devil on her shoulder. Rather than kick Jaz out, he could help her win this comedy final after all, she decided to see how this would all play out. Intriguing.

She was amazed to realise, as a perfect wife, she was disappointed it was so late and not likely to last long.

'Evening. Evening.' Lawrence's slight stutter came back with the situation he was finding uncomfortable. He then put his hand out again to shake Jaz's own.

Georgie saw a small smile creep onto Jaz's face. She knew he could pick her husband up by the skin on the back of his neck like a kitten despite his slight build. Comedy club life can toughen you like that.

'Jaz Jones. As you know.' He squeezed Lawrence's hand.

'Please just call me Mr Jones!'

Two beats passed and he laughed at his own joke, alone.

'I'm joking. Comedy is my business after all. Jaz. Just call me Jaz.'

Lawrence said, 'You are joking about that I presume. It's hilarious.'

Then he crossed his arms and sat down beside Georgie and Jaz at the kitchen table.

'Your other half did really well tonight. Didn't you Georgie? You're finding your comedy voice. It takes time but it's definitely coming.'

Lawrence snorted and Georgie shot him a look to shut him up.

'What the hell is a comedy voice? This is all a bit of fun by the way. No-one is expecting any great shakes of Georgie you know!'

She died a bit inside. Jaz saw. Lawrence didn't.

'Well, let me give you a demonstration.'

Georgie watched as Jaz slowly stood in the middle of her kitchen. It was as if he had flicked a switch to charisma because Lawrence and her were transfixed as he started to tell short, funny stories. He told different ones to those he used at his gig they saw all those weeks ago.

'I think contrary to popular belief English people are the rudest. My grandparents fought for you in India, then were invited over to live here. But since Brexit, it's now all 'Oooh you're in our country, you need to go back home'. To which I usually say, 'Yes, no bother but it's only two doors away Mrs Titchmarsh'.

'It reminds me of the time I was in hospital and had to

write down my nearest relative. I told them, it's my dad, he's in the waiting room next door.'

'There you see. My comedy voice. You need that to work against. Georgie.   You having a family who are teenagers is different to most comics on the circuit so that alone is something distinctive.'

Georgie said, 'I'm starting to feel comfortable telling jokes about that, rather than trying to talk about baking and all of that stuff.'

'Exactly. What you find funny is also part of finding your voice and..'

'Well, all this is fascinating but I have a big case I need to work on tomorrow so must head off.' Lawrence's eyes seemed to be sinking into his skull they were so deep in shadow. Georgie smiled to herself as she watched her husband clutch Jaz's elbow and remove his mug from the other hand.

'Of course. We're getting there, Mrs Chancellor.'

Then as he was headed down the hall to the front door Jaz whispered, 'Don't worry, you're doing fine.'

Her husband gently patted his wife's back as they headed up to bed.

'Hmmm. Can you smell cigarette smoke Georgie?'

'No. Don't think so.'

'Must have been your comedy friend. I'll give the hall a blast of the White Company room spray.'

Georgie felt relief as she flopped back on their bed. She picked up her alarm clock and was horrified to see it was now one in the morning. Six hours until she had to get up for work in the office.

A devil seemed to be on her shoulder who was going crackers with jokes, plucking totally inappropriate funny things out of the air. She made excuses about getting an aspirin and went down to the kitchen to type them up on her phone. There was no way she would have told Lawrence and hurt his feelings. She loved her husband but since the comedy course started, not in the same way. Despite her best efforts.

SEVENTEEN

The next day's teatime was business as usual for the perfect mother and wife. Cleaning, chopping, stirring. Only interrupted by boxing gloves flung onto the kitchen floor and bouncing to a stop. Georgie sighed and grabbed ice for her husband's nose. Boxing was always the panacea to masculinity's ills in their house and the 'comedy fracas' as he had called last night was definitely a trigger.

'Why d'you do this Mr C?' Her diction often went when she was exasperated. She pushed the frozen peas onto Lawrence's nose a little too firmly for his comfort.

'Look at the state of you.'

She knew, although he didn't, she could handle any potential assailant better than her husband, with or without his boxing gloves. Being the runt at a rough North East secondary school teaches you far more tactics than anything in the boxing ring. Although one of the best moves, she realised sharpish, was to run like the wind.

Lawrence looked at her, licked his lips nervously, sat down and made a pyramid of his hands and arms on the kitchen table. Georgie was non-plussed. Her husband of 18 years was never like this, looking as if he was about to reveal a secret.

The beautifully polished kettle did its high-pitched scream at the same time as the pan lids rattled to be put on to simmer. She noticed Lawrence close his eyes and control his breathing before he started to speak.

'I'm not sure I can do this anymore Georgina.'

'What. The kitchen noise?'

'No. This trying to be a macho man boxing thing.'

'Listen.' She was firm.

'Just stop it then. You were boxing, white collar fighting. Whatever. Long before we met. I love you without knowing you can thump someone good and proper. Just stop it. End of…'

'Good and proper.' He repeated and shook his head, carefully in case his nose hurt more.

A strange gurgle arose from his throat.

'Thing is, darling. I needed it.'

'What, a bloody nose?'

'No.'

She was now at a complete loss.

'Lawrence. Explain.'

She switched off all the pans and let the kitchen still. It was as if all the room was a living thing, holding its breath. Almost absent-mindedly she patted his hand to unlock the revelation, whatever it would be.

'My mother drank.'

Georgie stared at him.

'No way. We've been through this. MY mother drank. You never mentioned yours. Which to be fair, always suited me just fine.'

'I was 12 years old and just back from boarding school. The kitchen bin was full of empty sherry bottles when I went to put a chocolate wrapper in.'

Georgie nodded in recognition. *He is still putting neatly folded chocolate wrappers in bins.*

Lawrence said, 'My mother saw me staring and cracked me over the head with an empty bottle. It floored me and knocked me out.

'When I went back to school I learned how to box. I showed her my skills every holiday. Taking care to pull my punches within an inch of her nose. Then when we met, I knew you could've taken me out at any time so I kept it up. Yes. I knew. To impress, you see.'

'Lawrence, I'm so sorry. You poor soul. That's horrible. When you're poor you think rich kids are always having fun. I had no idea.'

She hugged him and held him tight like he held her when she was sad about her past.

Then a memory made her step back and she touched her cheek briefly. Lawrence had hit her once when they were first married. She had been really drunk and showed her true colours.

He had criticised her speech as being 'still rough round the edges' and she had said she hated him and their life. Always being on best behaviour. Never knowing what cutlery to use in restaurants. She finished by calling him a pathetic snob and tried to leave.

He hadn't known how to calm her down so he slapped her instinctively. The mortification on both their parts had meant it had never been repeated.

That thought also took her back to the time they first met.

Her favourite night club had been the floating ship nightclub underneath the world-famous Tyne Bridge. She had never even travelled abroad at that time and as she walked into it, she fantasised that she was in Paris.

In her daydream the gently decaying stone buildings on the opposite riverside were lining the Seine, in declining yet romantic splendour. As the dim Victorian-style lamps cast their ghostly pale light along the banks, they picked out the odd figure brave enough to walk along the disused warehouses and deserted former shipping offices. She imagined one of them was a French aristocrat.

He would see her at the ship's balcony and know she was the One.

Lawrence had not been exactly a French aristocrat, but he had been and was still, inherently middle-class or, put simply as she had, 'posh'. He had been in Newcastle to handle a Crown Court case and was on the disco ship with fellow solicitors up from York.

She had been drawn to him as his colleagues had been drunk and hassled both her friend Karen and her, trying to get them to dance. Karen, who was also an office junior at the marketing agency where she worked, was starting to get irritated and screechy. Never a good sign.

Despite her current, sometimes mixed, feelings for her husband, Georgie had a clear and positive memory of her first sight of him. He was the shortest of his party but in her inexperienced eyes he had something about him. Presence.

When he told the men to back off as 'these ladies were not interested in them and their 'high jinks', a phrase she had never even heard before, she noticed their immediate respect for his authority. One of them had even given a pretend salute and said 'Right boss' before apologising.

When his colleagues had gone Lawrence stayed for a moment as if unsure what to do next. He then took a step forward and stood right in front of Georgie, who was resplendent in a tiny, fluted, neon green skirt and t shirt, with a huge mass of white back-combed hair.

She had wondered what on earth he was going to say as he just looked at her silently for what felt like an eternity. Then she realised, he was plucking up Dutch courage.

He dropped his gaze for a second and then what seemed to be in slow motion said,

'You are the most beautiful woman I have ever seen.'

And for the first time in her life, Georgie felt as if she just might be. Although questions that leapt into her head were how could she get benefit from it and what would it cost her?

Back in her present life she knew the cost and had thought it was worth it. But things were slowly shifting.

*

The morning after Lawrence's boxing confession Georgie got up extra early, kissing him on top of his head before heading downstairs. She put an apron over her silk dressing gown cleaned the kitchen like a demon as usual. *Perfect wife. Perfect life.*

It was Wednesday so not only did she put her usual coq au vin in the slow cooker for dinner she popped a Victoria sponge in the oven as well. By the time the cuckoo on the Swiss kitchen clock popped out to declare eight o'clock, she was shattered but on track to have things on a more even keel.

The quick shower made her ready for the day. She swept through the kitchen checking Nat and Lily were eating something. Luckily her daughter was feeling well today. Morning sickness had passed.

Lawrence ate his cereal and drank his smoothie though she knew he would be much happier with a bacon sandwich.

He was leaning against the kitchen units, tailored suit fitting perfectly, albeit with a slight paunch. His dark, curly hair was feminine but suited him, just as he himself, generally suited her.

'I'm off to work now. Can you please put the dishes in the dishwasher Lily?'

'Okay. But you're going to have to stop asking me to do things in a few weeks' time. I'm. Having. A. Baby!'

Lawrence tutted and began helping her load it while Georgie finished applying her make-up in her pocket mirror.

'Packed dinners in the fridge.'

'Lunches Mam' said Lily.

Lawrence walked Georgie to the door and kissed her goodbye.

'Hope you win the case.'

'I hope Brett doesn't drive you mad.'

Georgie's boss was great but also prone to be disorganised. She never got a minute of headspace once she was in the office.

The difference in their two lives had never seen so great. Her husband on the legal stage at the Newcastle Courts and her the marketing firm's office manager and still the boss's gofer. Gofer at home.

Why am I suddenly bothered about this?

EIGHTEEN

Then

In the early days of their marriage, every Friday, Georgie and Lawrence had what he called an Eliza Doolittle session. She had no clue who she was until he explained, which was pretty indicative of the whole situation.

The idea was Lawrence's mother's. Apparently, Georgie ate like a labourer, talked like a market stall owner and drank like an alcoholic.

She told Georgie in no uncertain terms as the wife of a top lawyer she would have to entertain clients at formal dinners and events therefore needed to up her game, now they were married.

There was no way Georgie was going to mess up the chance to keep tight hold of this charmed life with security, so she got stuck in. There was just so much to learn about. Novelists, culture, artists, politics. What was right and left wing. The list went on and on.

'Bacardi and coke.'

Lawrence shook his head.

Georgie smacked her hand on the table, rattling her luminous bracelets in the process.

'Wine. Wine. I knew there was somethin.'

'SomeTHING'.

'Now Georgina. The million-dollar question. What type?'

'Chablis!' She flicked her permed fringe back from her eyes and felt proud.

Her husband, looked immaculate and couldn't have been more different to her past men.

'I feel like Rex Harrison.'

Georgie looked confused. 'Was he on that cookery show?'

Lawrence laughed so hard he nearly choked.

'My fair lady, Eliza.'

Georgie looked blank so he began to hum the main song about being loverlee in a cockney accent.

They then started to hum it together and held hands across the table.

'I get you. You know Lawrence.' In a fake posh voice she said, 'I would very much like a glass of Chab-il-ay Rex.'

She smiled submissively and willed herself not to muck up this opportunity. Georgie wanted a perfect life, in a beautiful house with a wealthy husband. This man, in ironed jeans and smart polo shirt was the best bet she'd had in her whole life.

Reuben could have been right for her. but she was not the right type of girl for him. That had been made perfectly clear by his family. The last time she saw him, well, the least remembered the better. Although in her bones she knew he was a bad penny likely to turn up again. Probably when it was least beneficial to her.

Georgie's heart always twisted when she thought of her first love. Then Lawrence was back with her wine. She would have loved a cider and blackcurrant but sometimes life just wasn't that straight forward.

These lessons had more low than high points such as when she said Gandhi was an Asian vegetable. That took some living down.

They lasted two endless months. But proved their worth.

She walked into Lawrence's firm's Senior Partner James White-Seymour's vast house with its long hall and stunning lounge wearing a Jaeger navy shift dress and clutching a Chanel bag. Her hair was gleaming and her make-up was flawless. Although she didn't feel it, she was able to pretend she belonged. Sort of.

The aperitif was pink gin with cucumber which she was pleased to realise wasn't a terrible mistake. Everything in the dining room was black, gold and glass with three feet candles lighting the grand mahogany table. Georgie began to relax, partly due to the gin. James and Katherine were perfect hosts, more like grandparents than a middle-aged power couple, which helped.

The starter was seafood which just a short time beforehand Georgie couldn't have eaten. Octopus, squid? She looked at Lawrence for a quick smile of reassurance then swallowed the whole plate in five bites to avoid looking at the creatures in detail.

A bloody blue steak with chips was next. Chips! She couldn't believe her luck so said so.

'I can't believe I'm getting chips. Here!'

'We sometimes indulge ourselves. And our guests. Don't we darling.' Katherine cooed.

And then before Georgie knew it, they were all drinking really disgusting coffee from tiny cups with a massive round glass of brandy.

She had managed to have a conversation about Georgian architecture, mainly by nodding a lot, name-dropped an avant-garde painter and recommended a Tuscan wine producer.

Once they were in the car, the new BMW, what else, she was over the moon with how Lawrence had praised her.

'When I saw the octopus, really Georgina, I thought, well it doesn't get more testing than this!'

He held her hand tightly before setting off.

I've helped him feel good about himself. A welcome change for him. Mainly due to his mother. What a cow.

And she also felt a bit better about herself and began to feel love for him as well. She now belonged somewhere. Every day there was food in the kitchen. Hunger was gone. Pain was gone. Forever, she hoped.

123

NINETEEN

Now

In her new comedy life, Georgie's most important date was gig-day-Friday and it came round quickly. Jaz had talked over her set in minute detail. Every pause. Every punchline. Georgie's five minute script was fixed firmly in her head and she repeated it over and over as she slowly examined the clothes she would wear.

She laid out an old black Nirvana t-shirt from her happy days of going to pubs' heavy metal nights. And black bootleg cords. Then decided to have a quick bath rather than shower, to thaw the chill her grating nerves had created.

Slipping her bony frame under the fragrant water, she felt the welcome slow closing of the warm liquid over her entire body. She gently pulled back her head until it rested against the very bottom of the bath.

Her hair floated to the surface around her pale face. She felt like Millais' painting of Ophelia 'incapable of her own distress', floating and softly singing, surrounded by beautiful wild flowers and reeds. White, translucent skin and bloodless lips slightly parted. Half living. Half dead. Lawrence was to thank for that imagery. A Tate Gallery Eliza Doolittle session.

Inside her head a cracked, dry voice suggested she stayed there, for just a couple more minutes, what harm could it do? It was her own cosy world. No telephones or television. No incessant shouts of Mam, Mam, Mam.

'MAM. MAM. MAM.'

Suddenly the bathroom door swung open and

Lawrence burst in pulling her up out of the water, followed by Lily, covering her eyes and shouting

'Where is my new Guess t-shirt? I am going out in five minutes. MAM!'

Lawrence ignored Lily and was shaking Georgie as if she had been Sleeping Beauty, unconscious for hundreds of years, 'Georgie, what are you doing? You could have drowned yourself!'

'Mam, this one will do that's on your bed. Mine are too small now. See you about 12. Just off out.'

Lily snatched the t-shirt and shot out of the door as Georgie was still trying to focus her eyes with the bright bathroom light and shake the water out of her ears.

At least I will get some peace on stage, although I wouldn't be surprised if they both turn up and stand stage right, hissing some request or demand at me. Not that I mind. Do I?

Lawrence stood in front of the old Victorian bath with its rolled top and antique clawed feet. Georgie knew he had bought it as a potential source of sensuous pleasure not a device to give him a heart attack.

'Why do you do that whole submerged thing Georgina? You know it terrifies me. I swear I saw no bubbles coming out of your nose just now. You could have died! It's just not normal!'

I'm not normal though, am I?

Georgie wondered if she would die on stage instead of the bath. She plunged herself back underneath the slowly cooling water. Tiny bubbles rose up to the surface, proving she was very much not dead. Eyes tight shut, she sensed rather than heard her long-suffering husband retreat. Feeling beaten.

She rose up. *That's given me more material. Good.*

TWENTY

Then

Georgie woke up with a clenched fist deep inside her belly. It rhythmically hit the walls of her womb as if it was trying to break them down. She screwed her eyes tight shut and, in that moment, she was tiny again, able to pretend she was invisible to people once her lids were closed.

With huge effort she tried to persuade her brain the last nine months had been a dream. Maybe her massive breasts were gone? Perhaps she was flat-chested and as boyish as her friends again. All this must be her imagination.

Her knuckles were hard and fixed as she pulled her age-worn, ballerina quilt over her head. The pale cherub-faced dancers now as disturbing as waxen Victorian dolls. She blocked out the light and breathed in deeply. Without warning she smelt Impulse on the pink, thin cotton. Sweet, sickly Impulse with the jaunty supermodel striding out into an exciting city dream. Every teenage girl's vision of perfection.

Then Georgie's mouth opened wide. She became Munch's Scream from the art class, purple bands of agony beaming out of her distended body, wave after wave. A distress signal with no sound. Her body was filled with demonic pulsing, as though the baby had begun to shred her womb into a thousand red ribbons.

Georgie cried quietly all the way to the hospital. Her father didn't speak to her and she felt compelled to hold in her pain to show him she wasn't weak.

She was left standing outside the maternity unit, while her father's car engine immediately revved aggressively into the distance. A few short steps can be as vast as the Sahara and she knew she was very much alone.

Then she also knew there would be no return to imaginary kissing of Batman or a popstar.

In the maternity unit all the midwives were very kind. She liked kind. It was strange like wearing someone else's coat, which she did sometimes at break time, when her constant shivering irritated her classmates.

Every time the delivery room door opened, her head turned in a split second. Maybe Reuben had been able to come for the birth after all? Her spirit died a little as the room remained achingly empty.

That was when the pain became terrifying. She wanted to be brave. Her fists clenched then unclenched. She longed for a someone to hold her hand and dry the tears which poured down no matter how hard she tried to stop them.

Beeping monitors reminded her of her own heartbeat. The baby setting the pace, one two, one two, come on, keep up.

'Time now sweetheart. Breathe out and big push,' said the midwife.

The gas and air made everyone sound so far away. She wanted to float off in a sleepy haze but her body was full of grit and pain. Then, like unblocking a drain, there was the baby. A pink scrunched up mess of blood and flesh.

Wiping the baby with towels the midwife said, 'You've had a beautiful baby boy, pet. Do you want to hold him before he goes away?'

She looked at the baby and felt all the misery of the past few months was now inside him. If she touched him, she might get it back.

But Georgie's son looked round at her with pinched eyes and dark pupils. Brown matted hair framed his face and round cheeks. His mouth made a small o shape and then a twitch of a smile. She was sure it was a smile. My baby. The words exploded in her head. *My baby.*

I need to hold him. I mustn't hold him. As I'll never be able to give him up.

The nurse seemed to understand as she had no doubt seen other young girls who knew they were unlikely to ever see their baby again once they were adopted.

"I know this time is precious so if you want to give him a bottle before he goes away, now's the time.'

Georgie's body was spent and she had endured the whole labour with just the midwife. For a few minutes she would have a family if she fed her son. She might feel a connection that had never been there with her own parents.

'Yes.'

Before she could argue with herself the baby was in her arms, flesh on flesh, warm, fat, new-born skin next to her own.

The sensation of her son nuzzling and exploring the bottle teat then taking a few drops was exquisite to her and made her want to feed him with her breasts. But she knew she couldn't possibly do that or look after a baby in her home with drunk parents and filth everywhere she turned. He needed to be safe even if she wasn't. She had looked after herself and it wouldn't be long before she could go somewhere else.

A midwife gently helped her lay back on the tough pillow. She thought the baby seemed to realise her smell was getting fainter as he was carried out of the room. For the first time she sensed a sadness that was not her own.

As she was drifting off to sleep Georgie was sure she heard Reuben's voice outside, but he must have been banished to boarding school by now. She had a black and white dream of walking on the nearby beach at Seaburn. Soft sand in her toes and icy water pulling her down and towards the horizon. She didn't know if she would ever surface or if she would ever see her baby again.

TWENTY-ONE

Now

Georgie had walked into her old boyfriend Reuben's club Baci several times before but tonight was so different. Not as bad as the first time when they met in their adult lives. Neither knowing what to say about their baby.

Lawrence's clients had been adamant the evening moved on to Reuben's famous club on the lively Newcastle Quayside.

Georgie had protested against it quietly and was shushed by her husband.

Reuben had recognised her straight away and a quick whispered agreement was forged that they knew each other vaguely from school. *What an understatement.*

Now two years on from the first meeting, they were now able to be civil to each other. Even so, she couldn't believe his club was where Jaz said the Stand-Up Star organisers had booked her in.

Her palms were sweating and every one of her senses was on high alert. She felt like a commando about to start a covert mission in foreign territory. Each sound was magnified.

When a customer placed a small glass on the bar it seemed to reverberate around the room.

Her nervous energy heightened as she was face to face with her own name, buried on the poster by the door.

She had arrived before Jaz and urgently needed his support.

'Hello! Are you on tonight as well?'

Georgie turned to find herself nose to nose with a strawberry blonde woman about her own age. She was dressed in a provocative bustier and pink pencil skirt, a slash of dark eyeshadow on pale skin completing the femme fatale image. She smelled deliciously of peaches.

'I'm supposed to be but I am just having second, or maybe, third thoughts.'

'Don't worry, you'll be fine. I'm Andrea.'

Andrea marched right into the room exactly as Georgie would have loved to do. Instead, she felt as if a demolition charge had been set off inside, collapsing her from the inside out.

Her head was exploding. *Why did I do this competition? And why here?*

Following in Andrea's slipstream and metaphorical tail feathers Georgie consciously tried to set her shoulders straight as she walked over to the bar.

 Reuben was standing with his back to them, wearing a navy blazer and washed-out denim jeans. On his left were a group of three wannabe comedians.

'Lovely bum, look at that.' Andrea leaned over and gave Reuben's bottom a sly nip and then moved back to the bar, signalling to the barman to get her a drink. As Reuben swung round in amazement, Georgie was standing still, jaw dropping.

'If I did that, I'd get a slap across the face darling!' He winked at Georgie, even more full of himself than he used to be when he was the school heart throb.

'It wasn't her. It was me. And you're welcome. Darling!' Andrea beamed at him and stuck her hand out complete with purple nail varnish and huge diamanté rings, 'Andrea. Comedian.'

'Reuben. Owner.' He raised his eyebrows but she was totally unabashed and continued to smile at him warmly.

Reuben took charge, as was his way. 'Come over here and meet the rest of tonight's comics. You too Georgie.'

He then leaned over to her and whispered in her ear 'Quite a surprise to see you on the list. But don't be scared. Actually, I was going to speak to you. Something, or should I say someone, has turned up who we need to talk about. But not now. Obviously.'

'What the hell. Reuben. I've got my hands full without you making these comments.'

He grabbed her elbow and ushered her to an empty table.

'It's about our baby. Do you ever think of him Georgie? I bet you do. On his birthday? Christmas...'

'Stop it. Just stop it. Please. We had an agreement...'

'Things change...'

'Not for me they don't.'

She shook him off and walked towards the other comics for safety.

Georgie felt as if every nerve in her body was being stuck with pins. Now her head was full of what Reuben wanted to discuss and their baby, instead of her script.

She was grateful for their presence stopping him saying any more and giving her huge smiles of welcome to their merry stand-up band.

'First time?' said one of them.

'Not quite. Early days though,' she answered, voice quavering.

Reuben was about to speak on her behalf but Jaz appeared and stepped in which was heaven for Georgie, but not the club owner himself.

'Tell them Georgie, you're doing well. Aren't you?'

Jaz and Reuben knew each other from the Newcastle nightlife scene but there was no love lost between them. Chalk and cheese. Georgie realised.

Reuben started to speak but Jaz cut him off.

'She's going to be just fine. You've got this one nailed Georgie, don't worry. You'll be great.'

'Hey, what about me?' piped a voice behind them, as Andrea stuck her head through the gap between Reuben and Georgie,

'Will I be great?'

The comedians quickly looked at each other, then back at Andrea and nodded in unison.

'Yep. You'll do.'

'You'll do me!' said one in a Fleetwood Mac t-shirt.

'I don't think I will.' Andrea smiled, wagging her finger at him.

A small table was set aside to the stage left for the performers. Clutching their beers, the male stand-ups, sat down. Georgie didn't join them straight away, she felt that would be even more stressful. She preferred to wait by the bar, sipping her cool wine and rubbing the glass against her overheated palms. Trying to forget what Reuben had said and keeping her nerves at bay.

Andrea linked Georgie's arm and marched her over to the comics table, pushing her into a seat by her shoulders.

'Don't you worry. These early gigs are always a trauma for people. We will get the crowd warmed up so they will laugh at anything. Slightly pissed, but not too pissed. Perfect audience.'

Georgie shivered and pulled out the sheaves of paper from her bag. Andrea stared at the pile with mock horror.

'Bloody hell, what's that War and Peace?'

The two women sat down and Georgie slowly read through her set notes. This gig was just as stressful as the others. Everything seemed to be not funny anymore and her stomach gurgled its worry in response. Her brain was bouncing. Then she remembered why she was doing this. *It's good not to be invisible and do something for me.*

Calling into the club toilets for a vital last-minute trip with Andrea, Georgie gripped the basin.

'I am a 42 year old mother of two for God's sake. This is mad. I won a chance to do stand-up sessions but this is becoming so stressful.'

Andrea thrust a shot glass full of vodka into Georgie's hand. She threw it down her throat as if it was poison. The sweet burn traced the outline of her throat as she persuaded her stomach to not regurgitate it. Then with Andrea firmly holding her arm, like an arrested robber not a stand-up comic, she was marched to the performers' tables and Jaz.

A comic was just finishing his act and Harry the MC puffed hard as he clambered on to the tiny stage, his builder's bum on display for all to see.

'Let's hear it for that fella, Jack Lott, everyone. The funniest small man in Newcastle, or at least this part of the

Quayside! Now our next act is going to be brilliant, she is a rare species up here. A female stand-up with teenagers who is going to make you all die with laughing, well not totally, at least not until the booze has all been sold! Can we have a big, Baci welcome for Georgie Chancellor please.'

Four firm hands, belonging to Andrea and Jaz, gave Georgie a decisive push on to the stage and before she knew it, she had picked up the microphone with her clammy, shaking fingers.

A quick gasp like a new-born baby and she decided she needed to just get this gig in front of Reuben over with. The hush around the room was terrifying again. The white spotlight blinded her and obliterated everything apart from the front few tables of people who were staring at her. They were neutral, which was better than hostile, with their arms folded and faces waiting patiently.

Georgie swallowed hard and gave herself a nanosecond to check out the expressions of the front row. Quite interested. Good.

She felt her pulse slowing and began. Georgie used her usual opening lines, repeating her gig script then added in some new family stories with a sassy attitude.

'You may think I look like a lovely respectable woman but I'm not. I'm a stand-up mam with a dark heart. Sometimes my family are so irritating I just want to talk about them up here to get it all off my chest.

Georgie began to feel confident. *There is no-where else I want to be, in the whole world, but here, telling my stories. I belong here.'*

'When I used to sit on my daughter's bed at night, and she would wait patiently for a story I would look at her excited eyes and say, 'Sorry, sweetheart, tonight is all about me!'

'When she was four, we were out in the country at a little café. We were about to drive off when two massive bikers pulled up alongside us. Our window was down and they smiled at my daughter who said hello and gave them a big smile.

'Oooh look' she said, 'Big shiny bikes.

The bikers smiled at her.

'Oooh look, lovely shiny jackets.'

Again, the bikers looked at each other and my cute girl.

'Look at the big, shiny earrings Mammy!'

Bikers still smiled back until she had the final word

'Just like Granny's…'

Before she knew it a red light was flashing at the back of the room and Harry was, once again, huffing and puffing his way on to the stage. 'A big hand for Georgie Porgie Pudding and Pie, made me laugh until I wanted to cry.'

There was no tumultuous applause but there was no scary silence either as the audience murmured general approval. Georgie felt a quiet surge of adrenalin and carefully took the steps down to the table beside Andrea and Jaz.

She felt a pinch of jealousy. Then he smiled and grabbed her hand to pull her down to the seat beside him. The green-eyed monster vanished as quickly as it had come.

'Good job G. Well done.' Jaz beamed. And she beamed back.

'That was spot on. I've got the fear now,' said Andrea.

'Thanks. It felt the best I've been. Nice change.' Georgie sat back in her chair and took a big gulp of her diet coke Jaz had waiting for her. *That's thoughtful and lovely.*

Harry announced the break before the final section and the two women made their way to the bar.

'For early days that was a really good set. How did it feel?'

Andrea leant on the bar trying to get the bar man's attention while glancing sideways at Georgie.

Her heart was still racing. She felt as if she had run a marathon.

'OK. That was such a lovely feeling of being accepted. Being me.'

But by the end of the night her happiness was blown out of the water. Reuben had insisted on seeing Jaz and her out of the door.

'I'll be in touch about what I mentioned Georgie.'

She wanted to shake him and stop whatever was in his head stone dead. But there was no time.

Then it was the usual, brief hug of congratulations from Jaz before she strode to her car.

Georgie realised she felt different as she left Baci that night. At five feet eight she had no need to delight in feeling taller, especially with heels, but she did. It was as if someone had put a hook in the top her head and was gently lifting her heavenwards. Passing Alec, a local, homeless man she offered him a couple of pounds.

'Here you go. Get yourself a MacDonalds.'

'I wouldn't eat that shite if you paid me, what do you think I am, desperate!'

He marched on, aloof for a few seconds, then thought better of it and returned, dirty hand open for her pieces of silver.

Snug in the security of her car, Georgie flicked through her phone and put on some heavy metal. Switching on the volume to ear-numbing proportions, she tore through the Quayside streets, windows wound down, by-standers gawking with amazement. The invisible woman was beginning to elbow her way through.

But there was the worry about Reuben's words. She needed to see him to find out, yet dreaded what could be coming.

TWENTY-TWO

The growing self-confidence of her family comedy routine and her friendship with Jaz were giving Georgie a new perspective on her life at home.

I'm absolutely exhausted. There has to be more to life than this thankless slog.

Lawrence was putting his new wine club delivery in alphabetical order in the wine racks, Lily and Nat were fighting about who had eaten the last Waitrose cookies. While Georgie stood at the kitchen sink scrubbing Jerusalem artichokes for a particularly intricate dinner, ready to kill all of her family.

There were several reasons for this. Lily had been really rude about there still being creases in her favourite dress after Georgie had ironed it. Nat was always furious about his sister's constant talking and interrupting his Xbox games. He never helped around the house either.

Lawrence was being particularly critical of her social skills again, even after all this time. This included her lack of ability to do the middle-class thing of making polite chit-chat while eating a meal. She always choked. What could she do? He was definitely becoming more like his late mother.

Georgie may be still the centre of all this family life but she was beginning to realise she needed to start and to stick up for herself. *Can I put them and their attitudes in my act?*

Maybe subconsciously this caused a shift in her life as everything began to change.

A loud knock early the next Saturday morning sent her nerves into a tail spin. She stiffened and knew in her very bones that something was very wrong in the world when she spotted Reuben at her front door.

Even though they had put the past behind them she dreaded hearing what he had alluded to at the club. She pulled herself up to her full height for confidence. Then she carefully smoothed down her t shirt over her jeans, ran her fingers through her hair to ensure it was away from her eyes so she could give him a long, hard stare. If needed.

She made her way down the final flight of stairs, gripping the rail hard as if it was going to arm wrestle with her. Lawrence, the early riser, had let Reuben in. The nightclub boss's usual self-assured, legs apart and planted pose was replaced with a half collapsed lean on the hall wall. *Strange indeed.*

'Well, this is a turn up Reuben. But come through. I supposed you'd better.'

Lawrence attempted to lighten the atmosphere by being overly jolly even though she knew he found their past, what he knew of it, both irritating and vaguely threatening.

'Georgie, my darling. Good old-fashioned manners. Eh?'

She looked at Reuben with all of the hardness she could muster, which for him, was a good amount. He, in return, smiled briefly and moved over, rested his hand on her shoulder and quietly whispered,

'Can I talk to you in private? Urgently.'

His hand was slightly shaking as he lightly touched her arm, gently moving her along to their front lounge and away from Lawrence.

'Lawrence. Please get some coffee for us. I wouldn't ask but you're much quicker with all of that coffee bean stuff than me.' Georgie smiled at her husband reassuringly.

He reluctantly agreed, looking back at them as he strode off down the passage to the kitchen.

Georgie was more worried than she had been for a long time as she pushed the lounge door open.

As soon as they were both inside the room Reuben

closed the door slowly and leaned against it, eyes shut and let out a deep sigh. Georgie stood stock still in front of him staring at his face and trying to fathom what brought him to her home. Yet dreading the answer.

They were standing so close she could smell his breakfast. Bacon. And eggs. His eyes were the perfect blue she remembered from all those years ago still framed with the golden eyelashes of the boy she thought was a God who had fallen to earth.

He put his hands on her shoulders and for a moment the absolute power he had wielded over her when she was 16 gripped Georgie like a sorcerer's spell. She was transfixed and similarly terrified. To her muddled senses Reuben's voice sounded as if he was speaking underwater.

'I've found him Georgie. The adoption agency has all his details.'

Her head had all of the blood sucked out of it and she would have fainted if he hadn't held her upright. All of the past 26 years scrolled in front of her. A silent film. A terrified schoolgirl. Alone in a hospital bed with a new born baby son's fingers lolling outside of the blanket and inviting someone to hold them tight to keep him safe for ever.

'He lives here. Can you believe it? He lives here, in Newcastle!'

Georgie's normally rigid frame began to collapse slowly in on itself. She took a deep breath and asked Reuben quietly the only question which was repeating itself over and over in her head,

'Why? Why did you try and find him?'

She couldn't believe he had broken their promise to try and forget they'd ever had a child, which had both welded them together and been a stone weight in their young lives.

Reuben composed himself and moved away from her to rest on the arm of the nearby sofa. Stretching out his legs he looked out of the window as he replied, his voice still low.

'I had a cancer scare a couple of months ago. It made me realise I had no real family. You know I wanted to see you after the birth but my parents didn't tell me that you gone into hospital until it was too late.'

She felt bile rise up and breathed out slowly to ensure she was indeed in the present day and not a schoolgirl again. Reuben shut his eyes again momentarily and she studied him. He was still as striking as he had been when he was the school sports champion and despite his greying hair, she knew why his commanding presence and charm had almost ruined her life.

Then he stood up and was almost nose to nose with her. She instinctively moved back to the door.

'Georgie. I never saw my son grow up due to my parents' wishes. Not mine. Which I accepted. I couldn't have been a proper father at that age with…'

She cut him off. 'As if there was even a talk about…'

'Listen Georgie. Please. Whether it's an age thing with that scare I don't know. But seeing you the other night also reminded me. It's raw. The need to find him was there with me every day and growing stronger. Now I know somewhere in this very city, there is a no-doubt long and lanky mixture of you and me. I think I see him on every street.'

Georgie said, 'I do too. All the time. But I've kept this hidden to get on with my life. My safe life. It's been hard won but it could get blown apart by finding him. I don't think I can cope with all of the hurt seeing him will bring. And as you know I DID see him when he was born, but to be honest,' she spoke in a whisper, finding it hard to get her words out, 'it wasn't the most pleasant of memories. Getting pregnant very nearly killed me and ruined my life.'

Reuben went to hug her to his chest in a bid to calm her and ease her distress. But she held herself taut,

Her tears were also held back. Just. 'I loved you so much. My heart broke that day. For not having my baby. Or you.'

She took a deep breath in and tried to calm down. The door handle was already in her hand as she turned to him and staring at him straight in the eyes said,

'I just wanted to curl up into a ball and die.'

Down the hallway Lawrence's chipper voice boomed, bounced off the walls and filled the room.

'Coffee's ready folks. And let them eat cake! Ha, ha, ha.'

Reuben was already at the front door.

'I'm finding him Georgie. What you do about meeting him is down to you.'

Before she could answer he was gone on his mission. Leaving a gust of cold air from the street outside. *What would the outcome be?* She dreaded to think.

*

Georgie couldn't believe it when she heard the Stand-Up Star organisers had picked Baci again for her next gig. Apparently, it was the only club with space for her that week. The whole comedy competition wasn't fun anymore. Jaz's company was the only thing keeping her going - that and his confidence in her doing well.

They were texting joke ideas or calling each other with funny anecdotes every day. More and more of her family life was pouring out and becoming jokes.

Every time his messages came in, she made sure there was time to sit down and savour them. Unlike everyone at home, he always asked 'How are you today?' *He cares. It's lovely.*

When she arrived at the club ready to talk to Reuben and prepared for the comedy gig, her stress levels were bouncing. The atmosphere seemed to be crackling like a live current being fed around its walls. Georgie wondered if it was just her and the impact of his announcement.

But Andrea, her comedy buddy, pulled up a stool beside her and whispered in her ear, 'There is definitely something in the air tonight. It is as if everyone has drunk a crate of Red Bull. This crowd is wired. I'm pleased I am on nearly last, at least they might all be quietly pissed and comatose by then.'

There was no sign of Reuben yet but Jaz was there already. He was wearing all black, drinking Jack Daniels and coke, relaxing at the bar.

When he saw Georgie, she could tell he knew something wasn't right.

'You don't look yourself. Anything up?'

'Loads. But it's more going down than up.'

'Well, whatever it is, you can talk to me. Or use it in your set?'

She gave a small laugh. Then decided the best thing to do was crack on with her comedy to take her mind off everything.

So, Jaz talked her through it and instilled some calm, but not much. He was also part of the head rush making her feel so different to her usual self.

Pulling her plain white top's sleeves over her hands Georgie tried to block out the endless chatter buzzing around the place. She wanted her set clear in her head.

She still hadn't seen Reuben since the morning at her house. *Where is he?* They needed the right moment to talk and both of them knew a gut-wrenching argument would likely ensue.

Tonight, despite herself, Georgie kept thinking of the warm baby bundle all those years ago. 'Our son.' She realised she had said the words aloud when Andrea spun round.

'Sorry hun, what did you say?'

'Scum.' I was thinking some of this lot are scum.

'Bloody hell that's judgemental. Take it easy!'

Harry, the regular MC smiled at Georgie and gave her a thumbs up sign, 'Five minutes and then you're on. We'll just let the last few get their drinks in.'

Georgie felt a cool chill move over her body. Someone is walking over your grave when you feel that, her mother would have said. She breathed deeply, concentrating on her lines.

Jaz said, 'I believe in you. You're special and don't even know it yet. But you will.'

For a moment she thought he meant to him personally but then realised it was as a comedian, obviously.

Back to the set, he said, 'Remember. You're ready for a bit of new material but keep it tight.'

Keep it tight. Keep it tight. And forget about my baby, for now.

There was a hush around the room. The last few were moving their seats into a comfortable position and she was on.

Harry the MC, started.

'Ladies and Gentlemen. Hope you all enjoyed a quick fag and wee in the break. Don't forget to avoid the nuts at the bar. They couldn't find a seat!'

A group of three men in their 20s were sitting right next to the stage and the tallest, skinny one in the middle, who was already quite drunk, began to heckle.

'You're not very funny mate. Could tell better jokes myself.'

He wouldn't shut up despite his friends trying to quieten him down. Harry got off the stage and sat on his knee and introduced Georgie from this unusual vantage point. He acted like he was the man's ventriloquist's dummy.

Georgie felt the now familiar rise of trepidation and her whole body pulsed with terror.

She fixed the noisy punter in her eyes square on. From somewhere she then found courage. From the side of the stage she shouted, 'That'll be the only lap dance you'll get tonight bonny lad, so might as well enjoy it!'

The whole club whooped and laughed at the gangly man.

It increased when the man squashed by Harry, suddenly seemed to sober up and stared, astonished she was the next act. She wondered if the MC's substantial weight had cut off his circulation.

'Here's another treat from a great new comedian from the other night. Hot off the block. In fact, hot full stop. And funny as well. Our very own Chancellor, Georgie Chancellor, only much more popular than the Government's one. Let's give it up for Geordie, sorry I mean Georgie!'

She strode out to the middle of the stage to clapping and had her customary nerves jangling about whether the microphone was on or not, until her voice boomed around the room and she knew she was good to go.

The first part of her set she repeated like clockwork. Then some new material was out of the traps.

'You all look like hard rock types, ready to salute the gods of rock like Iron Maiden and AC/DC.'

The crowd murmured assent and she set off again.

'As you can see, I'm a woman in her 40s but as well as having two kids I love rock music. My husband is a total classical music freak. But our son is into heavy metal and as a birthday treat our whole family went to see Iron Maiden at Twickenham. I'd rushed around the hotel, making sure they all looked the part. We were ready to rock. 80,000 people there, in black leather and studs. Shaved heads and piercings. A man in front of us had the Fear of the Dark album cover tattooed on his back.

'I had been so busy getting everyone else ready it was only when the gig started, I looked down. I was wearing a prim white cotton cardigan and white jeans in a sea of black leather. I was more like a damsel in distress than an Iron Maiden, maybe I should have 'run for the hills'! I stood out like a virgin at a bikers' rally.

'Way too old to be a virgin!' said gangly man.

Quick as a flash Georgie said, 'Says the man who probably still is one!'

The crowd lapped up the banter between them, apart from the man, who just raised his hand in defeat.

When Georgie had finished the rest of her set and come off stage there was a good round of applause. She had been in control rather than being overwhelmed by the crowd despite the trouble with the punter at the start. Sitting down with her usual post-gig thump on to the chair beside Andrea, she felt her body relax slightly.

'Here's your two men friends Hun.' Andrea put her hand on Georgie's knee and nodded over to Reuben and Jaz walking over, each with their own distinctive style. Jaz, cool and professional. Reuben, swagger and a touch of apprehension.

Jaz was helpful with feedback but in a rush as he had a gig himself in Newcastle later that night.

'Sure I can't tempt you to come along to the next club. I'll be good. I promise.'

Again, Georgie thought this could be taken two ways, then dismissed it as her brain playing tricks.

'Sorry. Too much on.' *Way too much to cope with.*

Jaz merely shrugged 'Your loss', but kissed her cheek goodbye. *Hmmm a kiss is new.* It gave her a small, surprising shiver.

She felt a strange mix of fury and fragility about being in Reuben's presence. Slowly this funny, daft competition had fired up her ambition. It had made her steel herself to come for this gig to test her set. All she wanted now was to enjoy a small post-gig glow then go home. She didn't want to think about past traumas that was for sure.

It was cold to have wanted to keep her first son a dark secret, but she had fought hard for her life's stability. There was a bubble around her. All normal feelings and emotions about him had been snipped, left to shrivel and die. Or so she thought. An unloved plant during the summer holidays.

Unfortunately, the stool beside her was free, but equally fortunate it was too small for Reuben who had to perch his buttocks precariously on the seat. He looked ridiculous.

Georgie continued to talk to Andrea as if she was oblivious to him. Placing the tips of his fingers on her knee to ensure he had her full attention he spoke above the room's babble into her right ear, sweeping her hair away from it beforehand as if she was his to own.

She found it strange that her stomach still reacted to him, more than her head.

'Great gig Georgie. You controlled the room very nicely indeed. Roll on the rest of your gigs up to the final.'

He went to put right the piece of hair he had placed behind her ear but Georgie grabbed his wrist firmly.

Then he leaned in to her other side. Her shoulder was stiff and unyielding,

'You can't avoid me forever. Let's go and have a grown up discussion about all this. The office?'

The thought of being in a tiny, windowless room at the

back of the club, was the last place she wanted to be alone with him.

'No. If we must talk about it, we'll go out on the Quayside, I'll need fresh air and plenty of it.'

Andrea raised her eyebrows as Georgie left. 'Everything OK hun? You look rattled.'

'I'm OK but not sure whether I'll be back tonight so break a leg. See you soon.'

They air kissed from a distance. Georgie joined Reuben who was holding the door open for her, where the cold river air grabbed her legs.

She strode out ahead of him, dodged the manic Quayside traffic and only stopped when she reached the iron railings on the river's edge. Staring at the Tyne, she remembered where she first saw Lawrence all those years ago.

Reuben joined her and was about to put his hands either side of her, pinning her to the railings, when she ducked out of the way.

Georgie spoke first, 'I need head room for all this so don't give me claustrophobia. Right. Walk. You stay on my left.'

They walked, stride matching stride, while Reuben sought the right words before stopping suddenly. Georgie came to a halt at the same time and they stood facing each other as he pulled out the white envelope from his pocket.

'These', he said, holding it front of her nose, 'are our son's contact details from the adoption agency.'

Something connected in Georgie's brain. 'You did see him, didn't you? When he was born?'

Rueben faltered, his voice faint. A confession.

'Yes. I never wanted you to know. Under close supervision from my father, I wasn't allowed to see you but I held him, tucked his fingers into my hand and breathed him in so I could hold as much of our baby as possible in me forever. The nurse had to prise him out of my hands. He never cried. But I did.'

Georgie stared at him. *He has never thought of anyone over himself in his life. If he did cry, I bet it would have been over soon enough.* She wanted to run. Jump into the rushing water and let it gorge on her, seeking out every crevice, until she disappeared. Problem solved.

Giggling teenagers with pink fairy wings and 'Carla's 18th Newcastle' t-shirts had stopped beside them and stared, just as she was staring at Reuben.

'Lovers' tiff?' said Carla, with a huge birthday top hat complete with candles perched on her head.

She jolted Georgie out of her trance.

'Has he told you he loves someone else? You're not bad looking for someone of your age. Just dump him!'

Her swaying friends all laughed in unison at this and picked up the battle cry. 'Dump him! Dump him!' Linking their arms together, they surrounded Georgie as if they were boxers in the ring. Poking her with their fingers.

Reuben grabbed Georgie's arm and shoved his way past them to march on down the Quayside away from the hectic bars and nightclubs. 'Bugger off you drunken cows. Leave her alone.'

They mimicked him, 'Drunken cows! Oooh listen to him, Mr Fancy Pants.'

Georgie was shaken but the irony of the encounter was not lost on her.

'So NOW you act like my knight in shining armour. Saving me from harm. It's a bit late Reuben. Way, way too late.'

She could still hear their laughter from way down the Quayside as she started a manic march away from them. An artistic metal bench was the nearest place to sit. She winced at the ice-cold.

'Sit.' She commanded. And he did.

This was a different planet to the start of their relationship. *He is not the Boy God of my teenage years. He's just a dad, with weepy eyes.*

'Now tell me everything.'

Reuben lit a long, French cigarette and she took one, even though they made her cough. She watched in the half light as he sucked in the nicotine rush. The smoke hung around him before it disappeared up his nostrils and was then blown out of his mouth in small circles.

'You always loved that when we were at school didn't you?

Georgie smiled at the memory of how impressed she had been by his silly tricks.

'Yep,' she breathed out and watched her own smoke get caught by the wind and take off seawards down the Tyne.

'I loved that very much.'

Reuben moved away from her slightly so his right hip was fixed in place by the arm of the bench, holding him in place, no easy escape. Staring straight ahead he started the story and Georgie similarly stared at the opposite bank so she could concentrate on his every word. Words she was intent on hearing yet at the same didn't want to take in.

'Our son, Paul. Is definitely here.'

'The Quayside?'

'No. No. But not far away. Newcastle as I said.'

'So I could have passed him. At any time?'

'Both of us could have.'

As usual things can never be just about me.

'What did you find out? *There's a big part of me really doesn't want to open this wound.*'

Reuben took a depth breath either for effect or because he needed to calm his own emotions.

'He was adopted by a Newcastle couple in their 30s who couldn't have kids. His name is Paul…'

'What is he doing, do you know?'

'Well, chip off the old block. Believe it or not.'

'A cocky snob?'

Reuben didn't even listen to what she'd said as he continued.

'Good at art. Doing a PhD in Fine Art at Northumbria University. Didn't find out he was adopted until he was 10 as his parents thought he might not understand what it meant.'

Georgie still stared ahead as Reuben paused for another drag on his cigarette, the perfumed smoke created their own room. A moment.

He explained again his health scare had in turn created a mid-life crisis. He sent a letter to the adoption agency pleading his case and was lucky. Paul wanted to be found, even though he was happy with his adoptive parents. Georgie gripped her hands and stared at them intently as Reuben continued.

'We'll meet up for the first time somewhere impersonal, a coffee shop maybe?'

Hardly an appropriate location for something so important she thought, forgetting for a moment, she didn't want to know about this baby, this boy, this man. Her son.

'We don't know if we'll meet after that Georgie but he has said he would like to meet you.'

'I can't. At all.'

'You must.' He got up and moved to the riverside railings, throwing his unfinished cigarette into the water.

'I must not.' Georgie whispered the words out as she got up.

'Every minute of every day I try to be the perfect wife and mother. This secret could blow it all up. You don't get it do you? I can't meet him. You can. Fine. That's your choice. I never had that when he was born.

'Our son broke me in two. His arrival meant I was kicked out of my home. It took me years to become even just a tiny bit human and successful. The devastation still haunts my life silently now, making me pretend, strangling my relationship with my kids, my hus…'

Why am I sharing these thoughts with him of all people?

Reuben pulled her toward him and they hugged in a silent embrace which felt like hours.

He spoke first. 'I'm so pleased we're getting the chance to talk about this Georgie. It's helping me so much. And for you…'

She didn't let him finish. It became too much for her and she turned her back on him and began to walk back towards the sparkling lights and illuminated bridges over the Tyne. Her pace got faster and faster and before she knew it, she was running, only pausing when she felt that her lungs were going to explode. It was then she realised she was alone. Glancing over her shoulder she saw he had stopped running after her and shouting her name. He stood still. His face in darkness.

Her hands were shaking as she reached her car. Home. She needed to be home.

TWENTY-THREE

What is my biggest fear? Georgie often thought that. Then she realised it was doing the stand-up competition which, although started by her family, now seemed to be of little interest to them, and having contact with her first baby.

It sounded like it could have been OK, giving your baby away when you've no way of looking after it yourself, just like giving your virginity away. Both were so inextricably linked, for her.

Despite never using her maiden name, the knock on the door from a no-doubt six feet, long-lost son remained an ever-present fear.

In her heart of hearts, she knew Reuben had been flaky. You don't run away from a pregnant schoolgirl girlfriend otherwise. But he was a similar age to Nat and with uncompromising parents who controlled him.

Reuben had definitely not wanted him. Never saw her again either, back then.

Until.

The knock at the door that was the nightmare come true.

Georgie's safe world was tied up with a ribbon. Reuben at her actual front door that morning, caused the whole package to unravel. 'Finding our son. It was an itch to scratch.' He said.

Only his nails were taking chunks out of Georgie's life not just his own. He was not giving up. He had found their son. And now he was going to see him, come hell or high water.

He had a name.

Paul.

He had a place.

Newcastle. Right here.

He had never really been far, like the lump in her throat. Not just in her throat but in her heart.

It twisted with a vengeance on his birthday, Christmas, which was when Georgie had to try oh so much harder, to be the most perfect wife and mother.

She always got up at six those days. Awake with a dark dread that wouldn't shift.   Such a contrast to the bright, shiny mother she pretended to be. Actually, had to be.

It wasn't that anyone in her family would consider giving her baby up for adoption as awful. She knew that. But it really wasn't the done thing as Lawrence said about almost everything in her past. It was because she struggled to deal with it.

She only coped by grabbing onto every part of her life with a firm control.

Scrub the cupboards. Forget the baby.

Have two more babies. Forget the baby.

See them grow into teenagers. Forget the baby.

Then. He's going to be 26 today. Forget, he's not a baby.

Reuben was going to set up a meeting. What the hell had he started?

*

Georgie did want to escape her life regularly. But Lily and her growing baby bump were such a constant reminder of her past it was even worse.

The heating was on full blast and she was alone in the house. Peace and comfort. Maybe she should try and write some comedy without Jaz's help?   It might help her to heal. Paul came into her head as he had been doing but she pushed him away again, for now.

Her phone pinged.

The next gig for Stand-Up Star booked. Jaz texted.

It was a new night at an established comedy club in York called a Gong Show. It was in two weeks' time and she had to have some great material for it. Andrea said these shows were like feeding the Christians to lions.

Material. She had to work on her an act to get more material to make the set hilarious but her mind was blank.

This was despite all the usual rituals being done before she sat at her desk. Washed up, tidied, scrubbed and polished. Everything.

She loved her home being this quiet with the only sound the deep ticking of the grandfather clock Lawrence had been given by his mother as a 21st birthday present. She had got an Argos travel clock for hers.

The stripped pine chair was pulled in tight to the desk. She balanced on her two hard sitting bones as she was taught in yoga, sipped builder's tea and scowled at the computer screen, searching for inspiration. Then she remembered all Jaz's instructions and heard him as if he was in the room.

'Right Georgie. Now is the time to get everything off your chest. Feel the rage. Feel the rage!'

At the time she had wondered how something which made you angry could also be funny.

Rants. Georgie was triggered by thinking of Reuben and started to make a list of everything she hated.

Out of no-where, the Devil on one shoulder knocked off the Angel on the other and let her tumble out vitriol and spite.

First out of the mental traps.

People who call their children names like Willow when you knew they were really a lumpy Oak. Lawrence had suggested that for Lily but luckily thought better of it.

Sucking the pencil, she stared into space until her Devil kicked into life again.

She fiddled with her wedding ring. *Ah, now I need to work on a whole new set of ideas about my family.*

Lawrence's bossy instructions on how to be a lady. And middle-class. Always wanting to be married to a version of herself that doesn't really exist apart from in his head. She remembered the first dinner party she'd prepared when they were newly married. And wrote it up in all its excruciating detail.

Then she wrote about men before him. Boyfriends that

promise one thing. Then disappear. Only to turn up again at just the wrong time. Wreaking havoc.

Just like a mother and a father who drink all the time. Embarrassing you at parents' evenings by falling off their chairs. Puking in neighbours' bushes on the way back from the pub. Forgetting birthdays. All the time.

And so, the set filled up.

*

Georgie hadn't had a real female friend for years as Lawrence's colleague's wives were not really her type. When her new comedy buddy Andrea had suggested a night on the town, the new Georgie thought, why not?

Andrea seemed to have a sixth sense of what she needed.

The Newcastle venue was a Geordie version of a Caribbean Island. Loud pumping music with a big bass beat. Cocktails with umbrellas on every table. And punters downing shots while filling their faces with huge bowls of jerk chicken.

She followed in Andrea's slipstream to their table. She picked her cuticles. Cooking Sunday lunch for Lawrence's new client the next day meant she had to be careful not to get hammered. She counted 10 different colours and styles of cocktail on the two tables beside them.

'Come on. Let's crack on. What you drinking?' Andrea thrust the menu at her. Drinks first. No sign of the food one, yet.

'Hmmm. I'm not…'

'Too slow. I'll order us a pitcher of Pomegranate Mojito.'

Georgie hadn't had one before and when the gorgeous glass of pink liquid was in front of her, she couldn't resist swigging it.

'You'll need to go a bit steady girl. I promised to get you home in good shape by midnight!' Andrea laughed.

Everything about her new friend felt alien to Georgie. She had never been out for a night like it since she got married all those years ago.

They ate their delicious fish tacos with their fingers while finishing off the huge jug of Mojito.

Georgie burped loudly and then slipped off her stool laughing.

'Hey gorgeous. Watch what you're doing!' A six foot man in his 20s, on his stag do, wearing a top hat with Lewis's Gang on it, put out his hand to lift her up. His friends all cheered in unison. 'Whoooo. Wait 'til Kelsey hears about this!'

'Thanks Lewis.' Georgie realised her speech was slurring.

A Bob Marley song began blasting out and before she knew it, Lewis and Andrea had grabbed her hands and were leading her to the tiny dance floor.

In her head she was flying through space. The beat was so insistent she couldn't help but enjoy the freedom of spinning, resting on Lewis's arm whenever she felt she was going to fall.

'I'm Georgie. When's your wedding?' She was on tip toes to shout in his ear.

'Two weeks. We're down from Glasgow. Newcastle is party central. We're having a great time. You local?'

'Yes. Never lived anywhere else.'

'They always say Geordie chicks are the fittest of anywhere.'

Georgie pulled herself up straight and smiled at him. Then winked.

He laughed. 'I didn't say you were. But you're definitely MILF.' Turning to his friends he said. 'She's proper MILF this one, isn't she?'

Andrea grabbed hold of Georgie's hand. 'Come on honey. They're even more pissed than us. Let's go move away from them and get some more drinks.'

Lewis blew Georgie a kiss which she pretended to catch and press to her heart as she was propelled to the bar.

Her head felt it had become disconnected from her neck. 'I'm not sure I can drink any more, Andrea.' Her stomach was twisting with the spicy food and the cocktails were definitely swimming around the top of it all.

Another burp erupted.

Andrea got her a big glass of water. With a spiced rum

cocktail. 'Here. Water will sort you out. It's only 11 and I promised you'd be home by 12 so we've loads more time for mischief!'

Georgie rested her head on the bar. The cool wood was lovely. Although it thumped with the music's bass beat.

'Maybe I should …'

'Don't you dare say go home. You need to live a little my friend. Knock these back and let's stand over there, away from the dance floor. I think I had better keep you away from your new friend Lewis!'

'I love you Andrea.'

'Love you too. You drunken daft thing. You really can't take your drink, can you?'

Georgie leant into her friend's shoulder then linked her arm and happily followed her lead.

When the taxi dropped Georgie off at home as the clock struck midnight, she stumbled up the steps, her stiletto shoe got stuck in between the path's paving.

'Sorry Lawrence.' She rested against the porch glass. Her face pressed against the coolness of it.

'Bloody hell. You're not the typical Cinderella are you, Georgina? Your shoe's down there and you're what our children would call wasted. My God.'

She stumbled up the stairs on her hands and knees with her husband following.

'I've had a really lovely… It's been so …. Ah no. I feel...'

Lawrence leapt past her and flung open the bathroom door as she threw up all over its floor. Some ended up in the toilet. Some didn't.

That was all she remembered until the alarm went off at seven the next morning.

TWENTY-FOUR

It was a very long time since Georgie had woken up alone and with a hangover.

Sunlight was pouring into the bedroom and Lawrence's side of the bed was cold.

She tiptoed downstairs. For her head's sake and because she was wary of the reception.

'Morning.' The kitchen door was wide open and Lawrence was staring at recipe books on the bench ignoring her.

'What. Do you. Have. To. Say. For. Yourself? Hm. Hm. Hm?'

Even though she was not at her best Georgie couldn't help feeling one Hm would have been enough.

'I'm so sorry. I don't know what...'

'Stop there. You were blind drunk. At your age. What a state. And now...'

'What about now?'

'The Winlaters are coming. And YOU need to get their lunch ready.'

Georgie flopped onto the kitchen seat. She lay her head on her folded arms.

'I can't Lawrence. Seriously. I need to go back to bed. Or somewhere...'

A Gordon Ramsay cookbook was slammed down, missing her head by millimetres.

'Just get on with it. They're coming in three hours. You owe me this Georgie.'

'Well, are you going to help me. You sometimes do.'

'I SOMETIMES haven't had to help you the night before.'

Georgie felt nausea rush over her and she grabbed a glass of water from the sink.

She began chopping vegetables, seasoning a joint of sirloin beef and making a fruit salad. Sipping water and resting her head in her hands every few minutes. Lawrence sat at the table, legs on a seat, reading the Sunday papers. At that moment she hated him.

Georgie was sick three times before their guests arrived. Lawrence had relented and set the table. This was mainly because she still couldn't always be sure to get the cutlery and glasses in the right place.

Toby and Jane Winlater were actually ok. They made appreciative noises about the food. They didn't mind hard carrots, flat Yorkshire puddings and very bloody meat. 'We like a blue steak.' They said in unison.

The sea of blood oozing from the joint when Lawrence carved it at the table made Georgie excuse herself. How was there anything else to come out of her stomach?

At least there couldn't be anything wrong with the fruit salad, she thought. That was until Jane picked out a hair from her dish. No words were said. She just quietly put it on her place mat.

'I'm so sorry.' Georgie couldn't have felt worse.

'And so am I' added Lawrence, giving her daggers. 'Can I get you a port and some Cornish cheeses to finish off?'

'We haven't got any Cornish cheeses Lawrence.'

Jane and Toby Winlater looked at each other. Toby tapped his watch. 'That's such a kind offer but we've got to call in to see our parents this afternoon.'

'I can go and get some cheese. It won't take long.' Lawrence was desperate.

'No really. It's been very … lovely. To see you both,' said Toby.

'Lovely. Lovely' said Jane, picking up her handbag.

'I thought we could have a crack on about doing a bit of business.' Lawrence was smiling and stayed seated to encourage them to do the same.

'Perfect, Give my PA a call. End of the month. Maybe.'

On the way out Jane touched Georgie's arm. 'You take care of yourself. I hate cooking and admire you giving it a go. Don't worry about today. Men and their port and cheese. Really!'

Georgie could have kissed her. But didn't feel able to be near her face in case she still smelled of sick.

They were on the doorstep in seconds. As the hosts waved them off Lawrence raged. 'Thanks for nothing Georgina. Not even any fucking cheese. If that deal doesn't come off it's down to you. And your new piss-head friend.'

She knew he would forgive her by the morning as he always did, when she cocked something up.

The difference was this time in her head Georgie thought *At least I've got a friend. And it feels lovely. Might also make a great story for my set.*

TWENTY-FIVE

Then

After their first meeting on the Tuxedo Princess nightclub Lawrence had asked her on a date. Obviously. Given his intoxication with her. He was making headway in his law career. He used to recount that date and how even then, with their very different backgrounds, he knew she was the one for him.

'Well.'

He always began.

'I knocked on this tatty door to pick up my date, (my now wife), and out came this blonde stunning vision albeit with a pierced nose and pink fringe.   And I thought mother's going to have a fit to match that pink fringe!'

Georgie mainly remembered trying on all of her jumble sale 10p dresses in various luminous satin-type fabrics, ending up wearing a black fish net clinging dress. When Lawrence knocked that night, her stomach actually flung itself about like a fish on a hook.

'Hello gorgeous' he said.

He's actually turned up.

'Hello Lawrie.'

No-one had ever called him that before and she was sure he liked it.

She kissed him lightly on the cheek, taking in his lemony aftershave and slight scratch of stubble that the razor had missed.

'Where can I take you in my chariot or should I say my BMW?'

Georgie wanted to feel confident and couldn't bear the

thought of eating somewhere with too much cutlery so they ended up at a Newcastle wine bar which she considered posh and, she could tell, he thought was a bit down on its luck.

'Tell me your life story.'

He held her hand with both of his, as if she might run off. That could have happened, as she did want to do just that. She realised how poor she was beside him, with a hole in her shoe, badly dyed hair, but this man was the best-ever chance of security.

She was 23 and working as an admin apprentice for her current boss wide-boy, Brett, who had been in her school and set up a marketing agency.

On that first date she said: 'I'm born and bred here. On that Gateshead council estate we passed.' The desire to lie and embellish was huge but she held back.

She was apprehensive of Lawrence, with his posh voice and white, immaculate fingers which she found both unusual and fascinating. She only knew men who had either nicotine-stained or work-battered hands.

'Can I have a pint please, if that's ok?'

He did a double-take but bought one anyway and a bag of crisps, finding her level.

'I've never been out with a lady who drank pints' he laughed.

Georgie made a mental note to never ask for another one. She was going to earn this lady moniker but was also going to have to learn fast if this escape-route-man wasn't going to slip through her fingers.

'What does everyone else drink then?

'Oh, wine, expensive wine usually, if I'm paying… Champagne when someone else is paying.' He laughed at that. So did Georgie. Champagne. That was the stuff of TV and films.

His thick, dark brown curly hair was short but got darker at the temples with sweat, as did his cheeks, as he drank his three glasses of Pinot noir. She realised she had also never seen anyone dress like him. Thick cord trousers not battered jeans, highly polished brown brogues and a blue shirt. *A shirt, for a night out!*

At the end of the night, she was torn between sleeping with Lawrence or pretending to be a lady, as she saw one, and the pretence won. Her fingers were crossed it was the right choice.

Lawrence walked her to the front door and she kissed him, slowly, expertly. All those awful lecherous men at her local pub made her value his hesitant manner even more. Had he even kissed a girl, she wondered?

'I'm sorry you can't come in. My landlady would go mad.'

His eyes nearly exploded out of his head, or that could have been her kissing.

'Oh my. I didn't expect to do that. Oh goodness.'

There would be another 10 dates before they slept together and Georgie took Lawrence's virginity as well as an opportunity to escape her life. He became a thoughtful lover and she appreciated the difference to her past men.

At the time she was living in a bedsit inside a dilapidated Victorian house in Newcastle's Jesmond suburbs. It has been grand in the 1920s and she had picked it for the small bit of kudos of the address. She ignored the other tenants, a polite ex-public school drunk, a barmaid with a lively night-life and a debt-ridden maths teacher. They, in turn, ignored her. Stuck up and down on luck, they surmised.

The toilet in the house was brown-stained and chipped. Georgie had the drunk Alcy Alf, banging on the door as she waited for the pregnancy test to show how her future might look.

Predictor – what a perfect name

'I don't know how that's happened.'

Lawrence sat stunned at the news. At least that's how she imagined it would be if she told him. Her calm, caring boyfriend didn't deserve this trap. The escape route had seemed perfect but for the second time in a few years Georgie was pregnant with a baby at the wrong time.

But when she had thrown up over her shoes in front of him one morning she had to.

'I can't have this baby with you. It has to be adopted.'

Lawrence cried. His tears soaked his shirt.

'We can't.'

Georgie also cried, soaking her one tissue and then a pile of toilet roll.

I caught him in a honey trap but this sweet man has been nothing but kind to me.

They had only slept together once and Lawrence had done the decent thing. What a contrast. Her mind did a mad dash back over the years and the frightening future she faced alone then. Even if Lawrence and her did split up he had pledged to stay with her at this point at least.

'Marry me.'

Georgie's tears picked up a pace with shock and relief that she quickly buried.

'Lawrence. I don't think…'

He held her hand and knelt on the stained, sticky carpet, she thought, against his better judgement.

'Please marry me, lovely Georgina.'

Bouncing balls filled her brain, each one more erratic than the last. They had all her doubts inside them. REJECTION. POVERTY. BABY.

'I need to get rid of it.'

Her tone was hard in a way she didn't feel.

'We can't do that. This baby is part of you and me. Marry me.'

Georgie made him stand up.

'I can't.'

She looked him in the eye.

'I wanted to catch you. But it's all gone wrong. For the first time in my life someone has done the decent thing.'

She started to cry again as the image of her baby boy getting taken away came back. Lawrence didn't know about him yet.

'I love you. And the beautiful woman I know you can become.'

Those prophetic words should have scared Georgie, or at least been an amber warning, but the lure of sanctuary was too strong. She tried to do the right thing. It wasn't in her will power to refuse support and longed for security.

It was definitely a romance that trucked along at a steady pace. But now with the added complication of a baby on the way. It was too much too soon.

She had read in *Teen Women's World* about the impact of bowling someone over. So, she wanted to bowl 'her Lawrie' over and catch him before he realised just what he was taking on by marrying her.

Overwhelmed and anxious were not the words Georgie had expected to sum up her wedding day. She hadn't wanted to invite her parents but Lawrence, who had only met them once, insisted, and her hormone ravaged body couldn't get her brain to articulate the words 'just no.'

The church where Lawrence had been baptised, his grandmother's life celebrated and his parents married, was huge. Its pulpit was so high you had to crane your neck to see it.

She was walked into the church with her father George Senior who was in a too small black suit, bought for drinking friends' funerals, of which there were many.

'God look at them. It's like the fuckin' Royal Family with them 'ats.'

'Don't swear or start anything, please.'

I'll do what I frickin' want. As you know all too well pet.'

The organ music soared and off they set, Georgie's billowing wide dress banging off the pews, her shoes tapping loudly on the floor. On their right were rows of ornate hats and bald heads. It looked like a flock of decapitated birds of paradise. And on their left was her mother. No hat. Dark, dyed hair scraped back into a thin pony-tail.

Second-hand grey coat topped off with a rainbow scarf, stolen from a department store.

Well. Your mam's scrubbed up champion.'

Could he speak any louder?

'Yes. Ssh.'

'Ah said…'

'I know. Shh.'

She felt quietly excited as she set off at a trot down the aisle until she was two pews away from her husband to be. Her feet suddenly seemed to be glued to the spot and she felt unable to put on in front of another. Lawrie turned round and gave her a taut smile. His head was cocked to one side.

He's saying well, are you going to do this or not?'

Georgie remembered seeing an old-fashioned film 'The Graduate' where the daughter ran back down the aisle from the altar. She at least knew where and who she was running towards, whereas Georgie would be heading straight to the edge of a precipice.

Her desire to flee was overwhelming when the decision was taken out of her hands as her bridesmaid, gave her a firm shove forward. It unlocked her feet from the stone floor and she was propelled towards Lawrie, marriage and family life, while hearing a quiet hiss from her right as his mother whispered,

'It's a wonder it doesn't have black dots all over it. Virginal white indeed.'

And they arrived at the altar. The delicious moment when responsibility shifted to Lawrence and she could hopefully shrug her parents off and never see them again. As if sensing this gleeful abandonment her father dug his fingers into fleshy part of her upper arm.

'We're always family, don't f'get. Ah, here we go.'

The vicar was posh and talked to a spot well above Georgie's head. And then with what felt like lightning speed, a ring was on Lawrence and her fingers and they were outside the church.

Photos done and on to the hotel.

More photos. More smiling and more worry about where her parents had gone. They had disappeared no doubt with the obligatory hip flask. There was still no sign of them right until everyone was about to sit down at the reception. They appeared.

'This wedding has got shot gun all over it.'

Lawrence's Aunt Dorothea, his mother's sister, was all in fuchsia and pinched tiny lips to match. She suited the hotel which was also pale pink and had chandeliers at every turn.

'That's enough'

Lawrence was cross and wanted to protect his bride.

'Come on Georgina. Let's get my gorgeous bride a glass of champagne.

He deliberately led her across to the silver salver of flutes.

'Lawrence, I can't with the baby coming.'

'I know that but we had to shut the silly woman up. Here take this and throw it in the nearest plant pot.'

The hotel was the most expensive place she had ever been in. Despite trying to be a lady she couldn't help scratching constantly at her own wedding dress waistband where it dug into her belly.

'Stop it please.' Lawrence pulled her arm. 'It's possible people might notice Georgina.'

He then smiled reassuringly.

'Best be careful.'

A tap on the glass by the head waiter made the 50 guests quieten down.

They all sat down at the crisp, white linen-clad tables.

Georgie was trembling as she sat at the top table with her husband, a new word, who held her hand, playing with her wedding ring. She shivered.

The flowers, a huge arrangement of pink and red roses gave her something to hide behind as everyone finally settled into their seats. Everything in the room continued the pink theme, shimmering in the sun which poured through the windows.

'Ahl right.' Her dad brought her back to reality.

Georgie heard him say it to Lawrence's mother as he sat beside her at the top table. She grimaced and pulled herself in tighter at the table. He then leant in towards her mother-in-law to whisper what? She dreaded to think.

Were there tell-tale signs of drink?

She couldn't see any but then they hadn't been topped up with the flowing champagne yet.

Her mother was wedged beside elderly Uncle Charles and Aunt Dorothea substituting for Lawrence's father, who had long since died.

It had seemed like a dream pretty much until that point. Waitresses in black with smart white aprons brought beautiful starters of prawns and seafood. She was ready to nibble new things she'd only recently tried, as Dorothea's husband Charles made chit chat about whisky and golf.

Chicken in cream sauce with dauphinoise potatoes and two stick thin vegetable portions followed. In her view the pudding was best, black forest gateau. She nearly licked the plate.

'And then my shares on the Nikkei fell by so much I had to take a heart pill … She zoned out.

'…. and the chairman said, 'Charles….'

And she zoned out again.

Once the meal was over and Oliver, Lawrence's best man, a friend from boarding school, had shared his embarrassing tales, which were not what she called embarrassing, he introduced her dad for his speech.

This is it. This is where my life unravels.

Georgie wondered if it was possible to crawl under the top table with a pregnant belly and a hooped underskirt, not to mention yards of satin.

'Well, yer ahll very differen t'me and my Mrs.'

At which point her mother burped. She always made the wrong noise at the wrong time. Although Georgie knew it could have been worse.

She put her hands over her eyes. She didn't care what it looked like but she didn't feel she could cover her ears in front of this audience. Then she realised people weren't listening to him so Oliver banged a glass loudly and the typically loud middle-class voices reluctantly slowed to a stop.

'…. and then when sher wus 12…'

Everyone missed Georgie's early years, thank goodness or so she hoped.

'Her Mam always said, 'She's got nowt in her heed but drawing and wurds. Wurds. Wurds. Wurds.'

The polite silence began to ebb. Then Georgie realised his voice was beginning to break.

Oh my God. He is really pissed and could totally collapse.

The subject of her anguish then took his champagne flute and threw its entire contents down his throat in one gulp.

His hands banged on the table and it was as if for once the alcohol had suddenly transformed him into something other than a mean-spirited thug.

'Her there's my lil girl. Am not the best fatha but….'

A loud sniff and mopping of his brow followed.

Georgie felt Lawrence squeeze her hand. Her head was down and her cheeks burned.

'…. She's amazin. Brought hersel up really, cos a do like a drink. I love yer our Georgina. I'm sorry. That's it. Needs to be said.'

The room stilled as his voice choked up. For the first time in her life her father looked at her with something other than quiet disgust. And it nearly broke her.

She pulled out her chair and Oliver told everyone to raise their glasses. As soon as the toast was done she grabbed a tissue and fled to the toilet. The rare emotion in her father's face was both overwhelming and repulsive.

Leaning against the wall outside afterwards the sun warmed her face and as she shut her eyes a hand was wrapped around her fingers. Lawrence kissed her.

'My gorgeous Georgie. That was quite a speech.'

She tried and failed to smile.

'Kill me!'

'No way. If I killed you, I'd have to die as well.'

His arms embraced her and she knew he loved her with all his heart.

I do love him I'm sure I do. This is me safe, forever.

TWENTY-SIX

Lawrence's mother slammed down her crocodile skin handbag on Georgie's kitchen bench and then flounced out of the house, when she had heard she was going to be a grandmother so soon after the wedding.

'I knew it.'

Early married life was bumpy and yet strangely solid. Having a baby boy six months after getting married was always going to be hard work.

When Nat was born Lawrence behaved in the exact opposite way to every man Georgie had ever known.

'Do you want a coffee Georgina?'

'Can I take him away in his pram for a walk to let you sleep?'

Treats of flowers and chocolates were also brought in after work most days. Sometimes it was food, other times it was a silk scarf, earrings, perfume.

Georgie was sure the other mothers at the baby club in an exclusive part of Newcastle would be appalled. Their own tales of middle-class husbands playing endless golf or going on work nights out with clients until the small hours struck horror in her heart.

Lawrence would sit with her and have 'his perfect Nathaniel' asleep on his chest.

'I'm the happiest man alive Georgina. Happiest Man.'

'I know. Love you. Happiest man.'

Georgie couldn't really begin to express the constant relief and gratitude she felt for him.

This meant when she had Lily, their second child. She sometimes thought how would she cope without him? There was no other support around her. None of her old friends liked Lawrence as they thought he was stuck up. And his friends thought she was very rough around the edges and tended to give her a wide birth.

On rare occasions she saw her parents, mainly in the city centre at a coffee shop, to ensure they didn't steal anything from her home. They had always stressed the importance of stashing things away on a shopping trip when she was small. A pair of socks in a coat pocket. Lipstick into a handbag. Not be missed, they said. She had never been sure exactly what that meant.

Lily was the apple of Lawrence's eye. He couldn't quite believe she existed.

'It's my baby girl.'

Then he would wrap Georgie up in his arms 'But you're still my number one.'

And as always, she would wonder why. She didn't see herself as a warm, funny woman who was also strong and beautiful. The mirror told her about imperfections, a strong, (manly) jaw line, pale blue eyes (creepy) and straight nose (pretty large).

The negative words were overheard by Georgie when Lawrence's mother in another room said them too loudly.

As if I need confirmation of my failings.

TWENTY-SEVEN

Now

When Georgie got up on a Sunday morning after 10 weeks of her comedy training, she put a theory to the test. Was she invisible? Jaz's attentive attitude made her realise often at home no-one listened to her or looked at her like he did.

Sun shone into the kitchen and she took pride in the spotless surfaces for an instant. But now a devil kicked in.

Go on, mess it up, see if anyone notices.

She smeared honey on the fridge handle, left dregs of coffee grinds by the sink and spilt cereal on the floor.

When Lawrence walked into the kitchen, he didn't look at her as he grabbed a banana and bottle of water before heading to pick up his weekend paper.

Lily gave a casual, half-hearted wave without looking up from her phone. When two huge thumps on the stairs signalled Nat bouncing into the kitchen. Georgie held her breath.

Her son briefly scanned her pyjamas, shrugged, then made a bowl of cereal, leaving spilt milk. And she resisted the temptation to wipe it up.

Georgie's face tightened, sick of being the perfect wife nobody appreciated. She gripped her now cold cup of coffee tighter.

The grim house she'd lived in when she was young was a world away from this. How she would have loved this home and never taken it for granted.

This place had always felt like perfection but now it was shifting in her mind. Life was getting ragged around the edges, like herself.

Her perfect family. Not noticing anything she wore, or what she did.

The list of domestic and general grievances grew longer until she thought her head would explode. Or at the very least give her some material for a new set.

She remembered an older secretary, Jenny, at the agency bemoaning the fact that when she hit 40 no-one looked at her. Ever. Then Georgie realised she couldn't remember if Jenny was still working at the agency. When had she last seen her?

Oh my God. It's true.

After everything she had done to get this middle-class life, she was disappearing from view, like in her childhood.

Georgie stuck her chin out. An old habit from when life got too grim.

The rest of the day she didn't tidy anything away. Family came and went, oblivious.

By seven o'clock she caved in and decided to make the tea, an intricate French stew with 30-day aged beef.

This was a tipping point. She knew it deep in her belly. What she didn't know was where this feeling of being rubbed out was going to take her.

Doing stand-up was going to help to transform her life but also lose what she had so carefully created and craved. Then there was also the situation with Reuben to contend with.

Creating the chaos in her home had distracted her from what was about to come. The image of her first-born was in her head from waking up to going to sleep. Being busy was the only thing that kept it at bay.

*

The next time Georgie walked in to Baci she hoped she looked like she had confidence. Reuben smiled and once they had ordered coffees, he laid the pieces of paper in front of her. She stayed standing.

He smoothed them down as if he wanted to meld them into the table.

Their eyes met and for the merest moment she was

catapulted back to the first time they were alone together at his home, that Sunday afternoon.

'Here's the letter I've back from the Council's adoption service and here's the note I got from our son about meeting up.'

Reuben had started to tremble slightly.

'God. I need a cigarette Gina.'

He called her by his pet name by accident, she assumed. It made her flinch. They were a long way from those times.

The lines around his eyes were darker than usual and his shave had not been quite so meticulous. Her fingers still itched to touch it despite herself. She made herself come back in the room.

'Well, you can't have one. It's illegal indoors. So, let's just get on with this shall we? You were saying…'

She got up stiffly and looked out of the club's windows at the hectic Quayside below. As usual when she was in the middle of a difficult situation, she couldn't quite believe the rest of the world didn't know about it. She almost expected everyone to be at a standstill looking up at her with a mass of bated breath.

'Look, here's his letter. Read it George, his writing is just like yours used to be as well. Remember that Valentine card? See how he loops his 'y' around and back. That's writing of real character. You can tell.'

Reuben was now standing beside her but she kept looking steadfastly out of the window. The roof of the Tyneside Baltic art gallery opposite was now strangely fascinating and the big banner down its front with a 40ft high question mark very apt, representing the millions of questions rolling around in her head.

'Look at me.' Reuben took hold of Georgie's chin and turned it sharply towards him as the barman approached their table and came to an abrupt halt. She shook herself free.

'Whooah! Really sorry guys.' He backed off quickly. Then Reuben continued.

'Paul has said he will meet me only if you're there as well. I imagine he wants to understand why we didn't, or couldn't, bring him up.

With a hint of menace, she said 'We had better dig up your father then hadn't we, so he can put his pennyworth in to the mix. The old bastard. I wanted to keep our son. It was horrific being separated. There's a lot at stake for me. No simple solution. None at all.'

'I know that but I want to see him Georgie. You're the key to all this. It is obviously important to him that he meets his birth mother.

'Anyway.' He wiped a damp corner of his eye with his sleeve. 'I've replied and said we'll see him next week, for a drink.'

Georgie's fury, mixed with guilt about how she felt, began to sear through her body. She fanned her face to try and cool down.

'I'll need to think about things. It's way too rushed.'

Despite her anger at being steamrollered into all this Georgie's immediate urge was to see Paul but it wasn't that simple. When she sat in her car to head home, she felt her spine had collapsed.

Oh my God. I can't do this. Not with Lily needing support for her baby as well

Paul would remind her of who she really was. Her real fear was that she was about to lose her security and also become a replica of her own crap mother. The worst of all. She also knew the time had come when she had to have the conversation with Lawrence that she had dreaded with her whole heart for so long

*

Georgie tried laughing out loud in front of her bedroom mirror the following evening to get in the mood for her comedy gig. It didn't work. She knew she had to tell her family about Paul but couldn't face it beforehand.

Jaz had helped her with some set tweaks again. She was going to start and talk about her family honestly despite the creeping fear of what would happen if they ever found out. The supportive texts from Jaz about it were the bright spots of a difficult week. She looked forward to them so much.

Then she was off to an arts centre in Durham.

Stand-Up by strictly screwed up she thought.

With its huge windows and thick black beams, the venue might as well have been an executioner's palace. Such was her pre-gig stress and feeling of misery ahead of her first Comedy Gong Show, where the audience decide who is the winner.

Even though she had arrived half an hour before the show started at 7.30pm the bar was already packed. Her overactive imagination thought the crowd of office parties and macho stags were like pacing wolves with wild eyes, ready to pounce and kill.

I have to do this. The pain feels right. If I do this show and survive maybe it will heal some of the hurt I've caused.

Jaz was there early. He had met her in the car park and cut through the crowd to find the backstage area with his usual, comforting confidence.

There were 10 comedians on the bill including her friend Andrea. Everyone sat round the green room like meerkats. Jaz said he would wait by the bar.

'I'm here for you. Don't forget. If there's too much going on at home, this gig can wait. Promise me. You'll tell me if you want to leave.'

He held her hand briefly.

Georgie stared at his long, beautiful fingers holding her own as she replied.

'I need to make myself feel better and it's not going to happen at home at the moment. It feels right to be with you.'

Then she pulled her hand away as it suddenly seemed to be far too intimate a moment.

'I'm off to the green room.' She smiled wanly at him.

'Good luck.' He rested his hand on her shoulder then gave it a squeeze before she headed off.

Mark Fat, the compere, was in the corner ignoring them all, reading his notes and writing them on his hand. A light and buzzer on the wall glowed red and made the whole room jump in unison.

The show's producer said, '20 minutes to show time people. Have that last wee. You know you want to!'

The voice stopped with a loud fizzing noise as the electrics popped and banged. It seemed to give Mark an actual shock. His baggy jeans hung off his huge backside and the black Metallica t shirt rose to form a frown above his hairy belly button. Without thinking he pulled fluff from its deepest recesses and dropped it on the carpet beside Georgie.

She clutched her notes which were now quite moist with sweat and twisted them in her hands until his pale fingers grabbed her wrist. His hands were as damp as her own.

'Stop doing that love. It's making me nervous.'

He leaned into her face until his belly was actually touching her breasts. She was sure he then deliberately brushed against them as he added,

'And we don't want that do we?'

His breath was rank.

Everyone seemed pleased to have something to look at rather than the walls or each other's equally white faces. Without exception they were all grasping their hands around their drinks and nervously rubbing the sides of the glasses. She thought they may be looking for their individual genies to come out and grant them a fantastic comedy career.

Andrea whispered in her ear,

'What a slob. I bet he's not even funny.'

Like a flash Mark was in front of her, leering down,

'I may be a slob, but I am not deaf.'

He went to walk away and then took a step back towards her and said, 'And I know I'm like an elephant so I never forget.' He then made his fingers into a gun shape and pointed them at her and mouthed, 'Boom! or should I say 'Gong!'

His gaze ran round the room quickly expecting everyone to laugh at his small joke. He was the Gong Master, so they did, loudly. One comedian even managed a shoulder shake. 'Creep', muttered Andrea looking at the culprit, determined not to be defeated.

Mark stood in the middle of the room like a ring master,

pulling his t shirt down over his stomach, in vain. His arm went out at a rigid 90 degrees to his body and he swung round pointing to each comedian as he moved his arm in a full circle.

'These are the rules people. I will give four members of the crowd voters' bats. If they all put them up, I hit the gong and you are off. The longest you can stay on is five minutes. This crowd is wired tonight so don't get your hopes up. Still. Good luck to you all anyway.'

He turned to Georgie and Andrea.

'Except you two! Only joking ladies. Have a drink with me after the show and all will be forgiven.'

He gave a hearty laugh and held his belly to stop it jumping as he swept out of the door.

The red light started to flash and the stage manager came in with the running order. Andrea was on in the first section. She had the last slot which wasn't that bad. The crowd was warmed up but not that drunk. Georgie was in the middle section and the second to go on. Like Andrea she was pleased - everyone was not likely to be too mortal. They seemed to be drunk enough. Any more alcohol and she would expect to see them all fast asleep or fighting in the aisles.

They could hear Mark introducing himself off stage right and they were all amazed by him saying he was a Comedy Winner at the Edinburgh Festival. He was getting the crowd to whoop for him to go on and the atmosphere grew even more lively. It sounded like the Wild West about to see a gun fight.

Mark seemed to be funnier when you couldn't see him. He had the crowd eating out of his hands in no time. The first three comedians made their way to the side of the stage and Georgie gave Andrea a high five. She still seemed to be excited about going on rather than terrified.

The first comedian was a tall, skinny one she now recognised from the gig at Reuben's club, as he was telling the same jokes. He lasted exactly 30 seconds and bang went the gong. Andrea was next and lasted much longer.

She had three minutes and got in some of her best

material as well as some applause. They particularly liked her stories about her dad's malapropisms. 'He was in an Indian temple filled with snakes and he said 'You will have to get me out of here!   I have got a fetish'. Her mam had shouted at him, 'They will kick you out you stupid bugger. It's a phobia not a fetish. They'll think you want to have sex with them.'

Andrea got a high five from the comedians when she came back into the now warm and slightly smelly green room. Nervous young men seemed to produce a lot of strange odours. Georgie was reminded of Nat and then tried to forget her children, all of them. Her brain needed to be full of her act. She read her crumpled notes over and over in the break and before she knew it, she was being called to the side of the stage.

The comedian before her had been gonged off after a minute and looked as if he was going to burst into tears. Four votes had come up after he started to tell a long, rambling joke about his first girlfriend which was obviously not the way to impress this crowd.

Mark Fat was in his element. He looked very full of himself as he was not being voted off himself. In fact, Georgie realised he was starting to look really drunk. When he walked on stage to introduce her, he began to do part of his own comedy set. Her nerves made her twitch. The crowd was in fits of laughter at his material and she knew he was going to be virtually impossible to follow successfully.

After what seemed like an hour but was only a few minutes, he left the stage with the crowd in the palm of his hand.

How can I follow that?

Her heart was beating as if it was going to explode.

Then she heard it.

'Here is our next victim. Sorry, comedian. She's Georgie Chancellor and she is one of those. You know. Funny Women. Give it up for her.'

Rather than giving it up for her, the crowd just went deadly quiet.   Apart from some people talking loudly at the back there was no sound at all.

Georgie remembered what Jaz kept saying about bouncing with energy and confidence. That was what she needed. And the courage to speak the truth. She tried to bound on the stage but if anything, it seemed to make everyone less interested. The exact second she was in front of the microphone someone in the front groaned loudly. One of the voters' bats was up and she hadn't even said a word.

'I am a stand-up mam with…'

She began and someone shouted, 'Couldn't care love.'

She said two more lines and the second bat went up. Her Adam's apple seemed to be growing with her panic and her voice was strangled by the huge lump in her throat. Tonight, more than any other gig, she felt as if every single person was in her sight and they were all looking at her with either pity or boredom.

Suddenly at the back of the room came a really loud heckle,

'Taxi for Georgie!'

This got a huge laugh and she knew she had totally lost control of the room. A commandment which should never be broken. She started the first part of her set and got no further than a few words out before the 'Taxi for Georgie' cry went up again, followed by more raucous laughter.

Two more voters' bats were up and the gong went. And so did she. Head down and utterly humiliated she left the stage and felt more crushed than she could ever remember.

Mark Fat was announcing her time on stage just as she went into the green room. Twenty seconds. Almost the worst twenty seconds of her life. But rather than feeling totally defeated, Georgie drew on everything she had overcome in her life, gritted her teeth and steeled herself. She started to feel furious rather than rubbish. Furious not just at this night, but at Reuben, her first son turning up and her family who had made her do this stupid comedy competition, then ignored her in real life.

In a flash she bounced back on stage and grabbed the microphone from Mark, who nearly fell off with shock as she shouted, 'You can all go screw yourselves!'

This, she found, got her the biggest cheer of the night.

Jaz had laughed at her sassy attitude but was disappointed in how it had gone. This made her sad although she understood.

'That was a shame. A real shame Georgie. You've got it in you to win those rooms. Every time. Just need faith. Yes, a bit more faith in yourself.'

Her head went down. She didn't need to feel any more rubbish than she did already. Especially now with Lily's baby and her first son on the horizon.

'I'm so sorry. It was hard. I failed. Just like I always do. Rubbish.'

Tears filled her eyes but she bit her lip.

'Come on babe. You can do this. I promise you. Just try and toughen up. We're a team. Next time will be better. Definitely.' He gave her a brief hug and it calmed her.

'Now. Text your fellow competitors and own this night.'

Her comedy competition friends loved her update when they sent their usual WhatsApp messages. Clementine, *Go girl*, Anna, *#braveheart*. Pat, *Eee by gum lass, tha's tough*. Will, *never doing a gong show now!* Matthew, *are you texting about someone other than me?* ☺

Now she had to go home and be herself and there was going to be nothing funny about it.

*

The house was in darkness when she got home with only the occasional flickering from the TV in the lounge breaking the gloom.

She expected Lawrence to be sitting on his own watching one of his dark Scandinavian crime thrillers. Instead, the whole family, complete with Jasper, Lily's boyfriend, were watching the Eurovision song contest in a huddle.

'Come on in Mam. This is hilarious', Lily shouted.

From the doorway Georgie could see a group from Ireland were banging huge drums, wearing a ton of baby oil and leather trousers.

Tears were determined to stream down Georgie's face so she stood stock still, holding everything in, when Lily shouted,

'Oh, come on in Mam. Don't get upset if you were rubbish. It's only a daft competition. Let's have a bit of family time. And you can tell us all about the gig.'

Jasper squashed up to Lily on the sofa and patted the seat beside him.

'Come on Mrs C. The baby's kicking. If you sit here, you can lean over and feel it. That little fella is going to be the next Harry Kane. I'm dead sure of it.'

He put both his hands on Lily's baby bump, gently making small circles. She chuckled with pleasure while Georgie felt as if each movement was a knife in her own stomach. No-one had ever touched her when she was pregnant apart from midwives.

Lawrence looked up and saw Georgie properly for the first time since she'd returned home and did a double-take at the expression on her face.

'You look like you've watched even more Eurovision than us. Come on and let's have a tea in the kitchen. Oh. By the way Reuben rang, apparently your mobile was off and asked if you could ring him back.'

It was at times like this she knew why Lawrence had swept her off her feet two decades ago. He bustled her along the hall and plopped her down on the nearest chair. He was at his best when he was taking care of her and usually knew instinctively what she needed. Before she could say anything a fine bone china cup and saucer, the Wedgwood one, filled to the brim with strong tea, was placed before her. Sitting alongside the saucer was an organic shortbread biscuit. Her favourites.

He pulled up a chair so they sat side by side as if they were on a plane about to take off. She could feel her breathing starting to slow down and her pulse quieten.

'Now Georgie. Tell me about the gig and what's going on. Get it all off your chest and let's sort it out.'

She blew her nose and took a sip of tea, enjoying the warmth snaking through her tubes. Then stood up in front of him. She felt she was going to do a stand-up routine. It seemed right to be talking about this with Lawrence seated. He would need to have support when she was finished with this tale, she was very sure of that. Her hand shook slightly as she picked up her cup to have one last sip before she began.

The sad tale of her first son took 30 minutes from start to end. Lawrence didn't speak. When she had explained about Reuben's quest to find Paul, Lawrence sat quietly and shut his eyes. His face was closed. There was no way of knowing if he felt extreme distress, hatred or nothing at all.

Her husband's silence not only filled the kitchen but seeped into the whole house, permeating every nook and cranny. It was ripe with anticipation, about to burst and cause devastation.

What was he thinking? What the outcome would be for her and their marriage? There were millions of questions to which she wanted to know the answer. There were also some she didn't.

Lawrence opened his eyes and his expression didn't change. She moved her chair to be opposite him. Now they looked as if they were interviewing each other. *A job for life? Maybe not.*

He dusted an invisible speck from his fine wool jumper before he spoke. 'Do you love him?'

'My son?' Even though in her head, for reasons she didn't understand, her thoughts went immediately to Jaz.

'No. Reuben.'

She pulled her chair forward so their knees were touching. He flinched as she did it. Taking hold of his familiar hands made her eyes become warm. By contrast Lawrence still looked composed, detached. She stared at his fingers without blinking as she spoke quietly.

'I have always been honest with you about Reuben and how I feel about our history…'

His voice seemed to come out of a throat of thorns at the mention of Reuben's name, 'Well. We know now that you've not been completely honest don't we? I bet he has wholeheartedly enjoyed having this secret with you. You may not have feelings for him but I'd wager he does have them for you...'

Georgie was going to interrupt him but he raised his hand to silence her. For a short man he was towering, filling the kitchen in a disproportionate way to his size.

'There's no way he would be so determined to find a son if he felt nothing for you. This son. Your first son...'

His voice was becoming quieter and he looked at the kitchen ceiling to compose himself for a moment,

'... is the link which will bind you two until death do you part. Perhaps. And now our Lily. She's repeating your life. You weren't honest with me. That's why you wanted her to keep her own baby. To salve your conscience.'

'Yes. I'm sorry. I couldn't let her have the pain I've had to ignore for so many years.'

Georgie thought her heart was going to actually break open with the pain of talking about her first baby. Tears filled her eyes. She quickly wiped them.

It appeared that the effort of keeping his dignity was overwhelming for Lawrence as well and his gaze rested on his hands. He then shook his head and looking at the floor walked out of the room slowly, banging into Lily who was coming in, engrossed with her phone.

'Hey Dad, watch where you are going. There are two of us here!'

Georgie saw Lily look at her quizzically and as she got a drink of water said, 'Shall I open the fridge Mam or do you think you have made the kitchen atmosphere cold enough? Some weird shit going down here by the look of Dad's face.'

Rather than hold her tongue Georgie marched towards the door

'Enough Lily.' Lawrence was firm for once with his daughter, as he made his way upstairs.

Then Nat bounced in, headphones on, and oblivious to her mood proceeded to spin her round the kitchen, singing a Bruce Springsteen track about dancing.

He stopped suddenly when he realised she was not

joining in the fun and knelt down beside her. His brown eyes were huge and luminous when they peered into her own. Her pupils were long corridors and he looked like he was trying to see the end. 'You OK Mam?'

A voice came from the depths of the freezer, 'When has she ever been less than OK and perfect. You daft prat. Grow up Nat.'

Georgie managed a faint smile and merely said, 'Bed, for me anyway.' As she traced a curl on Nat's hairline before leaving the room. Climbing the stairs her feet were leading to Lawrence and their bedroom but her heart was pulling her towards the sofa in the study. The implications of this seemingly small decision were scarily large. She loved her husband and the security he gave her and needed to know if her revelations had cast her adrift from him, her anchor, permanently.

Her hand paused on the bedroom door handle. What world lay beyond it? It felt like one of the biggest decisions of her life. Then, almost without thinking, her feet walked her into their bedroom to rest, as she was sure she would never sleep. Lawrence was still wide awake and held her tightly as though it was for the very last time. It felt good.

'We'll get through this Georgie. I'm sorry to have been so unkind. Reuben is such an awful guy. It's a shock.'

'I know. Should have told you years ago and…'

'Shhh. Let's sleep for now.'

She snuggled into him. But what unnerved her was it was Jaz's voice that was playing in her head to get to sleep. He was telling her to have faith in herself.

TWENTY-EIGHT

The pub room they used a rehearsal space was heavy with dust and tension. Georgie was nervous. Jaz had been stern but supportive with her about the gong show.

'We need you to up your game. I'm not having the next one like that. You've got this.'

'Yes Jaz.'

'We need the rhythm G. Bam. Bam. Punchline. Own the stage. Own it!'

'Yes Jaz.'

'And stop yes Jazzing me. Have an opinion.'

'Yes. Absolutely. I've got some new ideas.'

'Thank Christ for that. Let's hear them.'

They sat down on the two rickety chairs facing each other and she ran through stories of home.

Georgie felt the disgruntlement grow that she had refused to acknowledge at the time. Her brain, she realised, had a depository of small grudges against her family that were previously hidden.

'I can't say these out loud', she said after an hour of offloading 20 years of holding things in. Jaz patted her hand again.

'Oh yes you can. Let's work it up.'

Incidents, observations and one-liners tumbled out like a random rock fall of irony and anecdotes. Lawrence was in there. His dead mother was in there. Very much in there. Lily and her funny hormones were laid bare and she told the joke about Nat's obsession with food and sex, but not both together.

'I'm part housewife. Part slave. I do so much washing I'm surprised I'm not found dead under a pile of clothes with my feet sticking out.

'If I did die my kids would only take what they needed from the top!'

In no particular order they also touched on her true feelings about finding Paul, her family and how she felt, really felt, about each of them.

He smiled for the first time that session. 'This is the first time I've heard you speak and be really true to yourself. You're becoming funny. And brutal, to be fair. I like these stories. They've got legs.'

His hand rested on her own.

'Well done Georgie. You're getting there.'

I'm getting there. I'm getting there.

She felt fragile but had a glow at the praise.

When they had finished planning the next gig's set, she realised they were sitting so closely, their knees were almost touching.

They looked up from their notes simultaneously and locked gazes.

He leant forward and lightly kissed her on the lips. No, not really, in her mind he lightly kissed on the lips and said,

'I shouldn't have done that.'

In the real world he just stood up.

She rubbed her lip with the back of her hand and was wired and shocked at the same time as if it had happened.

What is happening to me?

'I'd better go Jaz.'

'Much better material. Ok. I think we're done. Until the next gig...'

The room felt busy although neither of them was moving.

Georgie made the first step, picked up her coat and walked towards the door. Neither spoke. Then she realised she wanted that kiss and it seemed funny, in a way that wasn't part of a comedy competition.

TWENTY-NINE

Lawrence was choosing not to talk about her first son and for now, it suited Georgie as well. She could concentrate on her stand-up. And the next gig came around quickly. Jaz's advice rattled around her head. She had to be on her toes. Short and sharp. Talking to the crowd. Acting out set pieces. Tick. Tick.

The place was packed as the owner had said on Facebook there would be pints for £2.

As she stepped on to the tiny stage tucked into the corner of yet another grotty Newcastle pub, Georgie could hear someone being sick beside the front door when it swung open and shut. The smell could strip the paint from the walls.

Jaz was helping her confidence but tonight it took some picking up. He gave her a high five as she left their table. Their fingertips fizzed for the briefest of moments, or was this only in her mind again, she wondered. Then she was on.

She tugged the mic from its stand. It came free like a silk scarf unwrapping from a 50's film star's throat. *I am getting the hang of this.* Her breath slightly faltered as usual when she started. The crowd was a mix of students and young couples, more interested in each other than a middle-aged woman trying to make them laugh, but her set was becoming more and more based on her teenagers and Lawrence so at least they had a bit of common ground.

'I'm old enough to be one of your mothers but I promise you I'm not! Although it probably does depend if your dad was in the Bigg Market regularly 20 years ago.' She got a small laugh. *And somewhere out there is my son. Who could even be here.*

'I don't get all of your initials for things, like WTF, OMG, BBF. But I got one over my son last week I said that CD is MOR. He had no idea what I meant. It is Middle of the Road music. See. We can teach you some things!

'So. I'm now going to give you all my motherly advice on driving lessons. I took my son out. We did manoeuvres in a supermarket car park. It was getting dark so he put the lights on and was doing three point turns. Suddenly he stopped.'

Georgie could tell she had the crowd's attention and even the smell of sick seemed to have quietened down. For the first time she had control over the audience, even the small crowd in this pub. She loved it. And the attention from everyone here. She could feel her day-to-day life loosening its tormented grip on her.

'I said what's happened? Why've you stalled? He looked at me like a rabbit in headlights.'

'Mam!'

'What?'

'Have you seen the other cars in the car park? They all have their lights off. I think they're dogging!'

'Imagine the humiliation. Dogging with L plates.

He said, 'Hey Mam, I've stalled and we are in MOR!'

'Just get your foot down in case they think I am MILF!'

There was a good gentle chuckle moving round the room and people started to make themselves more comfortable in their seats.

'The first dinner party we ever had. I had worked so hard to make it a success and had never even been to one before. We were about to sit down with our six guests. Finally. I had the food ready. I was about to flop into my seat and my husband Lawrence shouted,

'No napkins!. We've got no bloody napkins. What are we? Plebeians?'

'Everyone roared with laughter and I wanted to crawl under the table at first. Now I realise I should have tipped the whole lot off the table and onto the floor. I didn't even know what a plebeian was!'

The more expression and acting she put in to her set,

Georgie realised the better people enjoyed it. Even when her material was not hilarious, they were prepared to cut her slack if there was at least an interesting tale with a good punch line. And dishing the dirt on her family was the perfect revenge.

By the end she was getting a quick clap for her punchlines as well as laughter. She could swear she even heard a small whoop, when the MC got the crowd to give her a round of applause.

The customary flop into the seat afterwards was less pronounced than usual. Nearly graceful. Four other comedians who were sitting around the tiny table designated the green room stood up and also gave her a small round of applause.

'You're not bad Stand-Up Mam', said Joe, one of the Newcastle comedy circuit regulars.

'I liked the dinner party bit. That worked well. Punters love a family disaster don't they!'

Georgie smiled and realised she was looking slightly smug. She had won the respect of this motley crew, in their tatty t shirts and low-slung jeans. Then felt her usual amazement at how warm and friendly these stand-ups were. No matter how nervous they felt, every single one always had time to wish each other good luck and reassure the performer they had done OK. It never seemed to matter that it might not be the truth.

Jaz's notes were helpful as usual and tonight he hugged her tightly when she's finished her set. She was starting to enjoy being part of this team of misfits. And fitted right in, despite her middle-class home life. For the first time in many years Georgie was able to relax in her own skin. No pretending. And no pretension.

The last three acts found most of the audience had become comatose with drink just like the rough atmosphere the pub had most of the week. There was one old man sitting by himself and no amount of banter from Jeff, the MC, could shut him up. He didn't keep quiet even when he was told to SHUT THE FUCK UP. The man merely looked around as if he couldn't understand who

Jeff was shouting at and then started to rant again. Then at last it was over.

The Stand-Up Star finalists WhatsApp messages were all positive. Clementine. *I actually shut a heckler up!* Anna. *Did the first slot. Scary but ok.* Pat. *Died. Then did ok.* Will, *I think I hate comedy.* Matthew. *Brilliant as usual.* Georgie said. *First ever clap for a gag!*

I definitely had the best slot tonight she thought as she high fived the comedians on her way out. The stench of sick was now joined by a nose-burning mixture of fresh urine and sour vegetables. She thought of Lily and realised her sensitive pregnancy nose could not have coped with this stench.

Despite trying not to do so, her pregnant daughter and first son loomed in her head as she clicked open the car door to drive home. Music seemed to be the solution.

Meatloaf's music was absolutely perfectly appropriate. The frenetic riff blasted out of all four of the car's speakers round the riverside roads and through Newcastle. It left a slipstream of rock power pop strewn all over the city's dignified stone streets.

She was still humming it as she arrived home. And she had no fear that she would be damned. A bomb had gone off in her world. What was Lawrence really thinking about her revelations? Then her phone beeped, Reuben texted *Meeting Paul at the Glasshouse tomorrow, 3pm.*

Now she had to face up to even more music.

*

Compared to the grim pubs she seemed to be spending so much of her life in, the venue of Georgie's new performance couldn't have been more different. The light in the grand Quayside music venue's foyer danced with beautiful colours which poured into the building like a water. For a moment she was transfixed both by her surroundings and the rainbow of emotions enveloping her.

I must keep calm and sane. Relax Georgie… In an attempt to achieve the impossible, she forced her hands to cement themselves to the top of her thighs under the coffee shop table. Contrary to what her hands were trying to tell her body, she was anxious.

It wasn't just the head rush that was distracting Georgie, her gaze rested on the huge individual panes of glass to her left. She felt they were actually real windows on her life. It was as if God had put a giant scrapbook on display for her to see, even though she swore he didn't exist.

She screwed up her eyes as she knew this wasn't really happening but when she opened them again there were the same images. Her wedding day. Walking through the door to their house for the first time. Lawrence. Nat. Lily. She realised her mind was playing tricks with her and trying to take her thoughts away from the frightening horror of what was about to happen but she continued to go along with it. And there it was. The last frame and what should have been the first. Her baby son Paul, wrapped in a hospital sheet, reaching out his hand towards her. She could smell him.

Just at that moment the Chamber orchestra began their morning rehearsals and the whole building was bathed in colour and music. The chords ebbed and flowed like a holy mantra calling on the good people of Tyneside to worship at their magnificent sound cathedral. But today it was really only calling to her first son.

Her phone beeped and she was back in the real and present world.

Almost there. That was all Reuben sent.

Brace yourself. She thought. The music seemed to recognise her mood and began to climb with passion, getting louder and louder. Then, for all the sound continued, the whole lofty space was a silent bubble as two figures moved towards her. Even from a distance she knew who they were.

They were lanky automata made in the same factory. As they came closer, she couldn't believe her eyes. Breath came out of her mouth and it stayed open. She had expected to feel a whole range of emotions but not this jaw-dropping shock.

190

Her first born son Paul was someone she had seen before, part of the drunk, wise-cracking group at the gig. He was the one she'd told to shut up and ridiculed for being a virgin. Oh, the irony. But Georgie's shock was nothing compared to the young man now standing rooted to the spot in front of her, looking as if he was seeing the Devil Incarnate.

Whatever she had expected to see in her first son's face the first time, it wasn't this bewilderment and distrust. He kept looking past her as if his real mother, the homespun matriarch with freshly baked cookies in her bag, would appear magically. He was like a puppy version of Reuben but by the look on his face he was not about to lick her hand. More Pitbull than puppy.

His brain was refusing to acknowledge what was plain for both Georgie and him to see, and he was intent on walking past her. He began approaching the woman on the next table before Reuben put his hand in the small of his back and steered him towards Georgie, who was on her feet so quickly her cup rattled and crashed to the floor, reverberating round the building like an automatic pistol.

It was as if she had been shot. The pain in her heart was so intense she thought she was going to pass out. Georgie's whole body felt it had been plunged into the icy Tyne from its famous bridge. As he spoke his first words to her, she slowly rose to the surface but felt no relief.

Before Reuben could speak, Paul croaked out, 'You can't be my mam. You just can't. I can't take this in. Man.' He clutched the back of the nearest chair and then sat down gingerly as if he was expecting it to break.

She was engulfed by all this and his complete incredulity that she was his mother.

Instinctively she bent down to scoop up the shattered cup and saucer and almost bumped heads with the waitress who had rushed over to help. Without thinking the girl put her hand on Georgie's arm.

'Please don't worry, it wasn't your fault.'

She could have been talking about so many things and her kindness tipped Georgie into an emotional abyss, matched by the music which still throbbed around them. It was as if she was in some emotional film and not her own life. Her flight or fight instinct kicked in. She had to go outside and feel the Quayside air on her cheeks.

Reuben quickly mirrored Paul's movements, pulled out another chair deftly and went to yank Georgie down as well so they were all on the same level. She snatched her arm free and was about to say she was going outside but was mute with emotion. All she could do was raise a finger to indicate one minute and head for the external door.

Once there Georgie leant over the glass balustrade with its steep drop to the river below, and gulped down fresh air. Then despite herself, she began to sob without any control or thought for what she looked like. A tender hand was placed on her back by the waitress who had seen her distress and followed her.

'It's only a bloody cup pet. There're plenty of other cups!'

Georgie knelt down and leant against the cool glass rail. She closed her eyes and heard the waitress say as she walked away,

'You need to look after your mam, she is really not feeling well at all.'

Her eyes remained tight shut but she sensed someone standing beside her. The male smell was not Reuben's.

The disorientating feeling started to pass. Her eyes opened. She had company. A handful of curious Sage visitors could not help but stare at the peculiar sight she had created, as a strange man who she seemed to know, and yet did not know, knelt on the ground beside her.

She didn't speak as he turned round and sat down, staring ahead. She took in his battered white plimsolls sticking out of the end of washed-out baggy jeans from the corner of her eye. A big snotty sniff made her look round and face her son who was staring at her with ill-concealed dislike.

'This is so fucked up man. I mean. Really just totally fucked up. You're never my mam.'

He wiped his nose and then his eyes with his sleeve which distracted her from the business in hand.

A shadow loomed over both of them and Reuben handed Georgie a glass of water.

'This is not exactly going as planned, is it?' He tried to lighten the atmosphere.

It's too late for that. He should never have set this nightmare train in motion.

The strange effect of Reuben arriving outside was that he seemed to actually bring Georgie and Paul together, united in their rage at him for this outcome. He sat on the other side of her, taking care to keep his distance.

'What's going on Georgie? You said you had no idea about anything to do with your son and here you are. You both seem to know each other from somewhere and….'

Paul erupted, 'You ridiculous prick. This woman…' he gestured towards Georgie who was similarly overcome, '…. is only the stand-up comic I saw telling jokes about her fuckin' family.'

The flow of Sage visitors was now beginning to take more than a passing interest in this scene and a couple had actually stopped just in front of the three not-so-wise monkeys.

Reuben leant across Georgie to speak to Paul and couldn't help himself saying, 'You watch your language. There are other people here.'

'Who do you think you are? You're not my bloody fath….'

The word keeled over and died on his lips and his fury seemed to disintegrate instantly just like his face which became a distorted mask of grief. He pulled his knees up, hugged them in to his chest and wiped more tears from his face with his sleeve.

Reuben stood up and went to comfort him, hissing at Georgie as he passed, 'I'm amazed you didn't recognise him at your gig. He is the double of me. Look at him.'

At this point Paul seemed to collapse a stage further and he did a gentle moan as he rested his forehead on his knees. He was a tight ball, trying to stay in control.

Georgie stood and the resilience she had been forced to adopt her whole life and wore with some pride, rose up. *I'm not going to be a victim.*

She looked at Reuben with contempt, 'You started this path without my consent. You wanted your child. Well now you have one. Look at him, Reuben.' She took her first love's face in both her hands and forced him to look at the sad wreck at both their feet. 'Look. At. Him. This is your son. Our son. You've produced this horrible situation and we both need to help him.'

Her throat was stripped bare. She bent down to pick up the glass of water, suddenly desperate for a drink. After taking a long gulp of it she tapped Paul on the arm, forcing him to raise his head up.

'Here. You probably need something stronger but this'll have to do. We need to go somewhere to talk this through and we can't sit here.'

Reuben nodded. He suggested they went to his apartment. 'It is not far and at least we can iron this all out in private.'

Georgie got into her own car to meet them there.

She had just sat down and switched on the ignition when there was a gut-curdling cry from the pit of her stomach. The primeval noise had erupted without her will and engulfed her entirely. She collapsed onto the steering wheel and sobbed as if the awoken grief of being parted from her baby all those years ago would never end.

Her emotions were like a giant beast demanding to be released. A pre-historic monster rearing up through trees and smashing all in its path.

And this was just the beginning.

*

Reuben's renovated Quayside loft had been a Victorian trading warehouse. It was cool and dark which suited all of their moods. Paul stood not speaking. Georgie felt almost compelled to check that he was still breathing. It was as if they had abducted him and were going to demand ransom money.

She stood apart from him, trying to compose herself.

Reuben flung open the double doors to the lounge area and waved them through like a maître d'.

'Just sit where you like. I'll put the espresso machine on as I think we need something strong.'

Georgie sat on the nearest cream leather sofa to the door, handy if she wanted a quick exit. Paul sat farthest away.

The apartment was an archetypal bachelor pad. It had well-worn comfortable armchairs, an expensive wooden coffee table with a glass panel in the middle and a large theatrical spotlight lamp. There was a five foot square pop art style screen print of Reuben, like Warhol's prints of Marilyn Monroe and Chairman Mao, with the same size egos at work.

A few pop art cushions with POW on them were scattered along the sofa where Georgie sat and she instinctively put one of them straight. When she turned back into the room she jumped as Paul was standing right in front of her. *I can see Reuben and me so clearly in him.*

'What's your story then?' he said gruffly as though she was a schoolgirl late home after a party. Georgie shivered in recognition of the abrupt tone. Not again. *The gene pool couldn't throw up my father, surely?*

She was becoming upset and lost for words about this whole encounter. *Why did I agree to this?* A picture of Lawrence and his calmness pulled her homeward, meanwhile her bottom was perched on the end of this particular sofa. Paul leant in towards her, staring hard, trying to read her expression with the lack of maturity to do it at all subtly.

She met his gaze but couldn't find the right words.

He sat beside her. 'Sorry. It's all hard, you know. I just need to hear why you gave me away and never bothered to find me until now?'

He spoke to the floor and his sagging shoulders belied the sharp edge to his voice.

Georgie's voice was faint. 'When you were born I had a horrible home life and was basically thrown out. 'Reuben,' she didn't feel she could start and call him 'your father' without cracking open with emotion herself '…was sent away to boarding school. I didn't see him again until my 20s when we bumped into each other at his club where my husband takes his clients.'

Paul said, 'I'm sorry that's what happened when you had me. Sounds rough. Really rough.'

Georgie wiped her eyes and stared at Reuben.

'Yes. It was, but I survived. And here I am. A stand-up mam.'

'I know. Too well.' He gave her a small smile.

Georgie flushed. Part of her willing him to shrink to a pin prick and disappear.

The other half wanted to hold him and never let go.

'I wanted to keep you but couldn't. And now I've got to work out what is best for my family, and you, of course, in all this.' *And myself.*

She added, 'We need to take our time. Agreed?'

'Yes. Definitely. Agreed. One hundred per cent.'

He pulled her towards him and gave her a stiff hug.

Georgie had thought what she would feel if she was ever able to hug her first son. It burned. Her emotions were on fire. *I have suffered so much from giving him up as a baby. Now it's as if all of that misery is physically inside him.*

She moved back. In the pit of her stomach she thought this man-boy could destroy the person she was now. Yet she needed him. So much.

Reuben sat down on the other side of her with a satisfied sigh and patronisingly patted her on the leg.

'I know this is tricky but we're going to get there. Happy times to come. I know.'

He beamed at Paul while Georgie looked at him with disbelief and removed his hand. *Happy times?*

Paul's eyes were tearing up. 'All of these questions used to fly around in my head with no way of them being answered. Until today.'

Georgie stood up again.

'Well, here I am. A sad, teenage mother in all her grown up glory.'

Her years of pretending to be middle class fell away.

'Is that enough detail for you?'

Reuben flinched and refused to match her gaze. 'We have had more than enough of that historical stuff for our first meeting. Don't you think?'

Paul's eyes widened. 'So, we will see each other again? My parents, the other ones I mean, are very happy for me to see you both. They're dead straight, lovely people.'

She was desperate to escape and didn't want to begin to think about the family who had brought him up. *I've toughed this first meeting out as much as possible. I need to go now.* She picked up her bag and went to the door of the apartment.

'Will we? See each other again?' he said.

She was so conflicted and upset. 'Yes. I'd like that. I think.' Then continued walking to stop herself bursting into tears again. A last glimpse into the room showed Reuben and Paul had exactly the same stunned expression at her leaving so abruptly.

THIRTY

The whole story of meeting Paul came out in a huge torrent when she got home. Lawrence had scooped her up when she fell through the front door, despite trying to compose herself.

She had planned exactly how to tell him in a very precise, Lawrence way. It was going to be with a glass of his favourite wine, delicious food and the perfect, classical soundtrack. Instead, he made her a strong coffee which she still hated, the kitchen was cold as the heating had gone off. There was dirty dishes all over the bench. And the soundtrack was their children banging around upstairs which made their conversation stilted as Georgie didn't want them to know what was being discussed. Not yet anyway.

She was relieved with Lawrence's response to her seeing Paul with Reuben. His initial jealousy had faded and he trusted her love for him. Despite being shocked, he managed to be pragmatic and kind, compared to his first response to learning about Paul's existence.

'I'm not often lost for words Georgina but this whole thing is truly awful. You had to meet him. I understand that. You poor soul. A child yourself really. And the baby. Paul. Now a man. And Reuben. I still don't really know what to think about him. Suppose it was his parents' fault but…he's such an arrogant guy. It must have been so hard for you with the way Nat came along, unplanned. Now Lily's baby as well. The abortion idea was never going to happen. Truly. I never meant that to …'

Georgie cut him short, 'I'm so sorry I felt I needed to meet him in secret. It's been an awful time but I never

198

want you to think less of me. I didn't allow myself the luxury of ever thinking I might meet that baby boy. I wasn't sure what would happen. But couldn't see anything good coming of it. For anyone. Him, me, you, the kids. And what will happen now?'

She sunk onto the kitchen sofa, tears falling down her face and Lawrence sat beside her.

'We're rock solid. That's what you need to know.'

'Are we Lawrence? There's Lily's baby and how will this seem to her? I've been living a lie.'

'Nonsense. We'll take our time. Paul can meet us in due course. And the most important thing about it all...'

'Yes?'

'Is that my mother isn't alive to hear about it. Although I don't think she would've been surprised. She really didn't have a good thing to say about you most of the time, did she? Such a shame.'

Georgie didn't have a good thing to say about herself either. The only thing that made her feel slightly worth something was stand-up comedy. And Jaz.

*

A week later Georgie stood right in the middle of the stage in the tiny upstairs room of the Haystack pub, feet together. As confident and solid as she could fake it. She took her time when she lifted the microphone from the stand.

Jaz had been supportive with advice all week and managed to change his own gig bookings to be there. He gave her a quick thumbs up. His gaze held hers for just a second too long for comfort.

The spotlight was in an even worse position than the other gigs. She couldn't see the front row of the audience despite the venue being so small. It was hard to get any rapport going when you were speaking into a white void. For a second she thought this was what could be like at the pearly gates, explaining to God why should you be let in. Then she remembered she felt she sure was going to Hell.

The crowd laughed at her jokes, now coming out easily and they loved her impersonations of all her family. Her improved acting made her gags work so much better.

'I really don't like my family that much. I pretend to but they ignore me so here's my revenge. Call your son's current girlfriend the last girlfriend's name. Always goes down well as a punishment if he's forgotten to bring down his washing!' *I know the pain of this, from Reuben's father doing it to me.*

The crowd gasped at this and then laughed at her audacity. She then continued with her Mother's Day story, the dinner party and all of the family's dirty linen including Lily's pregnancy and her increasing demands.

A firm hand squeezing her shoulder was the first sign Jaz was right beside her as she carefully stepped off the stage.

'Hey girl.'

His breath was so close it tickled her ear.

'Your timing was better. The pauses are just as important as the gags. You did really well. Feel proud of yourself Georgie. Please. Treat yourself to it. You've earned every bit of success up there.'

He led her by her elbow back to the dark recesses of the room where all of the other comedians were sitting either waiting for their sets or enjoying a drink in peace because they'd finished.

They nodded at her and made encouraging noises about what they had enjoyed in her set. The nerves and tension in stand-up created a strong sense of community where everyone was entitled to mutual encouragement. It was a weird feeling and so different from the competitive world of marketing.

Tonight, Jaz sat a bit too close for comfort which was odd. She could tell the other comedians assumed they were a couple rather than a mentor and protégé. One by one they went to the bar or to sit nearer the stage, giving themselves some quiet time before they performed their sets.

'What would you like to drink? Are you ready for a Jack and coke?'

He leaned in towards her to whisper without disrupting the act with a loud voice. His hand rested briefly on her knee.

'Coke on its own is fine thanks. I'll be driving home.'

His relaxed self-assurance was such that he didn't even seem to notice she had lifted his hand off as soon as it had landed.

A few minutes later the glass of coke banging down on the table made her jump.

He laughed, 'Sorry Georgie, I thought you had nerves of steel!'

'I don't after this excitement. All I feel ready for is a crash out in bed to be honest.'

She had never wanted to cut her tongue out as much. Jaz raised his whisky glass to his lips slowly and deliberately, then sipped a mouthful.

'Really?'

She could read his thoughts and then deliberately chose not to do so.

'Come on then.' He said 'Let's get you home to your lovely, cosy bed.'

When they were out in the street, a dark cobbled alley off the main grandeur of Grey Street, Jaz spun round to stand right in front of her, making her come to such an abrupt stop she instinctively had to put her hand on his chest to stop herself from tripping up. This time it was him that moved back, making sure physical contact stopped.

'Truth or dare?'

He smiled down at her and she began to smile back. The adrenalin in her system and the warm, dark night air enveloping them seemed to be creating a new intimacy. It was like being in an old-fashioned phone box. No-one else could see or hear them. The street was deserted.

With the lovely, fuzzy buzz of the gig and this funny and gentle man standing in front of her, Georgie sensed her locked down personality open up. One by one the self-imposed clamps on her emotions were cracking free. Her heart began racing to a new rhythm. There was real relief after the pain and drama of the week, through speaking the truth out loud to strangers. It thumped so fiercely she thought it was going to burst out of her tee shirt and land slippery and flipping on the ground.

I have no idea where this game will go but I want to play it.

Georgie the-never-take-risks-perfectionist stared at Jaz in the eyes and decided to go home a bit later than planned.

'Dare! Go on, dare me!'

He burst out laughing and his normally composed face relaxed. His eyes twinkled. The street lights picking out their golden brown highlights.

'I dare you to run down Grey Street and back in less than four minutes.'

'You're on.'

She hitched her trousers up so they sat on her waist and took off down the street which was now beginning to fill up with people pouring out of the grand Theatre Royal. They parted before her like the Great North Run crowds on the way to South Shields.

She had forgotten how steep the rise back up the wide street was and was almost purple when she jumped to a stop with both feet right in front of him. Sweat formed on her top lip and made the white hair on the back of her neck curl and darken.

'Not bad. Not bad at all.'

She could tell he was amazed and quite impressed that she had actually done the dare. Impetuous acts in public were not Georgie's style but then who would have thought she would do stand-up comedy?

'Right. My turn.'

She looked around them for a good dare.

'I know. I dare you to climb up the Tyne Bridge and write my name on the metal.'

Before she knew it, he had grabbed her hand and she was running back down Grey Street leaving startled revellers in their wake and as they headed for the iconic metal bridge.

She was doubled up with effort by the time they got there although Jaz looked as if it was just a normal workout. He had torn ahead and was already working his way up the bridge's initial steep curve by the time she arrived.

'Stop. Seriously stop Jaz You'll get arrested. They'll think you're one of those dad protesters. Don't do it. I take back the dare.'

An elderly couple were walking past and looked at Jaz with horror.

'Oh, my dear', said the woman, 'Please take him back. Whatever he has done, you have just got to forgive him.'

The man merely looked at Georgie in a disapproving way and tutted before moving on. All the way across the bridge they kept looking back to check if Jaz was coming down or not.

A police car, sirens blasting out and blue neon lights illuminating the whole bridge came to a screeching halt underneath Jaz, now 30 feet high.

'Hey mate, what do you think you are doing?' The officer wasn't amused.

Jaz slid down the metal slope and landed like a panther at the officer's feet. He calmly dusted down his trousers and waved at Georgie who was a heady mix of breathlessness, dying with laughing and now in urgent need of a wee.

'My lady friend here dared me to do it. I know it was stupid officer but a dare is a dare after all. I profusely apologise for any time wasted here.'

He finished with a small bow.

The policeman who was obviously meant to be somewhere else at top speed, moved his not inconsiderable weight from foot to foot and then decided to cut his losses.

'Well, you have made quite a prat of yourself and could have injured someone below. You'd better not do it again. Understand?'

Jaz clicked his heels together and saluted the policeman with a solemn face. The policeman driving the car opened the door for his partner and Georgie heard him say, 'Prick' before it slammed shut and they tore off to battle crime on the other side of the bridge.

Georgie was standing crossed legged and still giggling manically.

I have never had a night like this in my life.

Every nerve ending felt filled with static energy. She couldn't remember a time when she had felt the thrill of freedom and confidence she had at this very moment. Jaz was smiling as he strode up to her and without thinking they collapsed onto each other in another fit of laughing.

A car slowed down beside them and the woman driver stared at her. It brought Georgie to her senses. She leapt away from Jaz, banging into the bridge railing.

In the nick of time girl. I was hugging another man in the middle of the Tyne Bridge. I'm going mad. This comedy euphoria is making me bonkers. And Jaz is not helping.

'Careful Georgie. You're going to hurt yourself.'

I am, she sensed it. Jaz walked up to her but she instinctively moved away from him and started a route march back to the car park.

'Hey. Wait. What's going on? We were just having fun.'

She realised she was not being professional or cool, or any of the things she wanted to be in front of someone who had the power to help her comedy and self-esteem. But she was out of her depth.

Within two or three paces he had caught up to her and gently tugged at her jacket to make her stop.

'We had fun. It was me up there not you. Please just chill. Comedy Queen.'

He had gone back to his normal, polite self and she sensed whatever the strange moment they had shared was, it had disappeared.

She deliberately tried to lighten the mood.

'I need to get home and I really need a pee. Probably a good shower as well to be honest. It's not every day I sprint around Newcastle!'

'It's been quite a night. The gig was fine and the after-show party was awesome!'

She smiled at him and he took her hand in his for a brief moment before she walked to her car. Talking very specifically to her hand and not the rest of her body Jaz said, 'It was a special night with you. Everything is coming together nicely, Georgie.'

She did not even dare ask what he meant. But was suddenly overwhelmed.

'See you around.' She replied with a small smile.

He merely raised his hand in recognition and headed back to the city centre but didn't look back.

I've no idea what has gone on this evening but I have a horrible feeling I have blown something.

She unlocked her car door, completely ignoring Alec the homeless man, who had to cough loudly to get her attention, which was not something he was used to doing, considering how he looked and smelt.

'Have a pound Alec. Don't mind if I do Mrs. That's very kind of you.'

He mimicked her voice and Georgie looked around in surprise.

'What! I didn't see you mate. Sorry. Here you go.'

She rummaged around the bottom of her bag and handed over two pound coins.

'You might have not seen me Hen, but I saw you well enough. And the other fella. Two pounds is not enough to keep my trap shut.'

He tapped his engrained palm with a long, curly index finger nail.

'I am not being blackmailed by you so just sod off.'

Georgie marched away towards her car.

'I am a bargain at three.' He shouted after her. 'I am starting to get dehydrated and cold.' A loud coarse cough was followed by spittle.

She winced but despite her better judgement, swung round and gave him a £5 note.

THIRTY-ONE

Jaz and the midwife Sally stood side by side at Georgie's front door.

'We'll have to make sure both of you don't get mixed up with your roles here today.' Georgie joked.

Jaz laughed as he caught her eye. The other night seemed forgotten.

'I'm definitely not father material!'

'Well, we'd better just crack on with our comedy material and see how that goes.'

Lily walked towards them down the long hall, rubbing her belly.

'Can we just stop talking about stand-up and how important Mam is for a minute and concentrate on my baby.'

The midwife laughed then until she realised, she was on her own and the rest of the trio were quiet.

Jaz broke the silence.

'We've only got a few weeks to go, Georgie, so we had better get going on our own special delivery.'

'Not long for you either.' The midwife smiled as she followed Lily in to the kitchen for her check up.

*

Georgie was pretending again. Lily had assumed she would love to go shopping for baby clothes. And she didn't have the courage to tell her the truth so off they set to Newcastle, which was bustling with the start of the Christmas shopping season all around them.

The meeting with Paul a few days earlier meant this wasn't going to be easy for Georgie to pull off. Every part of having a baby was raw.

In the middle of the main city square there was a gypsy selling lavender and offering palm readings. Lily grabbed her mother's hand.

'Oh, come on Mam. She's might tell me about my baby. Whether they are going to be a rock star or …'

'No. I don't think we should.' Georgie wasn't keen.

'Yes. Yes. Please. Please.'

Lily was told her baby would be a boy and he would grow into a strong, handsome man.

Georgie was about to move off when the gypsy grabbed her hand.

'I've seen you before lady. Many years ago. I remember the lines on your hand. They showed me things you don't forget. You have three children and they're all well…'

Georgie snatched her hand away.

'Three. That's hilarious.'

Lily was laughing. Georgie wasn't.

'Three kids.' Lily smiled as she rushed to catch up with Georgie who had rushed away.

'Come on Mam. It's all rubbish. We know that.'

'Yes. Rubbish.' She managed a small smile.

They stopped beside the best designer childrenswear shop.

Lily was tugging at Georgie's hand as they entered.

'Look Mam. These white babygrows are soooo cute. And there are some old pop songs on. Listen to that hilarious track.'

Georgie didn't hear as the music cut out Lily's words. Boombastic by Shaggy. Georgie froze.

'I'm. Sorry. Lil. But…'

She left the shop. Gulping for cool air and space.

'You ok Mam? It should be me feeling sick not you!'

Georgie leant against the shop window and closed her eyes.

'I don't know what came over me.' *Yes I do. After the gypsy. How can that tune that ended with Paul being in the world be playing today, of all days?*

Lily linked her arm.

'Come on. Let's go to John Lewis instead. We can always come back here.'

The store's maternity department was full of pregnant young women. The difference between Lily and the other blooming ladies with mothers was that they were all joined at the hip. When she got near to Lily, she felt like a magnetic charge was on repel. Memories creating barriers.

As she wandered through the racks of tiny baby clothes in all the pastel colours of a muted rainbow, she couldn't help touching them. Soft wool in the designer section. One hundred per cent cottons in the cheaper end. All of them waiting for a little bundle of mushy flesh to fill them out.

As she bent down to pick up a small set of white booties that had dropped off a shelf in front of her, she suddenly felt faint. At that moment she had a vivid sensation of being in her own skin all those years ago when she was pregnant with Paul.

I did this shopping trip then and I was in torment.

It had been 'Never Never Land'. Even though she knew she couldn't keep her baby, Georgie had been drawn to the department store. Against all of her instincts she had mingled with the women, most of them devoid of North East accents like hers, and also unlike her, seriously affluent. The warmth of other families wrapped itself around every fixture and fitting like dense mist on a beach. It seemed to gather her up. Then suffocate her.

She had started to pretend this happiness was her life. Her mother had just popped to the second floor cafe to order them both afternoon tea. It would be waiting for her after she'd finished selecting the baby's vests and sleepsuits in perfect white.

In reality, the grey sandshoes and washed-out sweatshirt stretched tight over her belly made her stand out as not being part of that world. Even Georgie couldn't keep up a pretence for too long, at least not back then. The kicks inside her stomach were matched with a dull thumping in her head.

Ahhh. Those small, white booties. Beautifully knitted. So tiny. How could feet be so small? She remembered an elegant shop assistant had bumped into her and they had fallen at her feet, just as now. Back then she had automatically bent down to pick them up but quickly realised her huge stomach stopped her. The assistant had scooped them up and placed them in willing hands before she could catch her breath from trying to bend down.

How could fine wool booties scorch like fire?

It was all she could do to not drop them again. In that split second all of her trying to not be sad about her baby being adopted dissolved like snowflakes on her tongue.

She wanted the baby. *I can't keep the baby. It will never wear these booties.*

Then there was a huge surge of power within her. The baby made a tiny movement, from this indistinct flicker there was a call on Georgie's heart which she was incapable of answering. *Hit it down hard*. In her mind she was physically pushing the baby down. The assistant had looked at her with warmth and pity.

She knows my life is unlikely to have any happy ever afters.

A hard slap against her arm brought her back into John Lewis. 'Mam. The least you can do is concentrate! Let's go and look at prams.'

With old-fashioned instinct Georgie put the booties in her pocket quietly. Shoplifting every now and then kept her right. *In case I lose everything, it's peace of mind that I can pull a small theft off.*

Lily linked Georgie's arm and hummed as she continued the unwitting torture of her mother.

She looks like she's going to literally explode with happiness with the baby coming out of her belly like The Alien movie.

'Oh Mam, Mam. Look at this nursery set. It's THE one. Look at the gorgeous white rabbits on it.'

Lily grabbed Georgie's hand and yanked it over to the mother and baby furniture section and away from the clothes. It was a huge relief as she was beginning to see hundreds of tiny babies' faces poking out of the top of them. It had become a scene from a horror movie with Paul's face as a baby smiling out at her everywhere she looked.

'Are you OK, Mam, you're still really white? It is supposed to be me that is washed out with all this baby shopping not you!'

'If you must know I was just thinking we're Yin and Yang.'

'Gin and what?'

'Yin and Yang. It's a Chinese philosophy where you believe that for things to be in balance there should be light and shade, fire and water...'

'Oh, you mean like opposites attract.'

'Or repel.'

Georgie could have cut out her own tongue but the words tumbled out without thinking or realising the impact on Lily, unlike normal. Her new stand-up mouth making her spout again. It was only when her daughter dropped her hand like a hot stone, she knew she had been tactless.

'Repel! You mean I actually repel you?'

'No, no, not at all, you silly thing. Not us. We are .... how would you put it. Rock solid.'

'Steady on, Mam. You will be telling me you love me next. Which I know you do, all the time, until it's actually really borrrring.'

If only you knew the truth of all I pretend to say and do.

A complete set of matching Moses' basket, cot and a tiny wardrobe with hand-made wooden hangers, all in the colour of Cornish butter, stood out from the rest of the natural wooden furniture.

'I love this Mam. Look at the little animals. They are gorgeous. Look.'

The price was at least twice what Georgie had expected to pay but, calling it guilt money in her head, she felt obliged to agree. The 20 questions from the assistant at the till didn't help her mood.

'When would Madam want it delivering?'

'About a month before do you think, Mam?'

'Perfect.'

Georgie's sick sensation came back with vengeance and as she punched her code number into the credit card machine to pay. All she could think of was her old bedroom when she was pregnant with her first son.

The damp, musty smell which hung in the air, apart

from the height of summer. It got so hot then she had to stand underneath the skylight, savouring every thin wisp of breeze. At least she had been given a bed when she was five months pregnant. The promise of one to replace the doubled-up blanket had gone on for so many years she had given up asking. How ironic it arrived so near the time she left that hated room for ever. The mattress still had its plastic cover on.

Now the assistant was beaming at her with a smile as big as Lily's grin and she forced a similar expression on her own face, knowing it wasn't very convincing.

'Food!' Her daughter announced. She tucked her arm through Georgie's elbow and marched towards the store's Brasserie.

A friendly manager in an immaculate navy t shirt and skirt escorted them over to one of Georgie's favourite seats beside the window with a view of everyone coming in. Lily, with her usual impatience, snatched the menu up and examined it with no thought of the cost.

'I could eat the whole lot with fries on the side. Ooh, I didn't see the pasta dishes on the back. How lush. What are you having, Mam?'

'I'd like a salad please.'

Her desire for sour food, with a bitter kick, throbbed through her body, as it always did when she was quietly angry with herself, or the world.

'Can I have the lime and chilli chicken one with vinaigrette on it. No bread, thanks.'

'Right,' Lily drew breath before she started on her marathon order, ending with 'Large fries on the side. Vanilla milk shake.'

There was no please or thank you. Georgie added them and even squeezed a small smile out to the waitress in apology for her sometimes charmless daughter.

'How are you feeling about the baby, sweetheart?

I don't really want to know the answer.

Lily cocked her head to one side and in one of her rare moments of perception, looked her mother squarely in the eyes. She didn't speak for a couple of minutes. This made

Georgie both apprehensive and curious about what was going to come out of her mouth. With Lily in full hormonal flow, it could be anything.

'What is going on with you and baby clothes?'

'Nothing is going on with me and baby clothes.'

'Yes, there is. Are you one of these people that gets the creeps around this stuff? Although I don't understand why, when you've two of your own.'

'I'm tired, Lily that's all. Sorry.'

'You're sick of me and baby stuff. I know you love Nat because he is the only boy and everyone knows mothers love their sons more than anything else. Fact. Nat is your beloved son. The favourite.'

'He is not my only son...'

The words flew out. Never to go back in.

The manic hustle and bustle of the Brasserie was suspended as though they were all actors on a film set and the director had shouted 'Cut!'.

It must have been an illusion but Georgie felt as if everyone around her had dropped their mouths open like Lily, who was staring in such disbelief, it was almost comical. But it wasn't.

'OMG.'

Lily spelled her horror which Georgie found very odd.

'What the hell, Mam? You're joking. Please tell me you're joking? The gypsy was right?'

Georgie could only think of Paul. It was as if he was standing behind Lily, calmly watching her. She knew this was not the right time or place to talk about her past but there was never going to be a right time.

'No. I'm. Well. You see. No. I'm not joking. I'm so sorry I blurted it out here, ...'

She gestured to the other tables, '...rather than at home, but yes, you have a half-brother.'

Lily made a quiet sob into a used tissue she found at the bottom of her bag. Her eyes were fixed on a random point on the tablecloth and stayed there while she asked a long list of questions. They were answered as calmly and truthfully as possible.

'When did you have him?'

'I was 16 and still at school. He was adopted as soon as he was born.'

'Is he Dad's son?'

'No. I'd never even met your father then.'

'Well. Who is his father?'

'I don't want to say at the moment as there is a whole heap of stuff going on with him at present and really Lily, it's not your business.'

'Not my business! Well, I'm telling Dad.'

'He knows.'

Lily's voice hissed across the table like a snake.

'So. Everyone knows but me. Perfect. I'll tell you what is my business. Having a mother who lies and is probably just pretending to love me and her perfect life.'

Georgie sat back in her chair aghast. The truth was there right before her eyes.

*

When they got home Lily went to her room and slammed the door. Georgie had a gig that evening. Jaz had texted some last minute tips as usual. Not something to fear any more, stand-up was now a welcome escape route from home.

She had wondered if she should stay in. But her life was taking on a totally different shape. Comedy was eating into her domestic perfection. It was slowly eroding everything she had made the centre of her life.

Her growing confidence made her also want the freedom to be herself. Instead of doing domestic chores she locked her en-suite bathroom door and spent the next hour preparing herself. Re-reading her gig set. Painting her nails just the right shade of violet and applying make-up as if she was a movie star. She added a flash of bright scarlet lipliner around her pink lips. And a touch of Electric Eel eye shadow, which was the most vivid blue she had ever seen.

The gig was in Gateshead's Brown Cow pub and the air smelled like mouldy plums. Jaz met her outside and walked her round the block to calm her nerves. She decided now was the time to tell him about her home life chaos.

He sat quietly while she explained why she'd been so preoccupied. The story of Paul's birth, Lily's pregnancy and Reuben's return into her life took a while. There was no judgement, only supportive understanding. After she'd finished, they both sat in silence for a minute, then he said, 'Use it.'

'What!'

'Use the bones of what you've told me tonight.'

'I can't.'

'Then you're not a true stand-up. You're always going to be a could've been.'

This gig was going to be the most difficult yet. Jaz told her she had to develop her comedy personality and tonight for the first time she was going to be herself.

I'll show him I can do this.

Georgie gathered her courage and stepped on stage at 10pm in the much-coveted third section, reserved for more experienced comics. And she briefly nipped her nose as she passed a punter who had been vaping, then took the couple of steps up to the stage.

Her set told the truth about how she felt about her children. She remembered hearing a successful TV comedian saying he had tried to be jovial and happy for months when he started his career and got no-where until on the night he had decided to stop doing comedy. He was himself, morose and grumpy. He brought the house down and never looked back.

I'm also going to be true to myself.

Georgie stood much more confidently than normal. She was centre stage, taking care not to blink in the bright single spotlight which obscured the crowd. Then she took hold of the microphone and looked out into the white space and deliberately counted for two beats before speaking, to make sure her voice was calm and controlled.

'You may think I look like a normal mam but I'm not. I'm a stand-up mam with a dark heart.

214

'I had a baby boy when I was a schoolgirl. That didn't end well. As you might have expected! But just like the eskimos have 100s of words for snow I learnt how many words we have for schoolgirl slag.

'There's a lot!

But my life turned round ok. Basically, I married rich. Totally recommend it. Only thing is you have to forget being poor. Don't ever think of not speaking posh or you'll be in the dog house for weeks. Or as I like to call it. The spare room.

'I'm going to be honest with you. I went on to have two more kids. And I don't always love them. In fact, I take delight in tormenting them. Sometimes.'

The audience began to chuckle.

'But I pretend it's all an innocent accident. Now they're teenagers I can torment them even more!

'When my son was ill, I asked if he wanted another pillow. When he said yes, I asked if he wanted it over his face or did he think he was going to get better?'

She pointed to a man in the front row who was wearing a smart shirt and waistcoat. 'And my husband. Yes. I've got one of those, short, plump, hairy. No sorry that's a character from Lord of the Rings, always getting them mixed up!'

When Georgie finished she felt the usual peculiar mix of relief and elation. She got good a round of applause and even on small whoop which she felt Jaz had probably orchestrated.

This comedy world is an illusion of confidence. I have to pretend to have it, in bucket-loads.

Tonight, she had used her version of Lily and Nat's voices again and it had definitely added to the humour.

Jaz was clear, 'The best yet. By far. Come over here and I will give you some notes while they're in my head.'

His hand nipped her elbow a bit too tightly as he manoeuvred her to a quiet table on the edge of the club. She enjoyed the nods and smiles from the people around them who were nudging each other and indicating they had enjoyed her set.

This feels like being a B list rock star and I don't care, B list is better than not being on a list. I'm not invisible anymore.

She knew if she had walked around this pub without doing the gig, no-one would have given her a second glance. Once she had reached 40 it was as if most women was automatically given Harry Potter's invisibility cloak.

Her lovely moment of achievement was interrupted by a voice message from Reuben.

'Have you heard any more from Paul? He said he would ring me but I haven't heard anything yet.' Reuben's voice was halting and fractured like a bad phone line.

She texted her answer. *Sorry*, a lie. *Not a text or anything yet*, the truth.

Reuben wasn't to know every time her phone beeped to let her know she had a message, her heart stopped. Meeting their son had opened a can of worms and she kept trying to convince herself it hadn't happened. *No news is good news.*

A reply from Reuben, *I hope we haven't rushed things with him.*

Don't worry it is a massive amount for him to take in. Seriously. I think by worrying about him you are actually jinxing it so please let him take his time.

Jaz was sitting, waiting for her to get the usual feedback, intrigued she wasn't as rapt as usual.

'I'll tell the Stand-Up Star producers you've improved and your timing's much better. You're not gabbling as much. People need a gap to take in what you're saying and get the joke. Don't forget for the final they'll have to get their ears attuned to your accent as well.

'Do you think so bonny lad?' They both laughed.

'I think you're ready for the next level. You're not 100%. But getting there.'

His voice was as warm as usual. 'You're ok aren't you, despite what's happening at home? Not wanting to chicken out? You've also got that big London gig coming up the producers lined up for you. And, we're OK aren't we, G?'

He took hold of her hand gently and laid it in his own,

not trying to hold it at all. It was as if it was a precious jewel likely to vanish in an instant. He looked her straight in the eyes.

She replied quietly, 'We're OK. Thanks. I really need to head off now. Quite a day. As you know.'

I would love to stay here with you and forget home.

'You're not stopping for a quick drink?'

'I need to make sure Lily is ok and tell Nat about Paul as well. Sorry, I must at least make a pretence of being a decent wife and mother.'

Jaz walked her to the door and swung it open confidently. The air outside was the normal welcome change to the pub's heat. He leant on the doorframe as she moved past. She was sure there was a delicate brush of his fingers across the back of her jeans.

The quayside down from Gateshead was quiet as she made her way up the steep bank to the car park. There was no sign of homeless Alec at his usual spot. She remembered now the last time she had seen him. He had made her think about her first son and if he had ever been close to living rough or in difficult circumstances.

Maybe it was best she at least knew he was alive and well. As she turned the corner and clicked her car open a dark figure shot out from behind it. She smelled Alec again before she recognised him.

'You nearly gave me a heart attack. Bloody hell man. What are you doing, lurking about here?'

He gave a chesty chuckle and stuck his hand out. In his rough brogue said, 'I thought I'd missed yer. Desperate for tea or something stronger, depending on your generosity.'

His joke entertained himself so much he cackled and made himself wheeze.

'Here you go. Don't forget you're the only person who I'm genuinely kind to, in the whole world so don't take the piss and ask for too much again, or it'll backfire!'

She was only half joking. As Georgie drove out of the car park, she took care not to knock him down as he made his way to the small corner shop, tucked away under the old railway arches.

Her mood lifted as she drove home and she blasted The Stranglers out to the world. She realised after all the years of difficulties and pretence she was finally being true to herself. With relief Georgie sang as loud as she could. Although she knew there would be music to face at home.

*

When Georgie opened the front door she could see Lawrence and Lily sitting in the kitchen. They were both silent.

'So, you know now.' Georgie got a glass of water and sat down beside them.

'Yes. I'm putting her mind at rest about everything. It's all a shock but not the end of the world. By any means. Is it Lily?'

'I know,' she didn't look at Georgie. 'Yes Mam. There was a good way of telling me about all of this and a bad way. I was having such a lovely time as well.   Really enjoying all that attention. Then whoosh. Away it…'

The front door burst open and Nat ran down the hallway and skidded into the kitchen as if he was on a skateboard.

He shouted, 'Here's…. Nat,' at the top of his voice. Then ground to a halt as he took in all of their faces.

'Oh God. Has someone died?'

Lawrence spoke first. 'No. Nothing to worry about. It's just your mother has something to tell you. Something important.'

'Is she packing in stand-up?'

'No, if only. Don't be silly Nat. Just listen.' Lawrence was firm. He made a grand sweeping gesture to Georgie to give her the floor.

'Mam?' Nat sat beside her.

'You've got a brother. An older brother.'

'That she had when she was even younger than me!' added Lily.

'I was so young I couldn't look after him so he was adopted.'

'Adopted. Oh. So where is he?'

'I never knew but his father found out and I've now met him. He's called Paul. He lives here, Newcastle.

'No way. Absolutely no way. You've got another son. Here, in the toon? That's mad.'

Lily added, 'Have you actually seen him yet Mam?'

'Yes. Once. A few days ago. It was heart-wrenching and so strange at the same time…'

Nat ignored any sensitivities. 'Well. Dish the details?'

'He's tall. Brown hair. 26. Studying art.'

Lily said, 'I hope I've never gone out with him. That would be so weird.'

Lawrence took charge. 'I'm sure you haven't. Now I think we all need to sleep on this news. We're a good solid family and this young man will see us all in good time. I'm sure.

Nat said, 'Hang on. We've not heard who the dad is yet?'

'Reuben. The night club bloke,' said Lily.

'No way. That's weird.' Nat was amazed. 'How did you even know him Mam?'

Lawrence shut him down, 'No more questions for tonight Nat.'

And Georgie was grateful. 'Yes, please no more for now. I love you both you know. This doesn't change anything.'

As Lawrence and her headed up the stairs Lily stayed in the kitchen with Nat. She heard her daughter say, 'It might not change anything but it explains a lot.'

THIRTY-TWO

Before Georgie had time to try and work out how her family really felt about her first son, she was meeting him again herself.

Paul was sitting in the retro Italian café-bar underneath Newcastle's art cinema, looking relaxed and more at ease in his own skin than their last encounter at Reuben's apartment.

Georgie had deliberately asked to see him at lunchtime when she had the excuse to go back to work if emotions overwhelmed her. The time until they met had seemed endless.

He stood up as she approached. Impeccable manners. She liked that. Felt proud. He was wearing dark green jeans, black Vans shoes and a white t-shirt, exactly like the bar staff.

'You blend in well,' she laughed, unable to resist touching his arm for a moment. 'Be careful they don't give you a job.' *I love him.*

At her attempt at humour, he looked down at his clothes quizzically then realised the joke and smiled.

'Can I get you a drink?' He pulled out a battered leather wallet which seemed full of coins rather than notes.

'Thanks. I'll buy them. What are you having?'

'I'll have an Americano, black, please.'

Interesting? I assumed he would be a hot chocolate type of man. Like Nat.

'What about food? If you're anything like my two, you'll have room for something.'

She was trying to be nice but had no idea if she was adopting the right tone. *I am not even sure if it is a good idea to mention my other kids yet. Am I being tactless?*

'Ah yes, the other two.'

He looked at her in a way which she found inscrutable.

Oh no, I can't blow this again. Losing a son once is awful. Losing him again is unthinkable.

Then he seemed to relax and smiled again. 'I'll have a triple meat and salad Panini, please. No mayo.'

This was weird. Nat and Lily were the only other people she knew who hated mayo so much they could tell if a sandwich had been within a mile radius of the 'Devil's sauce' as they called it.

'Excellent taste. Just like me.' *My son.*

She raised her finger to the waiter and ordered a blue cheese and pear sandwich for herself. Her sour and sweet craving was reaching fever-pitch.

'A tonic water. Lime, not lemon. Plenty of ice.'

The food arrived just before their small talk became so tiny it disappeared completely.

What we've to discuss is so huge I don't think either of us know where to begin. So instead, she concentrated on her taste buds bouncing with the ripe, smelly cheese. Paul ate his sandwich in six hearty mouthfuls and sat staring at her as she struggled to keep up. Eating and talking was still a tricky middle-class skill to master.

He said, 'I'd like to meet your kids if that's on the agenda. Like?'

Damn these social skills she thought as she choked on a piece of pear when she tried to reply. He was up in a flash and banged her on the back, not as gently as she would have hoped. The pear bounced into her digestive tract and she was able to speak again, albeit with a puce face. It did, however, calm her nerves.

She replied, 'I really want you to be part of my life. Forever. But this has to be done carefully. You've got to appreciate you're a big shock to them. To me. I tried to forget that time in my life but I never forgot you. Ever.'

He sat very still and stared at her intently with what could have been mistrust or just raw emotion, she couldn't tell.

She tried to weigh him up. But had her usual difficulty in reading someone. After a pause that felt too long to her, she decided. 'Actually I think it'd be good to have you come over for a meal to meet everyone. Took a while with Lily but she's coming round. Everyone is home tomorrow night, would that be ok for you?'

His face was still set in stone, trying to be tough but his eyes were magnified with held back tears.

If he goes. I'll be a weepy mess as well.

'I'd like that. To be honest I was thinking of myself when Reuben suggested meeting up. I didn't really think of the impact on your life, especially with your family. It must be different for him, being single I imagine.'

'Very different. He's a die-hard bachelor. Not sure what type of dad he would have been if he'd brought you up. I think you might have had a string of wicked step-mothers!'

A small smile flashed across his face and he quietly got rid of the damp patch from the corner of his left eye.

'Yes. Tomorrow would be very special. Thanks.....' he paused, *He doesn't know what to call me.*

'Georgie. Probably. Mrs Chancellor would be a bit too formal. Paul.' They both laughed awkwardly.

'Georgie.' he repeated quietly.

The finer details of the timings for the supper were sorted out and as they said goodbye both of them realised how strange this was. *Should I give him a small hug?* She gave him a light kiss on the cheek instead. He flushed with pleasure.

As he walked away she shouted.

'Nat's really chuffed he's getting a big brother.'

He turned round and gave her a smile which would have illuminated Wembley Stadium. And she gave him an identical one back. *That beautiful man is my son.*

THIRTY-THREE

The next morning Georgie's hands rested on the kitchen worktop, as if she was going to do a press up. She called the position Battle-Ready. The sun shone on the surfaces picking out the remnants of crumbs, never usually seen. She was still not back to her normal, immaculate housewife and mother mode. Instead, she was trying to gather her frenetic thoughts, some of which were what to cook for the Meeting Paul Supper.

Lawrence bustled into the kitchen and squeezed her arm as he grabbed a slurp of coffee from the pot on the bench.

'Oh. It's cold. Oh dear. That's a shame. You always have it just right Georgina...Is it because of tonight? What are we going to eat?'

'I'm thinking but still not sure.'

'It'll be. Perfect. As usual darling. Despite his provenance this boy or should I say man. Paul, yes Paul, must be made to feel welcome and I am sure the children feel the same.'

'Oh really?' Georgie moved away from the bench and turned to face him.

'Lawrence. Lily may be over the shock. But I think she's worried he's going to be a cuckoo in the nest about to push her out. Might be pregnancy hormones.'

Lawrence rubbed her arm reassuringly, 'You always worry so much about Lily. I know you love her to the moon and back.'

Sometimes. No. I don't.

'Yes. Lawrence. I do.'

'She loves you very much, Georgina. Don't ever forget it. And so do I.'

He went to kiss her on the lips and found himself attached to her cheek through a deft move on her part. She saw a fleeting look of surprise flash across his face as he planted his mug on the bench.

'See you at six.'

He didn't look back as he left the kitchen, picked up his briefcase and headed out of the front door.

Both Lily and Nat had stayed at friends' houses overnight so she had the kitchen to herself. This was not a good thing. She was brooding. Memories of Reuben. Images of him as a handsome school sports star came rushing into her head along with the same tight knot of adolescent lust in her stomach. Then Jaz. Never far from her thoughts.

She wanted this meal to be special so the complicated Ottolenghi cookery book was pulled out. To take her mind off the evening Georgie prepared home-made pasta, a slow cooked vegetarian sauce with 10 different ingredients and freshly baked focaccia bread. Then she cooked a huge pavlova for dessert.

*

The whole house smelled like an upmarket Italian ristorante making it seem warm and inviting.

Her family were trying to give off the same feeling when Georgie opened the door for Paul to come in and meet them. He seemed a bit taken aback by her appearance. She had dressed down to seem relaxed even if she wasn't, and had abandoned her designer-wear for a pale blue, baggy linen skirt and ACDC band t shirt. Her white-blonde hair was clipped back in a vintage jewelled slide. This evening she wanted to look like the mother she might have been if she'd not met Lawrence.

Paul handed her a beautiful bunch of hand-tied cornflowers. And a small part of her melted.

'Hi. Come on in.'

'Hello.'

He raised his hand as he said it as if he was swearing himself in to a court room.

Well, he is going to be judged.

She pointed ahead so he led the way along the hall to the kitchen. He had taken care with his clothes and looked smart, without being geeky. They were expensive denim jeans and a well-pressed white shirt, which she knew were unfortunately not likely to fare well with the pasta's sauce.

Lawrence was already in the kitchen setting the table. As usual with strangers he was both officious and friendly. Georgie saw Paul was surprised at how different he was to Reuben. Chalk and cheese. Her husband grabbed Paul's hand with both of his, to prove, without a doubt, he was welcome in their home. Georgie was not sure if this was a genuine gesture. *Is it for Paul's benefit or her own?*

'Lawrence. Pleased to meet you, Paul. Beer?'

'That'll be cool. Yeh. Ta. Thanks. Thank you. I mean.'

'Let's see.' Lawrence stood beside the beer fridge like a landlord in a country pub, then bent his head right down beside it, staring at the various labels. 'Peroni. Newcastle Brown. Sol. Where's my Budweiser gone? I had eight bottles. They have totally disappeared. That bloody Nat.' His head came up temporarily. 'That's your half-brother…', before diving back into the fridge.

Georgie noticed Paul was also at pains to put Lawrence out of his misery.

'Peroni would be great. Thanks.'

He took a huge slug of lager out of the bottle at the same time as Lawrence put a beer glass beside him on the table, causing pink to rise up his cheeks. He carefully decanted the lager into the glass as Nat walked into the kitchen.

'Oh you're posh. A glass! Just like Dad. No offence mate.'

The pink colour which had subsided flared again as Paul quickly stood up and put his hand out to Nat who duly gave it a sideways slap rather than a formal shake.

'I'll have a Bud, Dad.' Nat sat down and put his bare feet up on the table, where Georgie swiped them back down.

Lawrence's skin toned matched Paul's pink hue with temper, which he neatly grabbed in the nick of time before he exploded.

'Bud. I'll give you Bud mate.'

'Hey that's funny, Dad. Bud. Mate! It's the same thing.' Nat chuckled and winked at Paul.

'There isn't any Bud left' hissed Lawrence who almost forgot his manners in front of their guest, 'because SOMEONE. HAS. DRUNK. IT. ALL. Without asking.'

'Guess that'll be me then. Sorry Dad.' Nat was still smiling and not sorry in the least. He had automatically embroiled Paul in the situation by flinging his arm around his shoulder.

'We'll have another Peroni then if you please, kind Sir. You will be ready for another one soon won't you mate?'

Paul was staring at the floor. Georgie knew he was looking for a Paul-sized hole to disappear into when the front door swung open and made them all jump. They heard Lily before they saw her. She was being loud and brash.

Georgie gave the pasta a poke with a wooden spoon.

Is this going to be enough for everyone?

Then she turned to face the door to introduce Lily to her older brother but lost the ability to speak as she gasped at her daughter's outfit. Instead of her usual leggings and loose t-shirt she was wearing a skin-tight turquoise dress which showed every inch of her now pronounced pregnancy bump, including a very large belly button.

Increasing Georgie's dismay was the sight of a disheveled Jasper trotting along behind Lily, hair tied back in a pony tail and his goatee beard setting off his old blue boiler suit.

'Hey, Dude.' Jasper slapped Nat's back as he went to sit down in between Paul and him at the long kitchen table.

Georgie felt rare fury. Lily had turned up late and with Jasper. She banged the spoon against the pan as if she was a Judge trying to control a court with a gavel. They all immediately shut up and looked at her. This was not going to plan at all. She wanted Paul to see her as a warm mother.

'Right.' She definitely had their attention.

'Paul. This is Lily and her partner Jasper.'

Nat exploded with laughter. 'Partner. It makes him

sound like a solicitor in Dad's practice. Although as you can see, Paul,' he patted his sister's stomach as she stood beside him, 'He has had plenty of practise.'

Now it was Lily's turn to be outraged and she thumped his arm. Paul resumed looking for the sought-after black hole on the floor. For the third time in as many minutes his face was bright pink again. Lawrence stood up and raised his hand to quieten down the growing mayhem.

'Shut up, everyone. This is difficult for your Mam and Paul. A bit of sensitivity. Yes please. For Paul. We're not normally like this. I think your visit has got our children a bit over-excited, for want of a better word.'

Paul recovered his equilibrium and in a manner which was not unlike Reuben, he looked at them all square in the eye one by one before he spoke. 'I'm really pleased to be here. I didn't know what to expect as I don't have brothers or sisters with my…' he faltered not able to find the right word, '…. other family.'

Georgie saw Lily stare at him hard. 'Well, as Nat and me turned up out of the blue for you, who knows what other siblings might be out there courtesy of our mutual Mam?'

She gripped the spoon handle so hard it was a wonder it didn't snap. Georgie felt as though all of the years of battling to be the perfect mother where her own needs were always at the bottom of the pile, had been stored up and festered. They were now going to vomit over the kitchen. She saw Paul's eyes widen with disbelief.

'Awkward.' chimed Nat.

'Only because it's possibly true,' retorted Lily.

'Hey, come on people. This is way out of line.' It wasn't often Jasper came to the rescue in social situations but this was definitely his finest hour. Jasper gave Georgie a brief hug which she accepted but disliked, and he flicked Lily a dirty look, before addressing Paul.

'Take no notice of Lily, mate. She's all over the pace with pregnancy hormones. You could've had a far worse mother than Mrs C. Seriously. You should meet my mum. She drinks like a fish. Even early in the morning. You can smell it.'

'Enough already, young Jasper!' Lawrence was intent on making this evening a pleasant one for everyone, which Georgie felt was especially kind in the circumstances.

'Right, Paul. Tell us a bit about yourself so we can get to know the newest addition to our family.'

Lily added, under her breath, so Georgie alone heard it,

'It should be my baby who is the special new addition but don't let that worry anyone.'

'I suppose I'd a pretty happy childhood. Doing a PhD in Fine Art. No girlfriend at the moment. Love sport. Played basketball for the Uni team. That's it!'

His eyes lit up when he talked about sport and it was just as if Reuben had climbed inside his body and taken it over. Georgie was drawn to him and at that precise moment felt she'd truly opened up her heart to this stranger.

Even Lily was beginning to behave herself. Jasper was being really attentive towards her and stroking her belly. She was revelling in it then it began to make Georgie feel slightly sick so she concentrated on Paul again instead.

'And I got the note from Reuben sent via the adoption agency and my parents said 'You should see them and learn where you've come from. So here I am. Getting to know you. It's really overwhelming to be honest.' His voice faltered.

'I'd imagined all kinds of horrible scenarios, where my mother was killed or abandoned me somewhere. I never dreamt I would be sitting eating a meal with her family and me become a part of it. Welcomed by her husband and kids.'

He wiped an embarrassing tear then beamed at Lawrence, Nat and Lily who beamed back and ignored him respectively.

Georgie went to the bathroom before she too got caught up with her emotions.

Lawrence followed her out of the kitchen and as they walked along the corridor, they heard Lily start to tell Paul her view of Georgie. 'Don't kid yourself your upbringing would have been that brilliant ….' At that point Lawrence gave Georgie a pat on the arm and turned round.

'Not be a minute. You carry on upstairs.'

He shot back into the kitchen to shut his daughter up. Georgie continued to the bathroom and locked the door firmly before throwing cold water over her face and sitting on the side of the bath.

Suddenly through the floorboards she heard Nat do his impersonation of Lawrence and loudly laugh. This was followed by another giggle and then more raucous laughing. *What on earth was going on?* It was a while since an eruption of laughter had echoed through the house.

The hand towel was cold and damp. It smelled of Nat's feet. Despite this she was glad to rub her face with it and restore some colour to her cheeks.

As she went to turn at the top of the stairs, she stopped by the group of family holiday photos Lawrence had compiled into a big collage. There in the middle was the Cornish cottage from eight years ago. They were all smart in various combinations of navy, white and red.

Georgie saw the look on her own face properly for the first time. She looked haunted. Her face was making all the right moves but the smile was just as if someone had stitched the sides of her mouth upwards. A Batman Joker and just as scary, for herself, with hindsight.

As she approached the door she heard Lawrence saying, 'Your mother needs understanding. She is sometimes cold. But tries so hard not to be. Damaged. I fear.

I now know the true meaning of words being like a punch in the stomach. Damaged. I'm damaged goods. The memory of Lawrence's mother whispering the same thing when they had first gone to meet her over 20 years ago, came back to her from a dark cupboard in her head marked Dangerous, Never Open on Pain of Death.

Georgie was both horrified and furious at the same time. It was as if Lawrence was now colluding with the enemy even though his mother was long dead.

She'd matured. But now a different vision of her 16-year-old self repeatedly kept coming back to her, where she was a tough, street-savvy teenager. With one careless word Lawrence had suddenly stripped this illusion down to its bones. She again realised that being pregnant, pointed at in the street and giving up a baby, too scared to touch it, was not normal.

Lawrence slammed his lips shut as she walked in to a silent room. The laughing had stopped, that was for sure.

She had two options, either join the conversation which was obviously about her or ignore it altogether. Her three children were sitting in a row facing her. Their eyes all had the same expression of uncertainty. She was taken aback by how similar they looked despite the difference in hair colour. Their noses all had a small bump near the top and small, perfectly even nostrils. There was so little resemblance between both Lawrence and Nat or Lily she was amazed sometimes he didn't question their parenthood, although he had no reason to doubt her fidelity, for the moment.

She opened the kitchen door to the garden, letting the evening air soothe the atmosphere. It calmed her while she thought about what to do to mend this falling-apart family. Then with all of her acquired middle-class social skills, she started to assemble the pavlova and asked Lawrence to get more drinks.

'So, Paul, what are you going to do when you finish your Doctorate?' Georgie smiled at him to try and ease the tension in the room as well as herself.

'Reuben said he might be able to give me some work doing design work for the club but I don't know if that's wise.'

Georgie was slicing chunks of mango with a massive carving knife with little regard for her own personal safety. It made a resounding crash off the workbench, shearing the fruit open like a shattered skull.

Paul added, 'Are. Emm. Are you close? He quickly looked at Lawrence in case this was tactless.

Nat chipped in, 'Nahhh. Doubt it. No 'fence.. I know he's your Dad and everything but he sounds pretty up himself.'

Lawrence was quick to chide Nat but added, 'Reuben can be quite pompous, Paul.'

'Pot and kettle Dad', Lily smiled at him as she said it and he went to playfully cuff her ear. Lawrence started to talk about his own business but Lily raised her hand.

'It's not school Lily. You can talk when you want to.' Lawrence smiled.

'Ok. Well. This might not be the best time. But. I've got a big announcement. Sorry if I'm upstaging you Paul.'

You're not at all thought Georgie.

'Please don't mind me,' Paul said cheerily, trying not to feel uncomfortable.

'Well. Me and Jasp…'

Jasper and I…' interrupted Lawrence.

Lily threw her father a dirty look then continued, '… have found the perfect place for our wedding.'

'Somewhere appropriate for a pregnant bride I assume?' Lawrence looked stony-faced. Then realised they had a guest and painted a smile on his face.

'It's perfect for whatever your personal circumstances are Dad. Actually. And we're planning it for Christmas. After the baby's here. A really cute little barn near Durham. We've been looking at a few things on the internet and then went to see it with his dad, as he said he'd pay for it all.'

'He probably wants to just make sure his football pals can get in and there will be plenty of drink.' Lawrence laughed.

Georgie knew Lawrence thought Jasper's father, a self-made IT entrepreneur, was too working class to be a great addition to their family.

'Probably! We've got a possible date in the middle of the Christmas holidays. You and Mam need to come and see it obviously, before we sign things.'

'Lovely.' Georgie was relieved temporarily for the diversion from all of the Paul small talk.

But he was keen to talk some more about Reuben once the wedding details were finished. 'What do you think I should do about him?'

'I know he's very keen, almost desperate, to bond with you. How do you feel about that?'

Paul flushed and was irritated with himself for doing it, she could tell. So she went across to pat him on the shoulder in support. He gripped his glass as tightly as she had held her knife.

'I don't mind seeing him for an odd coffee but it's you. Your family which are special for me, having a sister and brother. I can't tell you how important it is for me to find out about them. Especially a mam who does stand-up comedy. I was a bit freaked out to find out it was you I had seen at first, but now I think it's pretty cool.'

'That's the only cool thing about her, everything else is hot-tempered at the moment isn't it, Mam? It's all the stress of her little comedy thing.' Lily added. She put her finger in her mouth and pretended to make herself sick. It backfired however and she had to excuse herself as it made her feel sick in reality.

He said, 'I thought you had plenty of good lines when I saw you. Didn't you all think the same?'

Lawrence spoke first, 'We've not had the pleasure as yet. Just a little taste of bits and bobs. Mixed up laundry, slimming club shenanigans, that type of thing...'

'But, when I saw her, it was all about...'

Georgie jumped in, 'There's plenty of time for my family to hear more about my jokes another time.'

'You are all going to see her though, aren't you?'

Lawrence nodded, 'Of course. There's just been quite a bit of activity in our house lately, not a lot of peace. Isn't that right Georgina?'

'Definitely, we need peace. But you're still welcome to text me any jokes you come across. Always need more material.'

'Really? Being here this evening, I would have thought you had plenty!' Paul laughed, not noticing that Lawrence looked perplexed.

'But we're not what she talks about...'

'Well, not always.' Georgie smiled. Lawrence thought she was being ironic. *Good.*

Georgie didn't ask Paul to call round with jokes deliberately. She was still working out how this scenario was going to end. If Paul worked for Reuben she did not want him tittle-tattling about her life. He seemed to sense the mood had changed and after a few minutes he pushed away his scraped-clean pudding dish and emptied his glass.

As he got up to leave, she felt another surge of sadness at being parted from him.

The sadness was also there at his birth but I just held tight to cope with everything.

'It's been really great to meet you all. Thanks for making me so welcome.'

He shook Jasper and Lawrence's hands, gave Nat a fist bump and went to give Georgie a kiss on the cheek which she avoided by a quick body swerve towards the dishes. Her ability to play happy families was starting to fray and she was sad it also gave her no pleasure.

She wanted to be on her own and have time to think. 'I'll be in touch.' She was showing him out as Lily emerged from the toilet and was walking carefully down the stairs.

'Ugh I have been sick. It was gross. It must have been that meal.' She glared at Georgie who shrugged rather than apologising as she usually did.

'See you around.' Lily continued on her way back to the kitchen.

'When is her baby due?'

'Eight weeks. Can't wait.' Georgie lied.

As her newly-acquired son waved bye and walked down the path his back view was so similar to Reuben she felt the age-old crushing feeling and was 16 again, miserable and at odds with the world.

The pathos of this whole evening was such a painful contrast to the promise of her new comedy life she could hardly believe it might be within touching distance. Seeing Paul disappear made her mind get back on track, concentrate on the future, thinking about her next gig in London, and Jaz

THIRTY-FOUR

The Joke House in Soho was a different level of venue to the series of pubs Georgie had performed in during her stand-up career so far.

Jaz and Georgie arrived early and sat quietly in the green room, going over her set. All of the gags were fine-tuned. Tyneside Metro trains references were changed to London jokes about the night bus.

She was terrified at the crowd who she saw arriving. All different nationalities and ages, with no doubt varying senses of humour and understanding of English.

A TV comic. Bob Brown, was the MC and got everyone warmed up with jokes about his family and friends with a smattering of politics thrown in. Mainly anti-Tory banter. The Prime Minister got ridiculed for all the reasons often on the front of the tabloid papers.

Then it was Georgie's turn. She wore her black jeans and t shirt, vivid red lipstick and dark eye shadow to build her confidence as much as possible. She felt sure of herself. Able to seize the moment. *Come on Georgie. You can do this.*

Microphone grab. Fine. Tick. Opening gag about London tourists. Fine. Tick.

The set's middle section continued at a good pace. There was a round of laughs and an all-important clap. Double tick.

She then talked about being from the North and how everyone assumed she met assumed she had a whippet and a flat cap. With the added bonus of a Greggs sausage roll. Then the truth started. She told them how she felt about her family and how the perfect housewife and mother was a really a make-believe dream.

'Can you think of any other time in your life you would be slaving away for three hours to produce something that disappears in five minutes without anyone saying a word of thanks.

'Well, welcome to the last Persian chicken feast I made, devoured before I had even sat down. As usual!'

Georgie was sure the lights in the room became darker as she began talking about her family and newly-found son. The tension and funny side of Paul eating with them. Lily being jealous and Nat loving the drama. She knew it was breaking their trust but every word healed a part of her that had been damaged for so long. No more pretending, she hoped and prayed.

The gig flew by. Georgie had a solid 10 minutes under her belt and Jaz, a happy mentor, by her side.

He was proud of her she saw that as soon as she stepped off the stage to applause.

'Well done Georgie. Not just for the gig but the stories about your family work so well. So dark but funny.'

'I hope they see the humour when I tell them how much material they've given me.'

'They don't know yet? Oh. Dear. That's going to be an interesting conversation.'

'It might never happen. Not sure I've got the bottle.'

'If you can say how you feel on stage in front of strangers I'm sure you can tell them to their faces.'

'I really don't exist to them.'

'Well, they're going to have to take notice of what you're saying with your set at some point.'

Georgie sighed and felt the confidence from the gig ebb slightly but she was still sure she was doing the right thing. For herself. For the first time.

They waved goodbye to the other acts. She felt pleased with how her set had gone as they headed back to the hotel.

The city air was oppressive; it was as if the whole city was at breaking point and about to pop like a giant, urban balloon.

Georgie stood at the edge of the road slightly ahead of

him, making him come to a sharp stop. Out of the blue he said, 'Let's walk back. It would be great to have some fresh air, we can go past St James's Park. There are some outdoor theatre events on until midnight. And, I've planned a surprise! A good way to unwind from your performance high.'

'I wouldn't go that far but I'm always willing to take a compliment.'

'I'll remember that...'

She was often unsure whether he was being deliberately flirty or if he was like this with everyone. However, soaking up the frenetic atmosphere and postponing sleep seemed a great idea.

'Lead on.' She saluted and clicked her feet to attention. 'I have no idea where we are so it's down to you. I'm intrigued!'

Her red pumps would rub like mad if it was too far but they were still way better than stilettos. Jaz's snappy strides made her feel like a little, fat maid scuttling to keep up with her mistress. The advantage of their disjointed strides was she felt less less like they were a couple.

He had stopped his occasional brushing her skin with his hand when he spoke tonight, which made her feel a mix of relief and disappointment. Lawrence had been cautious about her going away but knew they had started her on this competition journey and it would be unfair if he kicked up a fuss. He had offered to go. But it clashed with a New York deal being finalised. *Luckily,* thought Georgie, who didn't want her husband there for many reasons, some of which she refused to recognise, including being alone with Jaz.

She was well aware of her rock solid reputation for working hard in any field that was given to her. Perfect family life. Done. Perfect office manager. Done. Any wall which was put in front of her, the higher the better. Bring it on. As long as her husband approved.

And so she was in London, with Jaz, overnight. She had begun to chase a dream while trying to avoid her nightmares.

He stopped beside a shadowy gate, illuminated by dozens of fairy lights. 'Princess. Your surprise awaits.'

'I expected a London park at night to be more grotty, than grotto. Is it a comedy night?' Georgie smiled.

He also smiled. His dazzling teeth looked luminous against his brown skin while his dark eyes seemed to disappear altogether.

She took in his blue linen jacket and trousers. He looked like a prince. A not-unattractive one either she admitted to herself. Finally.

Jaz made a play of putting her hand on his as if they were courtiers going to do a formal dance and walked her into the park. 'It's not grotty I assure you. This is going to be spectacular feast for the senses. You'll be amazed!

'So not a comedy show?'

'No. Not everything in life is about being funny. Some things are deadly serious.' He grinned.

Georgie's eyes struggled to make out where they were heading and then through the trees she spotted it. A tiny space was cleared in the middle of the park and there was a row of seats on three sides where a crowd of people were patiently sitting.

He smiled at the steward on the entry point, whispered into his ear, put something in his pocket and the next thing Georgie knew she was being ushered to reserved seating at the front. There were only two spaces left and Jaz led the way past the crowd.

The man sitting next to them stood up and quickly shook Jaz's hand as if he was the most important guest in the world. He then reached across and lightly kissed her on both cheeks. No sooner had they sat down then there was a unified hush. The only sound which interrupted the atmosphere was the distant toot of a London cabbie. After the noisy, laddish atmosphere of the comedy club this dark park, with its sprinkling of fairy lights, was an enchanted kingdom.

The atmosphere was full of anticipation as the whole crowd held its breath.

A single piano player slipped into his seat and became

invisible. The first of the tango dancers appeared beside Georgie and wove her way around the performance space, setting the ground alight with tiny drops of oil and the music began. Two dancers, clad in skin tight black and gold dresses, danced together as if they were Siamese twins, fire flicking out from their bracelets and setting the earth around them on fire.

Georgie was spellbound. The smell of the burning oil, the wisps of smoke hiding the performers, then revealing them, was creating a sexy, dramatic landscape right before her eyes. Two male dancers entered, like gangsters at a shootout and the atmosphere changed again with the piano music spiralling into a frenetic Latin beat. The four dancers were entwined around each other and tiny spurts of oil were twirling around them, then bursting into flames as they hit the earth. The heat from the fire made the cool night air stick to Georgie's skin. She was shivering and hot all at once.

The show lasted an hour and by the end the crowd was on its feet with enthusiastic applause. As Georgie also got up, she realised Jaz's leg had been glued to her own without her noticing. Everyone clapped and clapped while the dancers took their elegant bows and curtsies, still shrouded by smoke and tiny pockets of smouldering flames.

'And now you can all have a go at the tango. Don't be shy. We'll help you.' The principal dancer stamped out the last of the fires and pulled up two couples, while other performers also picked members of the audience to dance. Sensual guitar music began to pulse around the park and the performers lit small torches marking the performance space, casting huge shadows around them all.

Before Georgie realised what was happening Jaz had taken her hand and she was in the middle of the floor with his hand pressed in her back and held so close to him there was no need for her to imagine what he would be like naked.

He threw her arm over his shoulder and swept her round and round. The trees were closing in and then disappearing as her head was forced to rest on his shoulder to keep her balance. Her heart raced while the music made her body pulse with a Latin beat which was as alien as the intense sexuality she could feel growing between them.

The floor was full of couples swaying and dancing, with the music getting more and more frenzied. Georgie was shaken from her trance-like state as the principal dancer took her hands and led her around the floor.

More dancers took partners from the crowd, the music's pace began to die down slowly and the few remaining flames dimmed. Georgie caught her breath as all of the crowd was gradually brought to a halt in the middle of the park. Sweat dripped down her back and as she wiped off small beads from her face, Jaz gently pressed a linen handkerchief against the base of her neck to cool her down.

'Grazie, Grazie. Good night, ladies and gentlemen. Bona notte. We were Tango Siciliana. Ciao.' The performers extinguished the final lights as they swept away into the furthest part of the park and the stillness descended once again into what had become a truly magic kingdom.

Jaz removed the handkerchief. 'You're a beautiful dancer Georgie.' The way he looked at her she realised he was not giving her a line. She had seen this look before with Reuben all those years ago and knew the night was going to need careful control.

Since Paul was born, she always tried to live her life where she had complete command of everything. The heat and emotion of this evening meant she could tell she was starting to take leave of her senses.

'We should get over to the hotel before it gets too dark or we could end up like Babes in the Wood, following breadcrumbs to find our way out of the forest!' She tried to lighten the mood and calm her breathing.

Jaz bent down at her feet and picked up an imaginary crumb and as his head lifted up his eyes travelled up her legs. The slower their gaze travelled the more a huge serpent seemed to be twisting around in Georgie's stomach.

'Found one!' He laughed and put the invisible speck in the middle of her palm, drawing a circle around it. When his hand fell back to his side, she felt an impulse to pick it up and hold it between both of her own.

'We need to go.' She sounded snippy to give herself a chance to get her head straight. Her legs marched her body out of the park and into the busy London street. Jaz had to give a quick hop and skip to keep up with her.

'Wait for me. Where's the fire? Oh wait. I know exactly where the fire is!' He said it suggestively as he caught up with her. They both said little as they briskly cut their way through the hectic streets full of tourists to the hotel.

She knew the silence belied their emotions.

In the close confines of the lift to their rooms, she thought their bodies were actually crackling out loud. Electricity hitting water. Jaz leant against the back corner and stared at her. Silent.

Another guest entered the lift and was a welcome barrier between them although when their floor arrived and the doors flew open Jaz deliberately moved within touching distance of her body to let her get past. His hand grazed the curve of her jeans. It was all she could do to not yelp out loud.

Think, Georgie, think. This is not the time in your life to cave in to your sexuality. You have the life you always wanted with Lawrence.

The streetwise part of her who had ruled her thinking with a hard heart all of her adult life, realised that there was a high chance if she slept with Jaz her life would change but not for the better. That could not happen.

Her key was in the room lock and his hand was on the door when he gave her the 'Get out of jail' card she had frantically been looking for. He just raised his eyebrows, questioning.

In a second the vestiges of physical heat were shaken off and skulked away down the long corridor. Jaz did not know the real Georgie yet. Despite her flats, she almost matched him for height and her eyes were fixed on his own. They were inches apart but she quietly shook her head.

He nodded and bowed in recognition of her decision.

'Good night Jaz. Thank you. I've had an amazing time.'

The key was in the lock, turned in an instant.

He had looked thoughtful and crest-fallen. She almost felt sorry for him. And herself. The attraction she felt for him had left its outer casing around her body, it tingled with anticipation that was not going to be fulfilled tonight. Her Devil kicked her shoulder in disgust and her Angel cleaned and stretched her wings as if the outcome of this evening had never been in doubt.

She leant on her bedroom door for good measure as she texted Lawrence, wanting his comfort and solidity. 'Extraordinary night. Great experience. Can't wait to be home. Love you.' It was a full minute before Jaz's footsteps moved from outside her door.

They were booked on separate trains home as he had a meeting the next day. It gave Georgie time to get her head straight.

THIRTY-FIVE

When she was back home Georgie made sure the house was pristine. Lawrence was relaxed and well-fed. Lily had spent all day leafing through baby magazines, making Georgie give her views. It was like nails down a blackboard but her daughter wasn't to know that.

'Don't skimp on anything you need Lily.' Lawrence boomed. 'I've spoken to Jasper's father and he said he wanted his grandchild to get the very best. Of everything. All sorted.'

Georgie shrunk inside, remembering his initial response when he had demanded Lily have an abortion. His first grandchild was something he could brag about now especially as there was a wedding planned.

Nat stopped playing his PlayStation.

'Can I have…'

'No.' laughed Lawrence. 'Whatever it is ask your mother to sort it out.'

Then the three of them laughed, as usual. When Georgie didn't join in, no-one noticed.

'I've got another gig tonight. Only a couple more before the final.' She said it into what she now considered to be a domestic abyss.

Never even looking up Lawrence said, 'Oh, it's that near the end of it all is it? Where?'

'Upstairs in The Ship. I think.' It was there but she didn't want to confirm it as this gig was The One where the truth of her feeling about her life was going to come out fully. It would build on her set where, with Jaz's encouragement, she had been transformed into a mother who almost loved her family but had had enough.

'Break a leg.' Lawrence shouted as she opened the front door.

The dark pub room was packed, mainly with students and couples. Jaz met Georgie at the door as always, sensing when she was likely to lose her nerve and bolt, never to be seen again. Although this had never happened. So far. There was no mention of London. He gently touched her hand. 'Stomach, OK?'

Georgie grimaced. 'It's my whole body.' Little did she know that at that exact time her family were getting in the car to see her and would soon be sitting tucked away in a corner of the pub.

When it was her turn the crowd sat politely, waiting as always for an older female comic to talk about the menopause and a love of shopping. They expected a slightly whimsical view of the world, and only slightly funny.

Georgie grabbed the microphone firmly, then rested on the stand to pretend to be nonchalant. She performed her set introduction. Then changed tack.

'I sometimes hate my family.'

Two students stared at their drinks, heads down.

'Hey you two. Don't ignore me. My stupid son does that and it's only because he's brain dead. I'll tell you the proof. He thinks you put a condom on BEFORE you go on a date.

'The secret to having a happy son is the F word. No, not THAT word. Food. If you run out you will have an internet gaming, World of Warcraft warrior raging around. And. If his sister eats the last of anything. There's the cry of…MAM she's hoovered up all the food in the house, like a Dyson powered by Greggs.

'He was nervous when he started school, hid in the toilets at lunchtime. Dinner nanny said 'Oh pet. How long have you been here?' He said 'Four weeks!'

Georgie added, 'Maybe I'd forgotten to pick him up! I'm a pretty shit mother to be fair. I try hard but always feel I could do better.'

She then moved on to two young women in the front row.

'And you. You're just like my daughter. Hate her guts sometimes as well to be honest.

'She's going to have a baby, going to be getting married, going to be…. Hmmm let see. Completely screwed, by too much actual screwing.

'And she's so rude about people. I took her to a café but she couldn't get the top off her coke bottle, I popped to get the cakes and it was open when I got back.

'Who opened the coke for you? I asked

'That fat man over there! She said this, IN FRONT of him.

Next Georgie had an older couple in her sights.

'And you.' She pointed to the man.

'Remind me of my short, bossy husband. So please leave as I'm really enjoying this time away from him.'

'And don't get me started about my now dead mother-in-law. She was helping Newcastle University with its memory research. But, wait for it, she forgot to go for the tests!

'No tact either, she asked her cleaner if she was pregnant. Then said, 'Well, someone had to tell her to lose weight!'

And so, the gig continued, gag after gag about her family.

As she walked off stage out of the corner of her eye, she spotted a group of three people coming over to her. It was Lawrence, Lily and Nat.

It can't be. I want to die.

Georgie started to tremble. She was gripped by fear and a strange strength at the same time. Although unexpected she was ready to face their music. And the consequences of everything.

She stood still by the stage, wondering if her life as she knew it was over. And also realising that this day had been coming since she started doing stand-up. Lawrence was first to reach her and grabbed her arm then pinned her to the wall beside the stage.

He hissed, 'We're leaving. Now. This shit show is what you've been working on? Hating your family. Sharing private things for a few cheap laughs. You're an absolute disgrace. My mother was right. You're damaged and mad. Totally mad.'

Lily wiped tears and shouted in Georgie's face, 'And you're not even funny.'

Georgie stared at them both expressionless. 'I'm sorry.'

Lawrence and Lily both snorted in unison, 'Sorry!'

Nat stood beside Georgie and patted her shoulder. 'To be fair, it is a shock but I thought the condom bit was pretty funny…'

Georgie shook off Lawrence's arm and was grateful for Jaz walking over to them, looking concerned.

'Everything ok here?'

Lawrence barked, 'What do you fucking think? No doubt you masterminded this to turn our marriage into a shit show and get into my wife's knickers. Isn't that what people like you do?' He had automatically put up his fists.

Now it was Jaz's turn to look angry, 'People like me? Want to explain that?'

'Dad!' Lily and Nat pulled Lawrence's arms down to calm him down.

He turned around and said 'We'll discuss this at home Georgina. Not in this dump, you've turned into your second home.'

'I am sorry Lawrence, Lily, Nat. Really. It's just…'

'Doesn't matter now. You've said all those things. In public.' Lily cut her off and marched out with her dad. Nat gave her a kiss on her cheek. 'It'll blow over Mam. Sometime soon. I think. Maybe.'

Georgie collapsed onto a seat when they'd gone and Jaz hugged her, which didn't make her feel better.

'On top of everything else, I'm sorry my husband was racist.'

'That's not the issue for you here. What do you want to do? Finish this or pack it in? Your choice.'

'I'm not packing it in. My life has never felt more fulfilled or happy. I'm going on. No matter what.'

'Good. But don't forget I'm here to help if things get out of hand.'

'I've coped with worse.'

The Stand-Up Star WhatsApp group couldn't believe all that she'd said in front of her family. And she'd lived to tell the tale. Almost. They all sent her a series of the monkey holding its head in its hands emojis.

THIRTY-SIX

From the moment she returned, the routine of Georgie's life changed. Lawrence and Lily continued to shout at her or ignore her depending on how they felt. In return she stopped being the house slave to perfection. Food was still put on the table but it was more basic, the food she'd grown up with, rather than intricate dinners. She was eating what she wanted and the family had to put up with it.

Lawrence and her still shared a bed for now but they turned away from each other. If one of them accidentally touched the other in their sleep they flinched.

After a week there were conversations about what had been said.

'Georgina. If you are still determined to do this comedy final. At least spare us all. Please stop talking about such personal things.'

'I'm speaking the truth and that's why it resonates with people.'

'But you were still funny doing the jokes about the dog and the wedding ring. All that type of thing.'

'I'm not going back to Mary Berry.'

'Jamie Oliver?'

'No. No chefs. They're not really awful stories. It's not like I'm saying you killed people.'

'You did say you sometimes hated us. I know that's not true but it's pretty terrible to say that. You must admit.'

It's the truth sometimes.

'I'm sorry for hurting your feelings.'

'Thank you. Will you think about Mary Berry then?'

Lily was still furious but Nat was the peace broker. He sat them down for a family conference.

Reluctantly Lily and Lawrence accepted Georgie's apology. She eventually promised to stop talking about them, after the final. They didn't see her fingers crossed behind her back.

Life went back to a form of normal but it seemed as if there was only three in the family. Georgie was on the outside looking in. Again.

Her focus was Jaz, gigs and she loved everything about it outside her home. He occasionally touched her hand to emphasise a point and inside she melted. Despite trying not to. She mustn't. So much was at stake.

Most evenings they spent either in the rehearsal pub, interrupted regularly by Lawrence on the phone, making his presence felt, or texting each other, fine-tuning her set before the final practise gig at Newcastle's Cackle Club.

Lawrence was now finding what he called her little comedy thing irritating and disruptive. The drunken night out with Andrea hadn't been forgiven either.

Georgie was glad to be out of the house more often and able to get some head room.

Paul's arrival in her life had shifted her views of motherhood and perfection. Not for the better of other people in her life, but definitely for herself. Now her comedy set covered every aspect of being a stand-up mam, from her newly-discovered hatred of all domestic duties to the general assumption at home that her needs were automatically not as important as everyone else's. Who knew?

To prove a point, she turned her mobile phone off and put Lily's whining about her stomach cramping, right out of her head. Since Paul had called round her daughter had raged round the house for what seemed to be all day and all night.

Georgie understood it was difficult for both Lily and Nat. He was taking it in his stride. Lily was definitely not. Tonight, the moaning had definitely reached its zenith and before she left the house Georgie thought she might actually kill her daughter, just for the chance of some peace.

The arrival at the Club marked the start of some serious stomach cramps of her own. The bouncer seemed amazed that this middle-aged woman was one of the acts as he opened the doors, although he quickly re-set his face to welcome her. Georgie was pleased Jaz would be there to give her support.

When she saw him by the bar her heart felt as if it had been squeezed tight. Her feelings shocked her. When he looked over and smiled, her cheeks flushed like a teenager.

Oh God. Oh God. I'm in love with this lovely man.

Tonight, was so near to the final it was terrifying. Jaz reminded her the audiences at Cackle were fussy about their comedians and nothing less than hilarious would do.

Jaz walked her to the comedians table, reassuring her and stroked her arm, sending more distress signals to her belly.

Andrea was already there, looking very much at home, a large glass of wine in her hand. Her big smile was like a beacon in the shadowy light. Georgie took solace in its beam and followed it, cutting through the drinkers.

'It's totally packed Georgie. Are you terrified?'

'You could say that. I am going to need a drink.'

Andrea pulled up a stool beside her and she could see her weighing up how she looked, then nodding approvingly to Jaz, before giving her a peck on the cheek. She patted the stool. Georgie duly obeyed and sat down.

I am really lucky to have Andrea and Jaz here.

'I really, really think I need a drink.'

She touched her chest and could feel her heart pounding even underneath her clothes. Its thump, thump, must have been visible to other people, she was sure. She put the A4 piece of paper with her set on carefully on the bar in front of them. None of it seemed fixed in her brain which was currently locked down like a high security prison. The set captured but not able to get out.

The place was becoming so hectic drinks were slopping on to this precious paper.

Georgie sipped a spritzer and the cool liquid only took a second to hit her stomach. It made it cramp even more but then it took effect and her adrenalin dropped a tiny portion.

Jaz was speaking to her but none of his words were really registering. Over and over in her head were the first lines she had to say. Her comic set piece. This reverie was interrupted by Bill, the MC who was trying to round up the straggling band of comics. He tapped Georgie on the shoulder, told her she would be first in the third section, pointed to the comedians' corner and gave her a thumbs up. She smiled and promised to go in the break before she was on. Sitting at the bar allowed her to pretend she was just a punter.

The acts in the first section were funny, a mix of local comedians and one teenager who had come over especially from Manchester. He was really cocky and full of tales of his search for the right girlfriend. His good looks and obvious charm went down well.

Georgie recognised him as a boy band type of comic, beloved of the TV stations. The crowd related to him and were eating up his every word. Despair filled her again. What would they make of material about motherhood and bringing up hapless teenagers who you don't even like very much?

This is it. Final gig before the final. Then Jaz patted her on the back and she was off to comics' corner to await her fate. As she walked, she noticed he was talking on his mobile and staring at Georgie with concern. *Whatever it is, it would have to wait.* She was relieved her own phone was off so there were no distractions.

The comedians who were already seated introduced themselves, everyone shook her hand and wished her luck. As she went to sit down she jumped as Jaz was by her side.

'Georgie. Your phone is off.'

'I know. But, as you know. I'm about to do a REALLY important gig.'

'But Lawrence has been trying to get in touch with you.'

'Him and his missing socks!' Georgie was trying to make light of it but Jaz's expression told her something serious was going on.

'It's Lily, George. She is in hospital.'

'She is such an attention seeker. It'll only be wind.'

'I think you need to ring Lawrence, seriously, he sounded really worried.'

Bill, the MC was finishing his drink and getting ready to launch the final three sets. She was next up. Georgie had a decision to make and quickly. The years of working at her relationship with Lawrence, Lily and Nat flashed before her eyes. Every fight and atom of love she had tried to create sat there.

But Georgie was desperate to succeed for herself. At something. She realised this summed up motherhood. It always found a way to erode your sense of self. No matter how important something was to her, the family always managed to get in the way and cock it up.

Jaz was still staring at her, expecting her to pick up her bag and rush out of the door. But Georgie did neither of those things. Instead, she gave him a huge hug, as if she was going to her death and would never see him again. She walked the long, lonely stand-up walk to the stage.

This was going to be her time to shine. Lily had Jasper and Lawrence, who would no doubt be a far calmer support for her.

I'll ring her when this is done. Until then, she goes out of my mind. Focus. I may be a rubbish mother but I am going to fight to be a great stand-up comic.

Bill introduced her and the crowd as usual were quiet and slightly non-plussed as to why one of their mothers must have decided to go on stage. Georgie was not going to let this opportunity pass by. Lily's predicament, whatever it was, had given her extra fire in her belly for success. If she was going to put this gig before her daughter's difficulties, it had better be good.

The lights were in the right position and as she thanked the MC and took centre stage, she could see the crowd well. They were like Madam Tussauds' waxworks, their skin pale and expressions fixed. The script was still stuffed in her back pocket. She deliberately took it out and crumpled it on stage.

'I was going to do a great, topical set for you tonight but my pregnant daughter has gone into premature labour, we think, and been rushed to hospital. However, I am such a crap mother I am going to stay here and talk to you all instead! Cue an appropriate pregnant pause from audience...'

Everyone chuckled nervously, assuming she was lying. She then went through her set, outlining the tales of bringing up teenagers and all her well practised gags.

Her last joke about a friend having the ambition to see the Grand Canyon and go down on a donkey, which must be two ambitions not one, got a clap of appreciation as well as a good few laughs out loud.

When Georgie put the microphone back into its stand, she saw Jaz sitting by the side of the stage, shaking his head. She didn't know if she had done well, but it had been her best, even if in real life she was a failure. Bill gave a high five as she came off and the crowd gave her a huge round of applause so she knew some of her set had worked.

Jaz spoke softly into his phone as she walked towards the door. Georgie rushed to catch up with him as he thrust the handset to her ear the minute they got to the entrance. Lawrence was in mid-flow.

'Lawrence, Hi, it's me, Georgie. Sorry my phone was off.'

'About time. We need you here at the hospital. Lily is pretty poorly and there are complications with the baby's heartbeat. I'll meet you in the maternity unit car park.'

His voice was breaking up with emotion as he spoke to her which almost melted Georgie's own heart. She handed the phone back to Jaz who looked at her quizzically.

'God Georgie. I have seen you become icy cool but this takes the biscuit.'

Georgie cracked back, 'What? No well done mate.'

The final comic had finished his set and saw them ready to leave. 'Oh yes, Your daughter's in labour. That was a good opening gag.'

Jaz looked at him quietly for a moment then said, 'I'll drive.'

What felt like a few seconds later they were outside the maternity wing and walking towards Lawrence.

He was so white and expressionless he looked spectral. The final waxwork of the evening. As they approached, he collapsed into their arms. Jaz knew it was time to go but Georgie wanted him there. The wrench was awful when he left.

Lawrence, Georgie and Jasper sat down in the reception area as midwives and consultants rushed around. Lawrence explained what had happened as they listened intently in case they missed a word.

Lily had felt severe cramps across one side of her stomach not long after Georgie had left for her gig. Lawrence had rung the maternity ward and asked for advice. Georgie pictured herself suffering self-imposed stress before the gig and felt a warm rush of guilt sweep through her body. She had been alone when she had her first child and would have given anything to have a loving mother to give her support. *Have I become my own mother?*

The hospital had advised Lily to go to the maternity ward to be checked out. While her thoughts were full of how to make people laugh, she learnt Lily had been terrified her baby was going to die.

I have to see her.

Never in her life had Georgie felt the need to hold Lily as much as she did now. It was like thirst. Real and insistent.

*

The waiting room was hospital white and stark. They waited patiently for more news as the medical staff were in and out of the side room in which Lily and the baby's fate were in the balance.

After half an hour of sitting and pacing, a midwife with a warm Welsh accent and broad hips came up to them. Georgie felt Lily was in good hands with her.

'You can come in and see your daughter now and we'll explain what we are going to do.'

'Is the baby OK?' Lawrence's voice was low, hesitant.

'Come on in to the room and we can explain things with a bit of privacy.'

Lily was lying very still against two huge pillows. Her face looked drained of blood. Lawrence was first to go up to her. Lily started to cry as they gave each other a tight hug.

Georgie did not want to have Lily and her current antagonism laid bare before everyone. She stayed beside the door even though some primal need in her wanted to close the gap. An invisible thread in her stomach was reeling her in. Before she could move the midwife adjusted the heart monitor on Lily's vast belly, rising under a sheet.

Lawrence nudged her towards the bed and Lily smiled wanly at her before shutting her eyes for a moment. *I don't blame her for keeping me out.* The consultant coming in to the room made the tension tighten. Even the baby's heartbeat on the monitor, seemed to freeze for an instant.

Dr Melanie Coutts was one of the hospital's leading consultants and she was already in surgery scrubs.

It was only when she began to speak that Lily opened her eyes. Georgie could see the fear in them and it was contagious. They closed the door behind them to hear the news in private.

She said, 'The baby is in difficulties and we need to deliver it as soon as possible.

'We're going to get Lily ready for surgery now and I do need to warn you that the baby will need to go to the Neo-Natal Unit. Please take a seat in the waiting room and we'll give you news as soon as we've baby delivered.'

Another medic put his head in to the room.

'We're ready, Melanie.' He shook Georgie and Lawrence's hands. 'Dom Mitcheson. Paediatrician. I'll be looking after baby while Melanie looks after your daughter.'

Georgie saw Lily was holding her stomach, her eyes closed tightly. She kissed her own hand, then placed this special token of affection on her daughter's forehead.

Lily did not open her eyes but said quietly, 'Don't let my baby die.' Georgie was willing the same thing.

'You are both going to get through this. I promise you. Lily. With all my heart. Your baby will be a fighter. Like you.'

'Yes. I'm a fighter…' Her voice faded.

Just like me.

Georgie squeezed her daughter's hand and kissed her cheek before she left the room.

The waiting area was quiet. It was pale blue and it made Georgie wonder if Lily's baby would be a boy. She had never really thought about what sex her own babies would be. *I was always just resigned to them coming.*

Jasper was frightened.

'Do you think they're both going to be all right?' He looked about ten years old, his eyes wide with anxiety.

Lawrence gave his shoulder a fatherly squeeze and looked at Georgie as he said reassuringly, 'One of my clients works here and she has told me Melanie is absolutely first class. She's definitely the right person to be in Lily's corner.'

He then ignored Georgie.

A further half hour passed by and they were all silent, staring at the NHS posters until they could have recited the slogans by heart. A young father in his early 20s walked through the waiting room looking as if he also had the weight of the world on his shoulders.

Georgie thought he looked a bit like Reuben and wondered if he had felt like that, despite not being in the delivery room with her, all those years ago. Was this how he had paced, under his parents' censorious eyes, after rushing to the hospital?

Every time the door opened, they all jumped. The minutes turned into one hour then two, their nerves were shredded.

Thankfully the face they wanted appeared. Dr Coutts looked as shattered as they felt. Jasper gripped Georgie's hand and without thinking she in turn gripped Lawrence's hand just as tightly. Only to find he dropped it.

'We've delivered the baby. You've a little boy in your family. He's in the Neo-natal Unit to be given the special care he will need for the next few days. He is 4lbs which is not a bad weight. He's getting oxygen and being scanned at present.'

Dr Coutts sat down beside Jasper and he unclenched his hands as he gave a long sigh of relief.

'Can I see Lily and him?'

Lawrence stood up, 'Yes. We really want to see our daughter as well as our grandson.'

She was shocked to see her daughter so white when they went to her room.

'Oh, my poor Lily.' Georgie stroked her face. She then held her hand gently.

'You're in the very best hands,' said Lawrence, 'and so is your baby boy.'

Tears fell down Lily's face. 'Oh Jasper. Our baby.' Lily's face crumpled.

'I know Lils. He's going to be fine. I'm sure. Really sure.' Jasper held Lily's other hand and squeezed tight.

All of her own birth experiences were haunting Georgie. Paul, Nat, Lily. Each baby had made her feel so sad but her daughter didn't deserve to feel the same.

After another couple of minutes trying to reassure Lily, Lawrence said they had probably better go, to let her sleep.

Lily's face lit up briefly when Georgie kissed her. It made Georgie's feelings for her daughter take another complicated turn which even she, herself, did not fully understand.

'We need to wait outside. Let you sleep.' Georgie was last to leave the room. Unsure what to say. It was silent apart from the occasional thump from a baby monitor in a nearby room or doors slamming shut.

Despite her woozy and tired state Lily said, 'I'm sorry, Mam. This is all a mess. I can't cope with it all.'

She started to cry quietly. 'And now he's in the baby unit and they're not sure if he's going to be all right. I can't bear it if he's not able to be normal. And it's all my fault because I had him too young.'

The tears flowed and Georgie wiped them again. 'Listen Lily. The important thing right now is that you keep calm and we get you home as soon as possible. We need to make sure your baby comes home soon as well. When you're well enough you'll be able to see him at the baby unit. They think it'll be the morning.'

The crying only intensified. Lily looked exhausted and had a haunted look on her face which reminded Georgie of how she felt after she had Paul. It made her feel sick to her stomach.

'But how can I go home if he's poorly?

'He's coming home Lily. I'm sure.'

Lawrence came back in. 'Georgie. 'I think she must rest now. We need to wait outside for any news.

Jasper, Lawrence and Georgie then sat dutifully and quietly back in the waiting room as the Sister came to see them. Lawrence had become more uptight and middle-class, attempting to be in control of a situation over which he had absolutely no control over. Georgie was trying to appear a normal mam, when she had no idea how a normal mam would react to everything that had unfurled before her.

The Sister said, 'Jasper, you can go over to see your son now, if you want to, now you know Lily is stable.'

Jasper shook his head.

'I want to see him for the first with Lily.' He was resolute.

'Fair enough, but he is a poorly baby. We suggest fathers go to the Neo-Natal Unit to get an update from the consultant over there.'

She then looked at Lawrence and Georgie who were sitting at opposite sides of the room. 'I'm sorry but you can't see him before Lily does. I hope you understand.'

'Of course. Of course. Thank you for all you have done.' Lawrence grabbed her hand and squeezed it with both of his own as if the baby's life depended on it. She gave a sympathetic smile at Georgie before she left which she couldn't quite understand. It could have meant I am sorry you have got such an odd husband or I am sorry you're such a crap mother.

Jasper sat down and held his head in his hands briefly. He looked so young and not up to the responsibility which the stork had dropped into his scruffy lap. Lawrence sat down beside him and patted his shoulder.

Georgie realised everyone had been patting each other or rubbing hands all night. It didn't come naturally but she had to admit there was comfort in it, even though Lawrence was not touching her at all.

He said, 'Jasper. We know this is hard to take in but you should see the baby and hear what is happening to him. Come on. I can't go in but I can at least go down with you to the baby unit and wait outside. It's only two corridors away. Come on my young fella.'

As they walked away from Georgie, Lawrence looked smaller than ever but she was pleased he was being kind and taking control. Jasper had his head down and looked as if he was going to his death.

Left on her own she wondered if she would be allowed to see Lily again but thought not. The nurses wanted her daughter to sleep. The thought of rest made her realise just how tired she also was. She lay down on the seat for a moment. Her eyes closed and a welcome blackness covered her like a fall of snow.

She was woken by her legs feeling as if they were giving way from under her. Lawrence had unceremoniously shoved them off the seat so he could sit down beside her. 'Seriously Georgina. Sleeping? Now?'

Her eyes were being pulled shut by gravity and she had to raise her eyebrows to get them to stay open. A frantic rub of her face brought her back to life and Lawrence thrust one of the hospital throat-burning cups of coffee into her hands.

Wiping tears from his eyes he explained, 'He's very ill, Georgina. They're scanning him as they know he has had some bleeding on his brain. Jasper's gone to pieces. Pieces. He told me there were tubes and monitors all over. He's getting oxygen and all they can do is do is wait and see how he responds.'

Georgie sat on the edge of the seat and looked straight ahead as she asked the question they had all dared not utter. 'Will he die, Lawrence?'

Her husband made a low guttural sound like none she'd ever heard. 'They just don't know. I can't bear it

George. That poor baby. And Lily. Our poor, little girl.' He got up to face the wall on the other side of the room.

Georgie knew she was ill equipped to cope with her normally formal husband but got up to stand beside him anyway. He continued, trying to regain his composure before Jasper came back in. 'We can see him tomorrow after Lily. Well. It is tomorrow now, isn't it? Later on. We need to see him later on.'

'I know.' She gave him a brief hug as Jasper came back in to the room with more news.

'I'm staying here with Lily until I can take her down to see the baby. Please go home both of you. There's nothing else you can do here for now. I'll let you know if anything changes. I promise. Go home.'

Georgie thought he had actually grown into a man in the space of a few short hours.

'I love you guys.' He pulled Lawrence and her close to him. Lawrence kissed him on the cheek and ruffled his head as if he was a child.

'You're right. I think we should go, Georgie, even for just a couple of hours. There isn't anything we can do here. At least at home we can ring and let people know what's going on.'

Georgie kissed Lily's forehead as a nurse checked her blood pressure. *Little does she know this does not come naturally to me but at least I am trying.* Lily made a small sigh in her sleep and said 'Night' just as she did when she was small, which seemed so long ago.

*

Lawrence was still not saying much to Georgie when they got home. They both fell asleep on the settees downstairs, too shattered to go to bed.

After three hours the sun streamed down on them. Georgie woke up feeling like she had a huge hangover. Despite this, they both knew there was no time to waste. It was time to get through the jobs which needed to be done, from buying a pram to spreading the word of Lily and Jasper's situation to friends and relatives.

The London Grand Final was also looming and the moral dilemma of whether she should go was bouncing around Georgie's brain.

Lawrence did the phone calls and texts. Georgie stayed out of his way with Nat, who was asking a huge number of uncomfortable questions which she did not want to think about.

'Will he go to a special school?'

The list went on and on until Lawrence sent him out to Costa Coffee with enough money to buy food and meet his friends.

When Lawrence rang the hospital for an update, the report on Lily was much better. She was sitting up and stabilised, but her baby boy's health still needed to turn a corner. They drove to see their daughter in silence, deep in their own thoughts about their frail grandson. All the time Georgie also wondered how she could broach the London final. The other finalists were texting her asking for gig updates. Each one unanswered.

All of her life she had had to fight for her self-preservation and to be perfect, to keep a grip on her life. Always struggling to do the right thing.

Lily told them she had been able to see her baby son earlier in the morning, even though she had to be pushed to the baby unit in a wheelchair, she was so weak. He had a mass of dark brown hair. Despite being covered in wires and tubes she had been able to touch his hand through one the small portholes in the incubator.

Georgie was pleased to see she had more colour in her cheeks and also glad Lily was pleased to see them both. It was often just Lawrence who got a smile. Jasper was still in the room, fast asleep on the hard armchair with his mouth wide open. Lily gave him a nudge and said he should take her parents down to the baby.

The unit was down a twist of corridors and had an intricate buzzer system to gain entry to the cots inside. After putting on the required sterilised white gowns and washing their hands to prevent infections, Lawrence grabbed Georgie's hand with apprehension.

They walked through the door to the intensive care room for the most poorly babies. The heat hit her like the emotional wall she was climbing over. It was as hot as an oven to ensure the babies were all at the best temperature for their well-being. Jasper led them over to an incubator at the back of the room.

And there he was, this tiny bundle of wires and thin, wrinkled flesh. Georgie could not bear to look at him, he looked so pitiful. They were invited to touch his tiny hand through the incubator's window. Lawrence's fingers gently stroked his grandson's fingers for a brief moment.

Jasper looked expectantly at Georgie who shook her head.

The nurse said, 'He needs another stable 24 hours and then we know if he will be OK. They're critical. We need to do our jobs and you need to be patient for this little fellow.'

As they walked back to the ward Jasper looked as if he had the weight of the world on his shoulders. Georgie felt sorry for him, torn between worry about Lily and his poorly son. Lily was looking expectantly at them as they went back in to her room, hoping for good news which they couldn't give.

'It is still a bit touch and go Lils. I'm so sorry.' Jasper sat down on the side of the bed and buried his head in Lily's lap. Tears filled her daughter's eyes and Lawrence followed suit.

Georgie tried to be strong but struggled to keep calm.

Lawrence said, 'The next 24 hours Lily. We just have to wait for that time, pray and keep our faith in the nursing staff. They are taking good care of him. He will be a fighter, just like you.'

The room door opened and a huge box of chocolates with bright purple chino legs came in. Lily dried her eyes and smiled at the face behind the present.

'Paul. How lovely of you to come. Wow. Some box of chocolates.'

Georgie could hardly bear to look at her first-born son. While he looked the appropriate mixture of sad and happy to see them all.

'Thanks for letting me know. I just wanted to be with

you guys. Show some support really. See if there is anything I can do. What's the baby called?'

Lily said, 'What did you want to call Paul, Mam? If you'd been able to keep him?'

Georgie froze for a second with the memory of picking a name she knew she would never be able to use. But also knew the answer.

'Zak,' she said calmly and clearly.

Lily and Jasper both looked at each other and smiled.

'Love it,' said Lily.

'Love it too, babe,' said Jasper, giving her a hug.

'What time will you come in tomorrow, Mam?' Georgie had hoped to be out of the door before she got asked this question. Her emotions were churning. She was in the middle of her worst nightmare, surrounded by babies and her first son appearing when she wasn't expecting him.

'I don't know if I'm able to come in.'

Lawrence looked at her with contempt.

'Explain?' was all he said.

'It's the Stand-Up Star final. You all know that. You encouraged me to do it. Remember.'

'I need you Mam. We all do.'

She looked at Jasper, who was leaning on her at the side of the bed, looking a spent force. Then to up the ante as she usually did, Lily stared at Paul, 'ALL of us need you Mam.' She was firm and stared hard at Georgie, who thought *She's not that ill if she can still assert herself like this.*

Lawrence stepped in and said, 'Your mam is not going and that's that.'

She saw Paul start to smile and quickly stop himself. Lily, who knew Georgie better, looked unconvinced.

Georgie didn't want to throw Lawrence up against the wall in front of all these people although she was tempted. She bit her tongue and realised she needed to get home. She also needed to leave home. As her self-esteem grew, her marriage was evaporating before her eyes.

They sat in silence all the way home until Georgie said seven words.

'Do not ever boss me around again.'

Her husband merely glanced round briefly from the looking at the traffic and put on Radio 4 to stop any further attempts at communication.

As they walked in to the house she said, 'I'm going. The baby is being looked after by specialists and doesn't need me. You all don't need me. And I'm so sorry but I need to do this.'

*

She went straight upstairs and began to put a few clothes in an overnight bag. Then decided to crash out in the spare bedroom.

The landing was full of washing which needed to be ironed, Nat's school bag and PE kit had tumbled out on to the floor and there was a huge pile of Lawrence's books.

I feel as if I am drowning again.

It seemed the accumulated rubbish was about to grow and grow until, like her family's constant demands, it covered her all together.

Her perfect mother act had vanished completely as had her home's domestic order.

I'm definitely going.

The messages constantly popping up on her fellow comics WhatsApp feed kept her resolve. It was as if the whole group was in a frenzy of excitement to see who would win this once-in-a-lifetime prize.

On the landing she bumped into Nat.

'Are you alright Mam?'

'Yes.' She lied.

By 10 o clock she decided to try and get some sleep but instead of the comedy gig all she could think about was Zak lying ill in the unit and Lily the only mother in the maternity ward with no baby beside her.

This newly-found empathy sat uncomfortably with her, like she had put on someone else's shoes. They rubbed. She remained wide awake despite her best efforts. At two in the morning Georgie admitted defeat.

I'm not going to get to sleep until I see the baby again. Only then can I go to the final.

She crept out of the house and closed the front door as silently as possible. The roads were eerie, as if everyone had been taken to another planet. This feeling of being all alone in the world continued in the hospital car park, with just a handful of staff cars scattered around the dark grounds.

She was buzzed in to the Neo-Natal Unit without question. Baby Chancellor was now Baby Zak, and a sleepy paediatrician was on night duty.

'It's late in the day, or early in the morning to see the baby, isn't it?'

'I know, I couldn't sleep.'

'Well. I wish we had really good news but I can tell you he's a fighter. He's certainly holding his own.'

The wired-up baby in the incubator was peaceful, the only sound the regular flow of the oxygen going in to his glass home. Georgie pulled up one of the hard, white stools and stared at her grandson, taking him in, inch by inch. This baby seemed to have no connection with her at all. She was desperately looking for something to make her feel a link to all her family and give her comfort, like she was now beginning to feel with Paul.

Then she saw. His smallest toes were disproportionately tiny and tightly tucked under the ones next to them. She knew exactly where she had seen this before. At the end of her own feet where her twisty toes were a source of amusement whenever she wore sandals. This baby had exactly the same toes as her first baby and herself.

Paul's tiny feet had stuck out of his blanket as he was taken out of the room all those years ago. Until this moment she had blanked out the horrible recognition that the bundle of bloody flesh being handed to some stranger was a part of her. Paul's toes had given her proof. She put her hand to her mouth and nearly fainted.

The paediatrician was oblivious to her distress and opened the ventilator porthole to adjust Zac's breathing tube. 'If you want to touch him, you're welcome but I'm afraid he's still too poorly to have a cuddle as yet.'

He left the small door open as he went to get some new tubes and without thinking Georgie's hand was gently stroking Zak's hand, no bigger than her thumbnail. His flesh was the softest thing she had ever felt. She was sure a small smile passed over his face for a brief second before the paediatrician returned and the incubator window was closed again.

She didn't want to wash her hands.

'You'd better get home to bed I think.'

The paediatrician looked concerned and she nodded, unable to speak. 'There will be another discussion with all the medical team in the morning. Wait for an update on his condition then. Try not to worry too much.'

Georgie took off her sanitised hospital gown in silence. Her heart and head were all over the place. The pent-up emotion she had felt when she gave birth to Paul had been ripped out of her by this premature baby.

Then she began to calm. There was hope. She could hope to build a relationship with Paul. Zak was healing her.

She was in Lily's room on a side ward in a matter of moments and wondered if she would now feel genuine warmth towards her daughter in the light of her feelings. The light was dim and the only sound the quiet pitter-patter of night nurses' feet on the floor, as they checked on the mothers and babies. An occasional cry from a baby pierced the air then vanished quickly, no doubt when its hunger was sated.

Lily was peaceful now. As she slept Georgie noticed the dark circles under her eyes had faded and her skin was back to its normal colour. The speech which had been going round in her head since she left the house was bursting to be said but it now had new meaning.

It didn't matter to her that Lily was asleep. She often picked this rare moment of tranquility during the night to talk to her.

Sitting quietly on the edge of her daughter's bed, with her hands folded in her lap, she calmly told her tale.

'I'm so sorry I haven't been a great mother to you. When I had Paul, it was so traumatic it made me shut down. Then when I had Nat and you the usual emotions just weren't there.

'Your first smile. Nothing. First tooth coming out. Nothing. Birthday celebrations. First day at school. I felt nothing and yet was surrounded by all these other mothers soaking up love from their children and giving it out.

But not me. I just kept pretending to be the perfect mother.'

And so, Georgie continued until she came to this night, where something bewitching had happened to shift her view. She was unnerved.

I feel the pain of separation for the first time yet I still feel the need to escape and be free. She stood up and looked at Lily, still sound asleep. A sense of love for her daughter surged through her, making the emotion she had felt with the baby come back anew.

It was time to leave. She had made her decision and hoped it would be understood. A gentle kiss was placed on Lily's forehead and a small smile played on her daughter's lips as it had on her baby grandson's minutes earlier.

'I love you, my Lily. For the first time. I love you and Nat with my whole heart.'

*

Lawrence must have heard the car pull on to the drive and was downstairs in the kitchen when she opened the front door. He looked as if he too had been awake for hours. This was a conversation she would have much rather had in the morning but she could not put it off when he was standing in front of her.

'Have you seen the baby? Tell me. Tell me.'

She scraped her hand across her eyes and followed it by a wipe of her nose with her sleeve. A long, slow breath out and she was able to speak at last.

'He's still poorly. They'll tell us tomorrow about his progress but it's still too early to tell.

'Lawrence. He could die and he's never have been hugged. Can you imagine? That tiny baby could die tonight and he would be alone. Oh God. It is all my fault. This is all because I am such a terrible mother.'

Her breathing made the words choke in her throat.

'Don't say that, Georgie. Stop it. Please, I beg you, stop it.' He shook her shoulders.

'See sense. The doctors will look after him and tomorrow we will get good news I am sure of it. We can go in the morning and hear the update first hand from Lily.'

He smiled at her for the first time in 24 hours but she didn't smile back.

'I'm not going to be here tomorrow.' She could hardly believe these words were coming out when they had been choked back a mere moment before.

'What do you mean you will not be here?' His tone was incredulous.

I need to be in London.' She could not meet his eyes.

'Why the fuck do you think you will be in London?' Lawrence rarely swore but there was a menacing fury in his voice.

'Is it that comedy guru? Mr Jaz Showbusiness.' His rage was building and for the first time in her life Georgie felt really afraid of him.

'I've worked so hard for the final, Lawrence. There's nothing I can do for Zak. I'm torn in pieces as much as you but I need to go to London and become a whole person. I've tried to be a great mother but all it's done is make me miserable. If I can find happiness through comedy, then maybe I'll begin to be the mother I always wanted to be. Like normal women. Can't you see that?'

The enormity of what she was saying made her cry again.

This Lawrence was no-one she knew. His jealousy of Jaz with Georgie's new assertive attitude, triggered him into a seething mass of rage.

'Ok. You go to London. Go and follow your dreams. I can't cope with this drama anymore.'

'It's a chance of a lifetime, Lawrence. I'm torn. This is a terrible choice to have to make.'

'Well, you've made it my darling.' Lawrence was sarcastic.

He turned away and punched the kitchen door with all the might his boxing training had given him. Then he seemed to age before her eyes as he walked slowly up the stairs away from her.

The grandfather clock chimed five. Each note seemed to ask Georgie a question. Are you going? Are you going? She stood with her back against the stair spindles and looked around her. She saw the heap of dirty dishes strewn across the kitchen table.

I can't do this anymore. She turned and took the stairs two by two. Her make-shift bed from earlier that night was still littered with bits of paper and her overnight bag contents.

She grabbed a plain black t shirt from the second ironing pile on the landing and threw in some clean underwear, black jeans and her red canvas comedy shoes. The script for the final was on the desk. It went on the top.

Georgie crept into Nat's room to say goodbye. The usual smell of teenage socks and sweat hit her but this time it made her pine, rather than gag. She quietly kissed him on top of his head and told him she loved him. He instinctively said 'Love you, Mam' even though he was fast asleep.

The kitchen was cold and quiet. Dawn was just beginning to break, casting long shadows from the garden across the floor.

Sitting on the table was Georgie's overnight bag, instead of the full fruit bowl, which she had neglected to replenish for weeks. A sign. She was going.

She knew Lawrence saw all of these changes in his usual domestic perfection.

Standing with her back to the room, facing the window and a new future, she sensed her husband before she saw him.

'You're going', he said.

When she turned, he stood still, instinctively blocking the doorway.

'I'm sorry. I need to do this. And I need to leave. You and here.'

She realised she hated this kitchen and the fact she had allowed herself to be its slave. Immaculate surfaces.

Immaculate food. Immaculate everything.

'I know. I know. London. Blah. Blah. Blah.'

'You encouraged me to do it. And now I love it. With all my soul. Love it.'

'Yes, but I didn't think you'd want to put yourself out there permanently and think you were ACTUALLY funny. Or turn into some kind of feminist.'

'Feminist. That's interesting. I'm certainly seeing what women can achieve with some encouragement, if that's what you mean.'

Lawrence made a small snorting sound. 'Is that what Jaz calls it? Encouragement. This comedy thing hasn't been much of a laugh for all of us, has it?'

'It's transformed my life…'

'At the expense of ours…'

'Goodbye Lawrence. I'm very sorry. You've meant everything to me but I've been so shaped by you. It's nearly destroyed me.'

'Shaped?' He was aghast.

'Yes. You've created me. This perfect, middle-class wife. Napkins. Fortnum and Mason hampers. The. Whole. Thing. It's not the real me. I'm so …'

'Don't say sorry again.'

So, she didn't.

Instead, they did a small side to side dance as he tried to stop her getting past.

She pressed her palm into his arm as she pushed past him. For a split second it reminded her of how secure he had made her feel. But she didn't need that now.

Then she was gone and her husband's shadow faded away behind her as she opened the front door.

Despite herself a line for a gig popped into her head, and it was pure stand-up mam with a dark heart.

THIRTY-SEVEN

Jaz had booked a hotel near the London comedy club and she arrived at midday.

The lift reflected Georgie's glinting eyes and dark shadows on her face. It was a perfect back-lit, stomach-lurching time machine catapulting her into a new life.

He was waiting by the bedroom door, holding it open with his usual immaculate timing.

'You're here. Wasn't sure you'd come.' His hand was out, palm up, inviting.

'Then you don't know me yet. Not really. Anyway.' She took that hand, enjoying the cool touch of his skin and stood next to him at the entrance to the room. As an equal.

'We're sure about being together. Aren't we?'

Later that afternoon, when the corridor was busy with families, chamber maids and their trolleys, they stood as one, oblivious. Faces lifted to the shower's cascading water. They washed away shame and their past lives.

Now to own the future.

*

A light kiss on her lips. A stroke of her hand. Jaz said 'I love you' and it made Georgie stir for a moment. Their fingertips touched briefly as he left to get the script for his part in the Stand-Up Star Final.

Her mobile rang at 5pm and her first thought was it might be news about the baby. But it was the Stand-Up Star producer to check Georgie was ready for the show's sound check rehearsals. She had to arrive at 7pm prompt to get the running order. No latecomers and no excuses.

Her head was full of everything but her script. Try as

she might she couldn't say it out loud without forgetting half her lines, or getting the punch-lines in the wrong place. She knew she was tough and determined but this Grand Final on top of the emotional tidal wave of the last two days was proving too much of a test.

The hotel's espresso coffee gave her a much-needed caffeine shot. Georgie was now wide awake. She checked and re-checked her phone to see if there was any news from the hospital. None came. *Do I contact anyone for an update or will that make things worse?*

It seemed very strange to be getting ready for such an important gig in total peace. She usually had one or both of her children diving in to talk about their problems or 'borrow' money.

The calm of her own room was wonderful in some respects yet extraordinarily alien at the same time. It felt as though they had all died and she was alone. Despite the fact she had craved this silence, now she had it, part of her still wanted her family. Most importantly she wanted baby Zak.

She decided she should ring Lawrence before she left for the final itself but he didn't answer.

The club was huge and the grandest she had ever been in. It was early but there were already big groups of people filling up the front tables. The good news was the crowd was all ages and types, not just the young groups of stag nights and hen parties. The back of the club had a balcony where people were already seated, making a racket, in for a lively night.

She recognised a couple of judges from TV stand-up shows and they were obviously enjoying being the established ones, not under pressure to be funny themselves. A stage assistant showed her to the green room where her fellow finalists were sitting.

Clementine, Anna, Pat, Will and Matthew were all tense, sitting in a huddle. There were the customary waves and 'Hi's' before they all shut up.

Dominic Duffer, a well-known comedy star came in and talked to them loudly as if they were two buildings away,

'Don't be nervous, you'll all be just fine. I'll warm the crowd up a treat. It will be a walk in the park. Promise you.'

He then went through the running order. Male, female comics were performing alternately. Georgie was in the middle, not a bad place to be.

'Everyone check your phone is off, please. You will get a two minute call before you go on so just wait here and try and relax.'

Georgie checked her mobile and even though her heart was in her mouth about Zak, she mustered her new strength. This was the right thing to do. She was here and it was no help to the baby to make a mess of this chance, after everything that had happened.

I need tonight to be a success so I can say. I DID IT!

The mentor comedians including Jaz were on first to warm up the crowd before the finalists. Georgie and the others waiting could hear part of their acts through the wall. What was particularly hard was hearing how well they all did. Jaz in particular. The laughter was fast and furious. Many of the jokes were even getting rounds of applause. Comics were coming back in pumped up and high fiving each other. The merry band of finalists gave Georgie a wry smile every time they did it.

She managed to get to the toilet just in time. The past two days were vomited out of her guts. A quick glass of water washed away the acid taste.

Her nerves were even more tight with adrenalin. She felt as if her skin was turned inside out, and every noise or clash made her jump. By the time the break before her set came, she was ready to admit defeat.

Georgie took a long sip of Diet Coke and decided to have one last look at her phone in case there were any messages about Zak. But there was no signal so far in the bowels of the club. She did a quick check of her watch to see if she had time to go out. The MC told her two minutes and she must be back.

Georgie shot out of the fire exit and the phone loaded up as if it had all the time in the world. Each second was precious. Eventually, it was ready. There was no message but it rang as soon as it was on. Lily's name flashed across her screen. Georgie thought she was going to be sick again. This could mean the very worst news.

'Mam. Mam. Are you there?'

Georgie was both numb and quiet. She just wanted the news to be out and over with.

Yes, it's me,' she replied softly.

'I just wanted you to know he's improved today. They're really pleased with him. Mam. It's all going to be alright. Isn't that great?'

'Yes. That's fantastic news.' Georgie was gulping back her emotions and wafting her face to ensure she kept calm.

'I understand why you had to go today, Mam. I love you and hope you do well.'

'Love you too Lily.' And with that her daughter was gone. Her words felt strange but full of hope.

The side of the stage was thick with people: hangers-on and the production team. Georgie took a deep breath in and kept her opening line in her head, saying it over and over like a mantra. Then the moment of truth came.

Can I make it as a stand-up comedian?

The final's host comic shouted, 'Ladies and gentlemen, let me hear you go mad for our very own Stand-Up Mam, Georgie Chancellor!'

There was a huge cheer for her. She had no idea how he had wound them up to that extent, but it was welcome nonetheless.

She could hardly make out anyone. Then, like apparitions, faces came into view. Paul, Jaz and Andrea. They were all raising their glasses and saluting her. She didn't know Jaz had arranged for them to be there. Her heart filled with happiness. *This is my chance to make a new Georgie. I can choose to be who I want to be.*

Grabbing the microphone with a firm grip, all of the emotion and fire she had felt over the past days seemed to erupt through her mouth. Her set was fierce and for the first time she was her real self on stage. Georgie was not some perfect housewife and mother. She was feckless, brittle, capable of being ruthless. But underpinning the whole act was also a new emotion. Love.

After all the tried and tested jokes there was extra pieces to her set.

'My daughter's vain. She's only 17 but planning to have Botox on her forehead to hide frown lines. I told her 'For God's sake. Just grow a fringe!

'Her brother's no better. He's applying for university soon. What do you think girls will see me as, when I get there, with being short? 'Hmm, I said, A friend…?'

This was the person the audience saw, with a vicious, sharp eye for anecdotes and cruel observations on domestic goddesses. But underpinned by love now. She brought the house down. There was no-one like her on the bill.

Have I won? I had a great response to my set. Please. Please say my name.

The tension in the Green Room was at fever pitch as they waited to hear who would get the Stand-Up Star Comedy Crown.

She was not religious but she prayed to win just as she had prayed for Zak to get well. They were all on the stage for the announcement. The moment she'd been waiting for.

The third place was announced and it wasn't Georgie's name. She picked her cuticles and rocked back and forth on her heels. All of the remaining acts were similarly showing off their nervous tics.

Then Georgie realised. She felt different. There was no need to win. She had taken control of her life. With Jaz's support she had found peace, self-esteem and true friendship. She also had her children firmly in her heart for the first time, all three of them.

It was unheard of, for a middle-aged woman, talking about family life and motherhood to win a stand-up competition. Some people had taken a quiet delight in telling her so.

She stared at the ground so there could be no chance the crowd could see she was disappointed when suddenly the MC pulled her forward.

'All hail. Georgie Chancellor. Official second place. Runner up. Second out of the whole competition. But a winner on so many levels.'

She was in shock and total disbelief.

It was only when she took hold of the star-shaped glass trophy that it all seemed real. She thought her heart was going to explode with pleasure. The whole room was on its feet cheering as though she was the actual winner.

Georgie held the trophy tightly then punched the air with it, like puncturing a balloon with her past inside and sending it off to oblivion.

The spotlight on the stage was blinding her so she could hardly see anything and only hear loud, hearty cheers.

Her support group at the front of the stage were on their feet and her Jaz was beside them. Matthew won, but she didn't care.

Then there it was, history repeating itself, the thin line of the stage, like a horizon spread out like the school roof all those years ago. And for the first time in her life, she was pleased she didn't jump.

About the author

Kay Wilson lives in North East England with her husband and has two grown-up children. She tried her hand at stand-up for two years alongside a career in PR and lived to tell the tale. That extraordinary experience inspired this novel.

Author photo by Christopher Owens

Acknowledgements

This book has had a long journey to publication and it wouldn't have happened without a great team of friends and supporters.

Firstly, I'd like to thank the author Stephanie Butland. Her advice and suggestions have made this book so much stronger than the original version.

This book wouldn't have been completed without the encouragement of my family and thanks to my husband Steve and children James and Freya. You are nothing like the characters in the book. I promise.

I am also grateful to my writing friends Vic Watson, Marie Ashurst, Sarah Jeffrey and Sarah Francis, who have spurred me on to complete this story.

The stand-up comedy community in the North East was a huge help and very welcoming to a middle-aged wannabe comic. I also want to pay tribute to my friend Andrea Whitaker-Lindsley who was on the stand-up adventure with me. We had the best of times.

Thanks also to my sister Sheila Hudson, Valerie Smith and Laura White who went along to the stand-up gigs with me and Gill Cowell for some funny anecdotes.

Proof reading and feedback were really important to getting this book finished. Kay Crone, Anna Korving, Cat Lumb, Linda McNamara, Alison McCann and Sylvia Whitaker were invaluable.

To find out more about Kay and to sign up for a regular newsletter visit

www.kaywilsonwriter.com

Printed in Great Britain
by Amazon